THE CASSANDRA FILES

Genesis

By

ROD PENNINGTON

epulppress.com
Jackson, Wyoming

The Cassandra Files

Genesis

ISBN13: 978-1-57242-043-4
ASIN: B08WPSJ6X1

epulppress.com
P.O. Box 8906
Jackson, Wyoming 83002

Cover Designed by: Kip Ayers
Interior Designed by: Jake Muelle

Chapter 1

ANYONE WHO HAD only known Cassandra Morse at the Naval Academy, or when she still had her flight wings, probably wouldn't recognize her today. For the first time since she had reached puberty, she had let her hair grow out. While not long by civilian standards, her blonde hair, that now reached her shoulders, spent most of its time pulled into a ponytail and sticking out the back of a Dodger's baseball cap. Lean and hard while in the military, in the past six months she had softened and added a few pounds to her five-foot seven-inch frame. And, much to her surprise, she had developed some curves. Her bust had gone from an athletic "A" cup to a tasteful "B". Dressed in a flowing linen summer dress, in her postage stamp backyard, she was tending a flower bed in the rear of her home which was on a canal in Venice Beach. She had, much to the annoyance of her four cousins, inherited the house from her grandfather, Admiral Henry Morse. She figured, since she was the only one of her entire generation to stay in the family business and serve in the Navy, her grandfather decided it was a part of her retirement package.

The view from her rear porch was amazing, and the narrow three floor house was far enough from any of the footbridges over the canals that it didn't get many tourists. The admiral had received the house as a wedding gift from Cassandra's great-grandfather on her mother's side, Malcolm Comstock, and it had been in the family ever since. The house wasn't much, but the land it was sitting on was worth a small fortune. Having been built between the first and second world wars, the plumbing was shot and the electric box still had screw-in fuses instead of circuit breakers. With its age and condition, it was a perfect "knock down" candidate to be replaced before someone nominated it for the National Registry of Historic Homes. Hardly a week went by without a realtor knocking on her door asking if she would consider selling.

That was never going to happen.

Cassandra loved the place because it was only a five-minute walk to the beach and the business district. What she liked the most were all of the quirky and weird people in her neighborhood and on the boardwalk. After a life of rigid military structure, first as a Navy Brat, then Annapolis, then as a combat pilot, it was a pleasant change.

When Cassandra saw the odd little man approaching on the sidewalk between her yard and the canal, alarm bells went off. He wasn't a tourist; his eyes were locked on her and he was purposely striding in her direction. After her performance the night before, he was most likely a reporter and she had no interest in talking to him. As she turned to go inside, she heard a voice behind her.

"Lt. Morse?"

That stopped her in her tracks. For the past six months she had done everything possible to leave the Navy behind. No one had called her "Lieutenant" since she had moved into her new life.

"I'm sorry, do I know you?" asked Cassandra guardedly. The man didn't appear to be much of a threat. He was two inches shorter than her and at least twenty pounds heavier. He looked like the effort of vaulting her rickety three-foot-high white picket fence and sprinting the twenty feet to where she was standing was more likely to induce a coronary on his part than any damage on hers.

"We've never formally met, but I was in town and saw the article about you in the newspaper this morning. That must have been some meltdown at the police station last night," the stranger said as he held up a copy of today's *Los Angeles Guardian*.

Not owning a television, never reading a newspaper and avoiding the cesspool that was the internet, this was the first she was hearing of the story.

"Crap," she muttered as she approached the man and snatched the newspaper out of his hands. Above the fold on the top of the front page was a banner headline:

"Dream Lady" Does it Again
Predicts Arson That Kills 2

Below the headline was a picture of Cassandra screaming while being restrained by several uniformed policemen.

Not her best look.

Cassandra felt her anger building again. As usual, she had been right. As usual, the police didn't listen. Now, two people were dead.

"It happened exactly the way you predicted it."

"Are you a cop?" She asked.

"No."

"Are you a reporter?"

"God no," the odd little man answered.

"Then who the hell are you and why are you bothering me?" Cassandra snapped.

"I'm just a guy who knows why you're having your dreams."

"What?"

Cassandra's heart skipped a beat. Could it be possible? Could someone actually explain the nightmare she had been living for the last six months? Then her skepticism began to creep in. Was this some kind of con man doing a cold read on her? He had read about her in the paper and now was telling her what she wanted to hear.

Her eyes narrowed. "Prove it."

"If you would like to find out the truth about what happened to you," he said as he started to walk away, "call the doctor who treated you at the USC Medical Center, Dr. Newman. Ask him if you looked like you had been adrift at sea for twenty-two days," the stranger said.

"How do you know about that?" asked Cassandra. "That's classified information."

"That's not important," the stranger continued. "Next, ask him to closely examine this part of your skull in an X-Ray." He touched the left side of head directly above the ear.

"After you've done that, we'll talk again."

"Wait!" Casandra shouted as she ran to her fence. "How will I find you?"

"Put a flower on your mailbox and I'll find you."

Chapter 2

AS THE MAN walked away, a series of high-resolution color stills flashed on a computer screen over three hundred miles north.

The man behind the oversized desk, with three 32-inch monitors in front of him, continued to work the joystick that controlled the camera mounted on the telephone pole near Cassandra Morse's backyard. As he feared, there was too much ambient noise and wind to pick up much on the microphone and he was only getting an odd word or two here and there.

Phil Levy was an overweight, pimple-faced computer nerd. While he worked out of a basement, at least it wasn't his mother's. He had been hired by a mysterious person on the dark web to keep a remote eye on a house in Los Angeles, and the money was enough for him to be able to afford his own place.

For six months, he had watched easily the most boring woman in history. Other than the occasional visits to her backyard, she almost never went outside during daylight hours. He had watched her many nights on the rear camera, as she got hammered on the porch overlooking the canal. On the front camera, he watched her leaving the house in the early evening and returning hours later obviously drunk and more often than not with a man. So far, none of the men had stayed for breakfast, and none had ever made an encore appearance.

He had specific instructions, if anything in her routine changed, he was to call immediately and report it.

He had a knot in his stomach. This was the sweetest gig he had ever had. After he had installed the motion detector software on both of the feeds, it took maybe twenty minutes a month out of his time. With what they were paying him, in cash, he figured, for the time he actually did anything, he had to be earning close to Jeff Bezos's hourly rate.

Levy compiled a file of the best pictures and sent them along to what he figured would be a world tour of computer servers before arriving at their destination. He was a pretty fair hacker but when he tried to follow the trail, he had gotten lost in a Chinese server farm and had given up. Next, he reached for the disposable mobile phone his mysterious employer had sent him, but he had never used. Levy dialed the only number available in its contact list, which he assumed was another disposable phone. His call was answered on the first ring.

"Yes?" said a female voice.

"This is Mr. Black. I need to speak to Mr. White."

"Hold."

There was about a two-minute delay then this time the voice was male. "Yes?"

"She had an unexpected visitor."

"How do you know he was unexpected?"

"She retreated when he approached and was agitated when he left."

"This is unusual, how?"

"She has never had a daytime visitor before. Every other man she has ever spoken to was on her arm after last call."

"I see. Anything else?"

"Yes," Levy answered as he cleared his throat.

"I had always thought this woman was a cold fish who never showed any emotion. This time was different."

"Do you have a video of the meeting?"

"Of course." Levy cleared his throat again. "The audio is really spotty, but I also took multiple still HD photos of the visitor."

"Excellent. Email the entire package to me."

"It should already be in your inbox."

The line went dead.

7 Months Earlier

Chapter 3

"KNOCK 'EM DEAD, Lieutenant," a female seaman offered as she pressed her back against the wall of the narrow corridor to let the two officers pass.

"That's quite a fan club you've got going there," Lt. Max Underwood said in his gentle Southern drawl as he slowed his pace to let his fellow pilot and fellow Navy lieutenant catch up. Underwood was over half a foot taller than Lt. Cassandra Morse and had a stride advantage to match. While it didn't help much on the tight turns and narrow staircases, it came in handy on the straightaways deep in the bowels of the USS Ronald Reagan. "I think every female crew member we've passed has wished you good luck."

Morse normally would have had a snappy comeback but currently she had her game face on. She glared at Underwood as she passed him, and then opened the hatch door to the pilot's ready room. Even deep in the bowels of the mighty ship they could hear and feel the subwoofer thunder and feel the "Gipper" swaying from the roll of the 30-foot waves breaking across its bow.

"No pressure," Underwood said cheerfully. "All you have to do is land a hundred-million-dollar fighter jet prototype onto the deck of an eight-billion-dollar aircraft carrier in the middle of the night in rough seas with half of the Joint Chiefs watching." With a twinkle in his blue eyes, he added, "What could possibly go wrong?"

"If I remember correctly," Cassandra answered tersely, "you were sitting about three feet behind me when I put the bird on the deck yesterday."

"True, true," Underwood replied with a chuckle. "But that was daytime and it was before this little sprinkle moved in." As if it were on cue, even a level down from the flight deck, they could clearly hear a rumble from a terrific clap of thunder. "The Weather Channel is calling this the storm of the century. They've never seen anything like it."

"Listen, if you don't want to tag along…"

Underwood knew his fellow pilot well enough to see from the expression on her face, and her body language, the time for joking had passed. In addition to being one of only a handful of female Navy combat pilots, she came from Navy royalty. Her father, grandfather, and great grandfather had all worn Admiral Stars on their shoulders, but she was on track to do something none of them had done, get her Lieutenant Commander gold leaf before her thirtieth birthday.

"Relax," Underwood said, suddenly serious. "The rest of the guys give you crap because of your glaring "Y" chromosome deficiency, but every one of them would take you for their wingman." A smirk covered Underwood's face. "Sorry, wing-woman."

His attempts at humor weren't helping to lighten the mood.

He leaned in close and tried a different approach. "We've done it dozens of times on the simulator. How could it possibly get any worse than some of those scenarios they threw at us?"

Lt. Morse shrugged but didn't smile.

The door to the ready room opened and a terrified fresh-faced ensign stepped into the room. With a slight squeak in his voice, he shouted, "Attention!"

As Lt. Morse and Lt. Underwood snapped to attention, Underwood whispered. "What's up with him? He looks like he's seen a ghost."

Captain Locke, commander of the Gipper, entered the ready room followed by a silver-haired, man in his early seventies dressed in a flight jumpsuit.

Captain Locke strode purposely up to Morse. "Both wind speed and wave height have exceeded the upper parameters for this exercise, Lieutenant. You have the option to scrub…"

"No sir," Morse answered without a moment's hesitation.

The Captain nodded then turned to Underwood. "You're dismissed, Lieutenant."

Underwood was a bit taken aback. "Sir?"

"Admiral Morse will be taking the backseat on this flight."

"Yes sir!" Underwood answered crisply. As he turned to pick up his gear, he whispered to Lt. Morse, "I stand corrected. It could get worse."

The elderly man looked around and said, "Can you give us the room." It was not phrased like a question but with the tone and authority of a man used to having his requests instantly responded to in the affirmative.

After the room emptied, Cassandra slugged the old man in the shoulder then gave him a hug.

"Grandpa, what are you doing here?"

"I didn't want to miss seeing my favorite granddaughter make naval history."

"First off, since I'm your only granddaughter, that's not much of a compliment. Second, I know you're a big mover and shaker over in Washington but the only thing you've flown in the past 20 years is a desk."

"Cassie, I've had over 500 arrested landings on twelve different aircraft carriers."

"Yeah, but none of them since I got out of diapers." Lt. Morse eyed her grandfather with suspicion. "How did you pull this one off?"

"Since I'm just going to be a passenger on a non-combat training exercise, I got a waiver."

"A waiver? From whom?"

"I have a friend."

"What kind of friend has that sort of pull?"

"One who lives at 1600 Pennsylvania Avenue."

Cassandra laughed and slugged her grandfather in the shoulder again. "So why is the president involved?"

"The United States spends more on defense than the next nine world powers combined. Our weapons procurement procedure could easily be called the 'Military Industrial Complex Full Employment Act'. We pay ten times more than necessary for weapons that take years longer than promised to be delivered and half the time when they arrive, they don't even work or they're already obsolete."

Cassandra rolled her eyes. "You've been ranting about that for as long as I can remember but it doesn't seem to ever get any better."

"That could change today."

"How?"

"I know everyone has been kept in the dark about the SV-1 you've been flying."

"That's an understatement," Cassandra said with a snort.

"We needed to keep it as much under wraps as possible since it may revolutionize weapon procurement technology. I convinced the president and a few key decision makers in congress to let me sidestep the normal appropriations process for the SV-1."

"How did you pull off that miracle?" Cassandra asked in disbelief.

"In Washington, money talks, and the SV-1 didn't cost them anything. It was financed and built entirely through private funding." Admiral Morse's eyes locked on his granddaughter and he leaned in a bit closer. He glanced around the ready room to be sure they were alone. While satisfied, he still lowered his voice to barely above a whisper. "By taking out all of the pork barrel spending and politics where anyone and everyone wants to get a taste, compared to the other weapons in our arsenal, the smart guys in Silicon Valley built your baby for chump change in months and not years. By not being saddled with a bureaucratic minefield in the Pentagon, they were able to put the best state-of-the-art technology into the SV-1. After the way you dismantled the E-38 and a baker's dozen Top Gun pilots at Naval Air Station Fallon with the prototype, you raised a lot of eyebrows. If you can land that aircraft on the deck tonight, it comes out of test trials five years early and will head straight to full production. That means $800 billion towards the prototype's manufacturer for a plane that actually delivers as advertised and $800 billion less to the guys who have spent a decade getting rich while building pieces of crap we eventually scrap." Admiral Morse smiled and changed the subject. "Your dad is so stinking proud of you, he's about to burst."

"That's nice," Lt. Morse answered with a disinterested tone in her voice.

"When was the last time you spoke to him?"

Lt. Morse shrugged. "It's been a while."

"Both of you are so pigheaded."

"Gee. I can't imagine who we could have possibly inherited that trait from."

The admiral laughed as he gave his granddaughter a hug and a peck on the forehead. "Nervous?"

"No sir. It flies like a dream."

Admiral Morse picked up a pair of fire resistant Nomex gloves and chuckled as he looked at the missing fingertips. "In my day, we had to cut the fingertips off ourselves," he said.

"We have some touchscreens in the SV-1," Cassandra answered. "Trying to fly with full finger coverage is a nightmare."

"Makes sense." The admiral picked up his flight helmet. "Let's do this."

Chapter 4

DESPITE THE AERODYNAMICS of the sleek two-seat combat jet, the occasional gusts of wind off of the Pacific buffeted it causing it to vibrate slightly. The wheel moorings complained but held firm. Lt. Morse was too engrossed in her pre-flight checklist to notice. Her fingers danced across a few laminated buttons on the touch screen of her control panel and all lights went green.

"Air Boss," Lt. Morse said into the microphone which was built into her helmet, "my panel is green. Requesting permission to launch."

"Affirmative, Valkyrie."

The jet rattled slightly as the wheel moorings were disengaged.

"The pattern is clear. Valkyrie has the ball."

Lt. Morse tapped her screen and both of the jet engines under the wings began to pivot until they were pointed downward. She looked to her left at the young woman in the yellow jacket. Morse saluted then gave a thumbs up.

The catapult officer returned the salute and dropped to one knee and motioned for her to take off.

Instead of barreling down the runway on the catapult, the engines revved louder, and the slick jet began to rise quickly off of the flight deck of the USS Ronald Reagan. When it got to a height of four hundred feet above the deck, the engines pivoted 90 degrees and SV-1 took off like a shot.

"Show the brass what the next generation of aircrafts should look like," the admiral said.

"Going up," Cassie answered as she pointed the nose of the jet skyward and gave the engines full throttle. Despite gale force winds and horizontal rain falling in waves, they were at 40,000 feet and above the storm in less than a minute.

For the next ten minutes, Lt. Morse put the jet through its paces.

"That's the entire checklist," Admiral Morse said as he reached between the seats and gave his granddaughter a pat on the shoulder. "Well done."

"Thank you, sir," Lt. Morse answered.

Through her headphone, she heard the Flight Boss. "The pattern is empty, Valkyrie, and the captain has requested a fly by before landing."

"Supersonic?"

"That's affirmative."

"Roger that," Lt. Morse answered as she allowed herself her first smile in days.

The SV-1 dropped nearly as fast as it had risen and banked into its approach.

"Wake 'em up, Cassie," Admiral Morse said in her ear.

"Yes, sir." Lt. Morse glanced down at her screen which indicated they were traveling at Mach 1.2. Less than a mile from the USS Ronald Reagan, she gave the SV-1 full throttle and the bird began to accelerate. By the time it passed directly over the flight deck and even with the top of the control tower, the air speed was Mach 2.1 and still accelerating. The whine of the engines combined with the sonic boom rattled the windows of the control tower island and drowned out the thunder of the storm.

Chapter 5

CONGRESSMAN DONALD "THE Duke" Warwick was relaxed as he watched the SV-1 roar past on the video screen in the officer's wardroom. Despite the Gipper being just a few miles off the coast from normally sunny San Diego he, along with everyone else, had been driven indoors by the foul weather. There had been an excellent turn out for the SV-1 test flight. Also in the room were three members of the Joint Chiefs alongside an assortment of other VIPs; including some of the major movers and shakers in the military industrial complex. On the other side of the mess, looking smug, were four representatives from the SV-1 manufacturing division.

Like so many congressmen before him, the Duke had a huge ego, modest intellect and suspect morals. When he arrived in Washington thirty-eight years ago, after a decade in the Ohio State legislature, he already had two ex-wives and didn't have so much as two nickels to rub together. Now, despite never drawing a private sector paycheck in his entire professional life, and never grossing more than $200,000 on his House W-2, his most recent congressional financial disclosure statement listed his personal net worth at between $10 and $50 million dollars. Anyone who saw the way he lived suspected even the top end number was probably way too low.

In a pork barrel town like Washington, keeping a guy like the Duke happy was a priority for lobbyists and contractors. After years of working his way up the ladder of the House Armed Services Committee, he was in a position where he could send literally billions of dollars of military contracts their way. To keep him smiling, a nice all-expenses paid junket to places with warm beaches and warmer hookers was a good start. A quiet stock tip or two never hurt. Also letting him buy in on a land deal that would turn a 300% profit in less than a year was always well received. Hosting a "K" street fundraiser or, better yet, setting up a PAC to juice the Duke's re-election war chest would assure your calls were answered personally.

Sadly, in modern day Washington, nothing the Duke did was considered unethical, much less criminal. This was pretty much what you would expect from a town where all of the laws were written by "career politicians" looking to protect their perks and privileges. You overlook my mistress taking home mid-six figures for a no-show job and I'll overlook your son stuffing foreign cash into his pockets.

Badly overweight, the only exercise he had gotten in the last three decades plus had been from chasing interns around the desk in his office on Capitol Hill. Having lost a step since his hip replacement, it had been a while since he had actually cornered a girl a third his age. Which was a good thing. His cardiologists had warned him that vigorous sexual activity might blow out one or more of the heart stents that kept his blood moving.

Normally, the Duke had a politician's smile and a mischievous twinkle in his eyes. As the SV-1 blew past the tower, he looked every day of his seventy-four years and was clearly rattled by what he was seeing. If those smart-ass kids from Silicon Valley could revolutionize military procurement the way they had with the internet and cellphones, the Duke knew his days of being the "kingmaker" were numbered.

To his left was Bradley Doorman, Senior VP of Bathmann Aeronautics and the point man for the E-38. Doorman was a fit and trim fifty-something with chiseled features and a full head of well-coiffed salt and pepper hair. His Italian cut suit, silk shirt and tie were immaculate.

Congressman Warwick leaned inward Doorman and said, "You are so screwed."

"Why is that congressman?" Doorman asked innocently while already knowing the answer.

"The people on the committee are getting restless. The SV-1 dismantled the E-38 in the head-to-head competition…"

"Which you will recall, I strongly advised against."

"Of course you did," Warwick answered with a laugh. "Because you knew what an overpriced piece of crap you were building. You're four years behind schedule and already fifty billion dollars over budget and still climbing."

"Let me remind you, congressman," Doorman retorted. "We provide an awful lot of good paying jobs in your district."

"So will the new SV-1," Warwick answered smugly. "Between constructing a new assembly plant and hiring all of the people you'll be laying off, it'll be boom time for my constituents."

Doorman's smile vanished. "You've already been in contact with the SV-1 manufacturer?"

"Of course I have," Warwick said as he licked his lips then ran his hand across his mouth. "I could use a drink."

Doorman snapped his finger twice in the direction of his stunning, twenty-something personal aide, Rachel Frey, who was hovering nearby and hanging onto his every word.

"Get the congressman a drink," Doorman barked in the dismissive tone he tended to use when addressing his subordinates.

Tall and curvy, Frey was only a year out of Stanford's MBA program, where she had been at the top of her class. Upon graduation, she had her pick of job offers. Doorman's boss, after seeing her physiological evaluation, had personally recruited her and selected Doorman to be her "Rabbi" and mentor. She smiled knowing now was the moment she would jump from the "Double A" farm club and straight to the big leagues. Soon it would be Doorman fetching coffee for her.

It had only taken Frey a few minutes to figure out the dead spots in the security camera's coverage. After all, this was the officer's mess and not the bridge, so the security wasn't as tight. She opened the oversized bag between her feet and inside were two nearly identical silver flasks. One was wrapped in a red cloth napkin and the other in white. She carefully picked up the flask wrapped in the red napkin, taking care to not actually touch it. Next, still using the napkin, she pulled out a cut crystal highball glass. Pretending to understand her place in the pecking order, she placed the glass and flask on a countertop next to Doorman and not the congressman. As expected, in full view of one the video cameras, Doorman picked up the glass, then with his thumb, flipped the flask open, poured about half of its contents into the cut crystal and passed it along to Congressman Warwick.

The congressman took a gulp which emptied nearly a third of the glass then slowed down to savor the whiskey. "Macallan?"

"Yes. And it is more than twice as old as our Ms. Frey here."

Congressman Warwick took another sip then glanced first at the golden liquid and then at Doorman's attractive young aide. "Both are lovely, but it doesn't help you with the matter at hand."

"You don't have the votes to cancel our contract," Doorman said with more confidence than he actually felt.

Congressman Warwick shrugged. "Not yet, but after today I don't think it will be a problem."

For the first time Doorman was rattled. His only job for the past ten years had been to keep the E-38 cash cow putting cream and butter on the Bathmann Aeronautics table. Now, all of his hard work, scheming and the occasional well-placed bribe was starting to unravel right before his eyes.

"You, of all people, Congressman, know there is nothing more permanent than temporary military spending," Doorman stated calmly as he picked up the flask and refilled the congressman's glass.

"I've always liked you, Brad," the congressman said as he patted Doorman on the shoulder and took another sip of his drink. "Bathmann Aeronautics is out and the new guys are in."

Rachel Frey had a keyring in her hand. When she heard Congressman Warwick's comment, she pushed a button that normally would lock the doors of a car. A moment later, an alarm bell onboard the USS Ronald Reagan began ringing.

Chapter 6

A FEMALE PETTY officer, who was manning a radar station, turned towards the Captain, "Sir, we have an unidentified bogey."

"Range?"

"957 kilometers."

"Could it be a weather anomaly?"

"No, sir," the crewwoman said with a hint of panic in her voice. "The bogey is headed straight at us at Mach twelve."

The Executive Officer slammed a button on his console and an ear splitting bosun's whistle began blaring throughout the USS Ronald Reagan and all of the other support vessels in the area. The XO leaned into a microphone. "General Quarters. General Quarters. All hands, man your battle stations! This is not a drill. Repeat, this is not a drill."

Captain Locke, with the steadiness in his voice which the situation needed, calmly said, "Get the Aegis Weapons online."

"Coming online now," the Weapons Officer answered. "Weapons are hot."

The captain glanced at his Radar Officer. "Where the hell did that thing come from? Sub launched?"

"Unlikely, sir," the Radar Officer answered. "We first picked it up at the top of our range."

"A space-launched weapon?" The captain asked.

"That would be my guess, sir."

"Why didn't the Space Tracking and Surveillance System see this coming?"

"Unknown, sir."

"What's going on, Captain?" Congressman Warwick demanded as he barged on deck followed closely by Bradley Doorman and Rachel Frey.

The captain turned to his XO. "Get these civilians off my bridge."

"Yes, sir."

The Executive Officer motioned toward the door, but the congressman balked.

"Do you know who I am?" the congressman demanded as he put his glass down on a nearby table. His color was awful, and his breath was coming in short puffs. "I'll…" he never finished his sentence as he suddenly gasped and clutched his chest. As his knees buckled, Bradley Doorman caught Warwick and helped him to the floor.

Doorman shouted, "We need a doctor, now!"

In the midst of the confusion and chaos, Rachel Frey used the cloth still in her hand to pick up the congressman's drinking glass. She was careful to not add her fingerprints to the glass or smear the prints of Doorman or the congressman. With her other hand, she pulled a large plastic bag out of her oversized purse, placed the glass inside it then dropped it back into her bag. Next, she did the same thing to the flask Doorman had poured the drink from.

"Launch intercepts," commanded the Captain.

"Captain, whatever it is, it will be here before we can get any planes in the air."

"Get me Lieutenant Morse," said the Captain calmly.

"Online, sir"

"Lieutenant, we have an unidentified object headed toward the Gipper," the Captain said.

"I see it on my tactical screen," said Admiral Henry Morse.

"We don't have time to launch any additional aircraft. We need you to intercept it," Captain Locke said.

"This aircraft is rigged for a training exercise, Captain. We have limited offensive capability," answered Lt. Cassandra Morse.

"We have no idea what we're dealing with here, Lieutenant, and we need eyes on it and you're all we've got," said the Captain.

"Roger that," said Cassandra.

Lt. Morse banked the SV-1 and started to climb. As they broke through the top of the storm clouds, headed directly toward them was a blinding point of light. Even at over 700 kilometers away, the light was so intense Cassandra had to avert her eyes.

Admiral Morse checked his screens. "Bogey is approaching at Mach 12."

"Captain, we have visual," Lt. Morse said calmly. "Activating front camera."

"We see it, Lieutenant," Capt. Locke answered. As they closed the distance, the unidentified object was growing larger and larger.

"Those bastards," Admiral Morse muttered as his eyes were locked on his tactical screen. He tapped one of the instruments. "Captain Locke, have the Reagan and every ship in your battle group fire the heaviest metallic projectiles you've got at that object with the widest possible dispersal. The more metal you can get in the air the better. Then point your bow in the direction of the object and be ready to get hit with a shockwave followed by a potentially tsunami-sized wave."

To his credit, Captain Locke didn't ask any questions, instead simply stated, "Yes sir."

In the distance, for the first time, Cassandra got a clear view of the object. It was crackling with lightning and pulsating like a Tesla plasma ball.

"Cassie, we need to get the hell out of here."

"You know what that thing is?" Cassandra asked.

"Unfortunately, yes," the admiral answered.

"Will it knock us out of the sky?"

"More than likely," the admiral answered calmly.

Cassie shook her head. "We're not going to make it? Are we?"

Admiral Morse reached around the seat and gave his granddaughter's shoulder a squeeze.

She reached back and at the same moment their fingers touched, the first wave of missiles launched from the USS Reagan Battle Group made contact.

The sphere exploded and began to expand until it completely engulfed the SV-1.

Chapter 7

THE BRIDGE OF the USS Ronald Reagan was in night mode. The lights were dimmed and there was only a skeleton crew on deck. The XO was in the Captain's chair when the warning signal chirped. His head whipped around in the direction of the sound. "What have we got?" he asked as the entire staff on the bridge was suddenly wide awake and alert.

"It is a distress beacon, sir," a young seaman, who was so low on the seniority list he had the graveyard shift, answered.

"Location?"

"Twenty-two kilometers off of our starboard bow, sir."

"What?" the XO demanded. "That puts it just outside our defense perimeter."

"Sweet Jesus," the seaman muttered as he rechecked his console.

The XO took two quick strides to the console and his jaw dropped when he read the message on the screen. He flipped back the cover on a button and then slammed it with his fist. Immediately horns began blaring throughout the ship. He picked up the ship wide microphone. "Captain to the bridge. Repeat. Captain to the bridge. Prepare to launch rescue helicopters with medical staff onboard. This is not a drill. Repeat. This is not a drill."

Slowly the Gipper began to light up and through the windows the XO could see sailors starting to scurry around on the flight deck. Captain Locke entered the bridge while still buttoning his shirt.

"What have we got?"

"A distress beacon, sir." The XO's eyes locked on the Captain. "According to the beacon's signature, it belongs to Valkyrie."

"That's impossible," Captain Locke answered. "Valkyrie has been MIA for twenty-two days."

As soon as the heavy ordinance had made contact with the object, it had lost its integrity and released a massive electrical pulse that had knocked out some of the unshielded electronics on the Gipper and its support ships. If much of its power had not been dissipated by the storm, the wave it had created could have been much worse. It was speculated to have had the power of a two-megaton nuclear blast. The USS Ronald Reagan carrier group was far enough away from the epicenter that it only experienced minor damage.

The SV-1 wasn't as lucky.

Within minutes of when the unknown object had made contact with the SV-1, the entire incident had been given top secret classification.

With no trace of the aircraft being found, it was speculated the prototype was vaporized. After three weeks of investigation and one of the largest air/sea search operations in history, nothing, not even a paint chip had been found of the SV-1. There was no debris field. No oil slick. Nothing.

"Are you sure it is Valkyrie?" Locke asked.

"Affirmative, sir," the XO answered as he pointed to the console.

Locke read the screen and shook his head. "I want Lt. Underwood on the rescue helicopter."

"He has already been notified," the XO answered.

Racked with guilt that he should have been with Cassandra Morse on the day of the incident, Underwood had been an eyelash away from turning in his wings. Considering the situation, certain allowances had been made. Because the Navy didn't want to lose him, after the search for Valkyrie had been called off, he had been given a week's leave to spend time with his wife and son and given time to grieve. He had requested to be assigned to the Gipper, and his request had been granted.

The XO pointed out the windows. "Lt. Underwood is on the flight deck, sir." They could see the distinctive lanky lieutenant as he sprinted in the direction of an HH-60H Knight Hawk helicopter.

Chapter 8

UNDERWOOD AND THE medic accompanying the doctor helped the senior flight surgeon, Commander Clifton Johnson, onto the helicopter. Underwood was glad to see that the head of the department was responding and just not one of the staff doctors of the USS Ronald Reagan. Once the doctor and medic were safely onboard, Underwood clambered in behind them. A yeoman handed Underwood a helmet with built-in communications so he could speak and be heard over the engine and rotor's noise. On cue, the twin turboshaft engines began to whine, and the rotors began to turn.

There was a thirty second delay, which seemed like years to Underwood, before the rescue helicopter lifted off the deck. While Underwood wanted to do something, anything, his years of military training had kicked in. He stayed in his seat and let the crew do the jobs they were trained for. He watched a pair of fit men in their late teens or early twenties as they pulled on wetsuits. Next, he watched as a pair of sailors prepared a gurney and checked its complement of first aid supplies.

Underwood closed his eyes and muttered a silent prayer.

"Please, God. Make this a rescue and not a body recovery."

Since the rescue beacon had gone off so close to the Gipper, they had not bothered to close the side door. Glancing through the open space, with the wind whipping in his face, Underwood could see the sun was just starting to come up and the seas were calm.

After about ten minutes of tense silence, Underwood heard a voice in his ear. "Thirty seconds out," said the pilot.

"I have a visual," stated the co-pilot. "Flight raft with…."

Underwood's heart stopped.

"With one person onboard."

The sailors in the wetsuits hooked themselves to the lowering cable and the other crew members moved the gurney closer to the door.

The helicopter slowed and then started to hover over the raft. Underwood looked out the open door.

It was Cassandra.

But she wasn't moving.

His heart sank.

The sailors in the wetsuits were out the door and were descending fast.

Underwood watched as they landed in the water inches from the raft. Not wanting to risk capsizing the small raft, one reached in and put his finger on Cassandra's neck.

"I have a pulse," came a voice in Underwood's ear.

Immediately the doctor and medic Underwood had helped on board began setting up a triage area in the cargo bay.

The gurney vanished through the open door and a lifetime later it began to rise.

When it reached the door again, strapped lifelessly to it was Lt. Cassandra Morse. Her helmet was missing, and her flight suit was covered in soot. The skin on her face was sunburned and her lips were badly chapped. There was dried blood flaked throughout her hair.

The medic instantly began cutting off her flight suit with razor sharp scissors, while the doctor checked her heart rate with his stethoscope. Knowing everything he would say would be recorded, he began his examination. "Good pulse rate. Breathing thready. The subject presents signs of head trauma and appears to be severely dehydrated."

The medic attached a blood pressure cup. "Pressure 95 over 58. Pulse 57," he announced.

The doctor lifted Cassandra's left eyelid and shined a bright penlight in her eye. He did the same in her right eye. "Subject appears to be suffering from a concussion. Severity unknown." The doctor turned to the medic. "Let's get some fluids back into her."

"Doc?" Underwood asked softly.

The physician ignored him as he continued to check Cassandra for other injuries. "Subject presents with mostly healed, minor contusions to the torso and extremities consistent with injuries inflicted twenty-two days ago. Subject presents no sign of fractures."

"Doc?" Underwood asked again this time with more urgency.

The doctor nodded and Underwood moved closer to Cassandra and held her hand. Next, the doctor turned his head in the direction of the front of the helicopter. "Do we have sufficient fuel to reach the University of Southern California Medical Center?"

"Yes, sir," the pilot answered.

"Take us there and please inform the ER that we're en route with a head trauma patient and we will need Dr. Daniel Newman available when we arrive."

"Normal protocol calls for us to go to the VA," the pilot answered.

"This is anything but normal."

"Sir?"

"Do you know who this is?"

"No, sir," the pilot answered.

"We have Valkyrie onboard."

"Roger that," the pilot answered crisply.

One of their own.

The helicopter immediately banked into a new heading then its nose dropped as it began to accelerate to its top speed. A few moments later the pilot said, "The FAA is clearing the airspace for us and we'll be coming in hot. ETA is twenty-six minutes."

At supersonic speed he saw them before he heard them. Four F/A F-18 E Super Hornets were closing fast. They roared past the helicopter, each tipping its wing in a salute as they went by. An instant later the helicopter was hit with multiple sonic booms.

"What the hell?" the medic muttered.

At the familiar sound of the war birds, Cassandra stirred for the first time. It wasn't much, she just shifted her weight slightly then gave Underwood's hand a gentle squeeze.

Then they heard a new voice in their headsets. "Underdog, this is Bronco."

"This is Underdog," Lt. Max Underwood answered.

"Compliments of Captain Locke. We're here to escort Valkyrie to Los Angeles. Our orders are anything short of Air Force One gets in the way we persuade them to be elsewhere."

"Roger that."

"Status?" Bronco asked softly.

Underwood looked in the direction of the flight surgeon.

"From the neck down from a preliminary examination she appears fine." The doctor glanced over at Cassandra as the medic was tucking a blanket around her naked body. "She has suffered head trauma which exceeds our facilities on the Reagan so we're taking her directly to the USC Medical Center." The doctor patted Underwood on the knee. "Dr. Newman is the best in the business."

Chapter 9

CASSANDRA'S EYES FLUTTERED open and she touched her heavily bandaged head. She blinked a few times and looked around as she tried to reorient herself.

She was in a bed.

Looking behind her she saw a bank of machines making odd sounds. Lifting her left arm, she saw an IV attached in her forearm.

Hospital.

Not her favorite place in the world, but better than the alternative.

From the dim lighting, and seeing the rosy glow through the window and the quiet surroundings, she concluded it was early morning; just before sunrise.

Next, she took a personal inventory. Her mouth was dry, her head was throbbing, and she felt like every muscle in her body was knotted. When she shifted slightly to try to relieve a cramp in her back, she felt a pain in her groin.

Catheter.

"Lovely," she thought.

"You look awful," said a familiar voice.

A smile broke across Cassandra's face as she saw her grandfather in his full-dress blue uniform. He was unscathed.

Cassandra tried to speak but her mouth and throat were too parched to form words or even sounds.

"Don't try to talk," the admiral said. "You're probably wondering what happened."

Cassandra tried to clear her throat without any success as she nodded her head.

"As I suspected we were hit with an old Star Wars weapon called 'Icarus'."

Cassandra motioned for him to continue.

"It was basically an array of solar cells that over time fed into capacitors that could discharge their energy all at once." The admiral chuckled. "While it looked impressive, it was a classic DOD boondoggle. Contact with anything metallic would cause the integrity of the sphere to disintegrate and turn it into nothing more than a powerful and noisy light show." The admiral shook his head. "A twenty billion dollar weapon that could only fire once without a thirty-day solar recharge. Then it could easily be defeated by a single surface to air missile." The admiral shook his head again. "Typical Bathmann Aeronautics Bravo Sierra."

"But," Cassandra croaked.

"But," the admiral continued with a smile. "It was able to take out the SV-1." The admiral's eyes twinkled. "Which begs the question. If it couldn't do much damage to the Gipper, why launch it to begin with?" A master of the Socratic Method, the admiral's eyes locked on her as he gave her a moment to process his question.

Cassandra closed her eyes and rubbed her forehead. It hurt to try to think.

Then it hit her.

"Crap," she said softly.

"Exactly," the admiral answered. "While the Reagan could absorb a blast from the Icarus device with minimal damage, at close range, the SV-1 never stood a chance." The admiral smiled. "The SV-1, and by extension you and I, were the target."

Cassandra tried to slide up further on the bed but in the process dislodged one of the electrodes wired to her body. Immediately one of the monitors on the wall behind her began to beep.

A nurse started to enter the room but pulled up short in the doorway when she saw Cassandra was awake.

"Welcome back, Sleeping Beauty," she said as she reached under Cassandra's hospital gown and reattached the electrode.

"How..." Cassandra tried to ask but her vocal cords were still uncooperative.

"Let me get you some water," the nurse said as she grabbed an empty pitcher and carried it over to the sink.

Cassandra smiled. She guessed there was no reason to have water standing by when a patient was unconscious.

The nurse filled a cup and inserted a flexible straw then held it next to Cassandra's lips. Cassandra took a sip and she felt her entire body relax. She had never tasted anything that wonderful before. As she leaned forward for more, the nurse pulled the cup away. "Let's start off slow, okay?" She put the cup on the bedside table and headed back out of the room. "Dr. Newman is doing his pre-surgical rounds. I'll let him know you're back amongst us and get you some ice chips."

The admiral smiled down at his granddaughter. "I'm afraid you're going to be in for a rough patch. The smart play will be to claim you don't remember anything."

"I don't," she answered.

"Perfect."

The admiral took a step back as Dr. Daniel Newman entered the room. The doctor ignored the admiral and focused exclusively on Cassandra.

The doctor was a serious man in his late forties with a receding hairline balanced by his progressing waistline. His quick gray eyes took in Cassandra and he leaned across the bed. "I'm Dr. Newman. I'm the neurologist who has been treating you for your head injuries," he said as he shined a light in her eyes. "What's the last thing you remember?" he asked.

"A blinding flash of light and then waking up here," Cassandra said.

"What's your name?" asked the doctor.

"Lt. Cassandra Jean Morse. Why?" she asked.

"You experienced some severe head trauma, and we want to be sure it hasn't affected your cognitive or motor skills." He flipped back the end of the blanket and took her pulse in her ankles, first left then right. He had the soft hands of a surgeon. He ran a finger along the bottom of Cassandra's foot which caused a reaction.

"That tickles."

"Excellent," Dr. Newman said in a flat, professional tone. "Wiggle your toes."

Cassandra complied.

"Now your fingers."

Cassandra rolled her eyes and shook her head. "Is this really necessary?"

"Yes." Newman answered flatly. "We're going to raise the head of the bed." When the bed reached about a 45-degree angle it stopped rising. Cassandra was too low in the bed and was now at an awkward angle. The doctor glanced at the nurse who went to the other side of the bed and, with the doctor still on his side, they lifted her into a more comfortable position.

"How long have I been here?"

"You came in yesterday," Newman answered.

"How long was I in the water?"

"They claim for twenty-two days."

"What?" Cassandra shook her head. "How is that possible?"

"We were hoping you might be able to help us with that question."

Cassandra Morse glanced in the direction of her grandfather. "I don't remember anything." The admiral gave her a double thumbs-up.

"What day of the week is it?" asked the doctor.

"If I was at sea for twenty-two days and here for one day, then it is Thursday," Cassandra answered.

For the first time Dr. Newman showed the slightest flicker of emotion as he let a smile form on his face, and he patted Cassandra on the knee. "Excellent. Remarkable actually."

Cassandra looked around the room and could not locate her grandfather. "Where's the admiral?"

"Your father has been informed you're awake and…"

"Not my father. My grandfather."

The smile vanished from Dr. Newman's face. "Your grandfather?"

Cassandra leaned to the side to look around the doctor for her grandfather. "Yes. I was just talking to him."

"You saw and spoke to Admiral Henry Morse? Here, in this room?" asked the doctor with a concerned expression on his face.

"Yes. Where did he go?"

Dr. Newman turned to the nurse. "I want an MRI scheduled ASAP."

The nurse immediately turned and left the room.

"What's going on?" asked Cassandra. "Where's my grandfather?"

"Lieutenant," Dr. Newman answered gravely, "I'm sorry to have to inform you but your grandfather is still missing and is considered to be MIA."

Chapter 10

THE NIGHTMARE HAD started almost immediately after Dr. Newman had completed her MRI. Within hours, a naval doctor had shown up. Since she was conscious, stable, and ambulatory, he had insisted Cassandra be transferred to the Los Angeles VA hospital. Dr. Newman had balked, but the decision was up to Lt. Morse. Other than a serious headache and massive body tightness and cramping, Cassandra was itching to get back in the game. Over Dr. Newman's strong objection, she agreed to the transfer.

Big mistake.

It didn't take her long to figure out what she had done wrong in her initial debriefing by an NCIS field agent. Instead of following her grandfather's advice and claiming she didn't remember anything, she casually mentioned the word "Icarus".

Within an hour after she had uttered that word, she had been transferred from the rehab ward to a private room and a guard had been placed outside her door. Whenever anyone entered the room, the guard would accompany them. The only visitors she was allowed were family members and she got the distinct impression that if her daddy hadn't had Admiral stars on his shoulder, he wouldn't have gotten in either.

The first visit from her father had been a grim affair. They had barely spoken since Cassandra's mother's funeral. After a tense five-minute chat, he left and said he would be back after he had been briefed on what was going on.

After her father's visit, things got even uglier. There seemed to be an added sense of urgency to the questioning. Since it was already on record that she had seen and spoken to her grandfather, a series of increasingly more aggressive interrogators had questioned her. Since she had stated that her grandfather had visited her in her hospital room, they wanted to know where to find him. When she said she had no idea where he was, they didn't believe her.

The wheels began to completely come off when they grilled her about her knowledge of Icarus. When she stated she first learned the name from her grandfather after regaining consciousness in her hospital room, all she got was a frown and an eye roll from her interrogator.

"I don't think you realize exactly how much trouble you're in, Lieutenant," the interrogator stated flatly.

Cassandra eyes locked on the man. He was probably closer to sixty than fifty. He seldom blinked and his face showed no emotion. He looked like he would be no fun to be sitting across from at a poker table.

"So far, I've been interviewed by a Field Agent, then a Senior Field Agent, then the Special Agent in Charge of the San Diego office. Now across from me is Melvin P. Johnston, Assistant Director of NCIS." Cassandra's eyes narrowed. "Should I be expecting Leroy Jethro Gibbs or the SECNAV later today?"

"Look," he started to say until he heard a tap on the door and turned his head as it was starting to open. "I gave instructions that I was not to be…" He stopped dead when he saw Admiral Hank Morse striding through the door in his dress blue uniform. Among the cluster on his chest was a ribbon for the Navy Cross, a Purple Heart, and a Silver star. Behind him was a fierce looking female Lt. Commander with salt and pepper hair, also dressed in blues, who appeared to be around forty.

She stepped past Admiral Morse and barked, "This interview is over."

Cassandra swallowed her smile. Despite their recent differences, she had to admit, her father knew how to make an entrance.

The Assistant Director of NCIS chuckled. "Been expecting you." He nodded first at Admiral Morse, "Hank". Then at the Lt. Commander, "Sandy".

"You want to give us the room, Mel?"

Assistant Director Johnston, rose to his feet, held his hands up in mock surrender and left the room without protest.

The Lt. Commander extended her hand in Cassandra's direction. Her grip was strong and dry. "I'm Lt. Commander Sandra Sutton…"

"JAG Corps," Cassandra finished for her.

"Correct."

"Do I need a lawyer?"

"I'm afraid you do," she answered as she sat down in the seat recently vacated by the Assistant Director. "The Navy has a pretty compelling case against you."

Lt. Cassandra Morse pulled back in disbelief. "On what charges?"

"Espionage, treason…"

"What?"

"How and when did you first hear about the Icarus Project?"

"When my grandfather visited me in my hospital room at the USC Medical Center after I regained consciousness."

"And that's the problem," said Sutton.

"Why?" Cassandra demanded.

"You have working knowledge of an eyes-only DOD project."

"Yes."

"You know, of course, The USS Ronald Reagan has more powerful communication equipment than the SV-1. They track and record pretty much everything that is broadcasted on or around the ship."

"Of course."

"While you could not hear them during the attack, they could hear and record everything you and your grandfather said," Lt. Commander Sutton added.

"Okay."

"Your grandfather, Admiral Henry Morse, made no mention of the Icarus project while you were in flight."

"I've already stipulated that in my statements and interviews."

"Yes. Which means you either already knew about Icarus before the flight or learned about it later."

"And? I've stated I learned about it from my grandfather after the encounter."

Sutton sighed. "You claim he was in your room in dress blues?"

"Yes."

"If an admiral in his dress uniform marched into a civilian hospital don't you think someone would have noticed him?"

"Probably, but it was pre-dawn."

"The Navy has interviewed everyone who was on duty at the hospital the morning you regained consciousness and none of them remember seeing your grandfather. Including the doctor and nurse who were in the room with you when you claim he was there. Also," Sutton continued, "there are cameras all over the hospital, including one which shows the door to your room at the USC Medical Center. There are no videos of Admiral Morse entering or exiting the building and no video evidence of him ever walking through the door to your room."

Cassandra shook her head as the reality of her situation began to dawn on her. Her grandfather's visit had just been a hallucination. She leaned back as she felt a cold chill go down her spine. "What am I up against?" she asked firmly, an analytical edge to her voice.

"The Navy believes you had prior knowledge of the Icarus Project and possibly were involved in the assault on the USS Ronald Reagan."

"That's absurd," Cassandra protested as she felt her blood pressure rising. "What would be my motive?"

Lt. Commander Sutton shrugged and opened her briefcase. She pulled out a document and handed it to Cassandra.

Cassandra's eyes and mouth both flew open. "Resign my commission!"

For the first time, her father spoke. "Your navy career is over, Cassie," he said softly. "Even if you fight this and win, they will never let you fly another aircraft again and you'll top out at Lt. Commander; maybe even where you are now. Then they will try to run you out of the Navy by giving you the worst assignments they can possibly come up with."

"Ah," Cassandra said softly. "That explains the urgency of the interrogation." She nodded her head as she had a moment of clarity. "The Navy was trying to get as much information as possible so they would have the maximum leverage to make me go away without a fight before you made the notification." Cassandra's eyes locked on her father's. "Well? What are you waiting for?" she asked. "Make the notification."

Admiral Morse glanced at Lt. Commander Sutton then sighed. "They've found your grandfather," he said softly. "His body was recovered by a fishing boat this morning and has been positively identified."

For only the second time in her life and the first time since her mother's funeral, Cassandra Morse felt tears forming in her eyes, but she fought them back. "He went down fighting," she said softly.

"Yes, he did," her father answered as he started in her direction to give her a hug but halfway there, he decided against it. "He had been in the water since your crash, so it is impossible you saw him in your room."

"With the severity of your head injuries," Sutton added, "we could plead you were hallucinating but that would not explain your knowledge of the Icarus Project. With your sworn statements already on the record," Sutton continued, "they have you by the short hairs." Sutton sighed. "Fortunately, the Navy simply wants this to go away with as little publicity as possible."

"Take the deal, Cassie," her father said. "It will be an honorable discharge and you will get military medical retirement and pension."

"Or," Cassandra said as she glared at her father.

Lt. Commander Sutton answered for him. "Or. You spend years in a high-profile court martial proceeding which you are very unlikely to win. Then spend the rest of your life at the Naval Consolidated Brig in Charleston."

"The Navy has been in CYA mode since the Reagan incident," her father added.

Cassandra snorted. "And, since they thought they had seen the last of me, I was the perfect scapegoat."

"Unfortunately for you, yes," Sutton answered. "They have their story and they're sticking to it. Your knowledge of Icarus gives them the perfect tool to discredit you, but they prefer to not use it."

"If I go quietly, they'll buy me off and leave me in peace. If I fight it, I'll go to prison for likely the rest of my life?"

"That's pretty much it," Sutton answered.

***

Two days later, Lt. Cassandra Morse, along with the President of the United States, six cabinet secretaries and every member of the Joint

Chief of Staffs were at Arlington Cemetery. Among the well-wishers, along with her father, were a handful of cousins she barely knew and a great-uncle, William Comstock, who was the admiral's brother-in-law. She had met Comstock a few times previously at family functions and thought he was a charming kook and never understood why the admiral had always liked him.

When she got back to her bedroom in her father's house, with tears in her eyes, she placed the folded flag the honor guard had given her on the dresser. Next, she hung her full-dress blue uniform in her old closet next to her dress white uniform, an old flight jacket, ancient prom dresses, and musky civilian clothes that had been there since before her Annapolis days.

She straightened a wrinkle out of her uniform's sleeve and squared it up on its hanger.

She knew she would never wear it again.

That night she had her first dream.

6 Months Later

Chapter 11

THE FILE TITLED "Valkyrie" had been so inactive, Tom McMahon, a middle manager of one of the security divisions of Bathmann Aeronautics, had to open it and read the summary to refresh his memory. He shrugged, yawned, and queued up the video Levy had sent.

He was less than impressed.

The interplay between Valkyrie and the man looked to be pretty harmless and the audio was worthless. If he had to guess, it was some tourist who had wandered into the wrong place and had been chased off by the homeowner.

He quickly flipped through the still photos and picked the best one. He entered the image into the facial recognition database and clicked a few buttons.

He yawned again, leaned back in his chair and intertwined his fingers behind his head. The FR software was much better than it had been even a few years ago, but if someone wasn't in the system, then it could take a while to get name or it could come up empty.

He felt his eyes starting to close when the facial recognition program beeped.

"That was quick," he said as he felt his pulse quicken. To get that kind of response time the person had to have been in the Bathmann Aeronautics "Search First" files as either an employee, past or present, or a person of interest to the company. "Crap," he muttered when he saw the name pop up with a 97% certainty rating. He reached for his phone. Any thought of napping had completely vanished.

"Ms. Frey's office."

"This is McMahon. Is she available?"

"I'm sorry. She's in a meeting with the CEO."

"We just got a facial recognition hit which is less than an hour old on Dr. Tanner Dawson visiting one of the people we have under surveillance."

"Hold."

Less than thirty seconds later, Rachel Frey, recently named Senior VP of Bathmann Aeronautics, was on the line. "Location?" she asked abruptly.

"Venice Beach, California."

"Venice Beach," Frey said with a hint of panic in her voice. "Did he make contact with Valkyrie?"

"Yes, ma'am."

"Shit. What assets do we have in place?"

"None currently in Los Angeles, but six in San Diego."

"Put them all on a helicopter."

"Yes, ma'am," McMahon answered.

"Move this to the top of your list. I want Dawson found."

"What about Valkyrie?"

"Take her to Level Two surveillance and I want a complete dossier on everything she has done for the past six months on my desk within the hour."

"I'll have my team in the air and in place by mid-afternoon local time."

The line went dead.

Tom McMahon drew in a lung full of air through his nose and slowly released it through his mouth. Former Special Forces and two tours in Afghanistan, few things in this world scared him, but one of them was Rachel Frey. He had done a preliminary background check on her when she was still at Stanford. Clinical sociopath with an IQ of over 160. She was exactly the kind of person Bathmann Aeronautics liked to recruit. In an organization built by backstabbing ladder climbers, never in his wildest dreams did he see this coming. In her first five hundred days, she had gone from trainee to number three in a company that had over 200,000 employees worldwide. The vivisection she performed on Bradley Doorman, who, up until the moment he had taken Frey as his assistant, was one of the most feared men in the company, was already the stuff of legends. Doorman's swift downfall was the subject of much wild speculation around the company watercooler. It had ranged from child porn on his computer to Frey having photos of him having carnal knowledge with a farm animal. One day after the events on the USS Ronald Reagan, Doorman had gone from being king of his domain to "retired" to his Villa on Lake Como and Frey was sitting behind his desk. No one, other than the CEO, the board of directors and possibly the president of Bathmann knew what she had on him or how she had used it. Whatever it was, the way she had delivered the shive in the back to Doorman, the only two people above her on the organizational flow chart had both hired food tasters.

After making the necessary calls to reallocate assets, considering Rachel Frey had personally requested the six-month report of Valkyrie, McMahon decided to do it himself. He had a feeling the fewer people in the loop on this one, the better.

McMahon squared himself in front of his keyboard and started with a Google search for "Cassandra Morse." At the top of the list was the article from this morning's *Los Angeles Guardian*. He closed his eyes and rubbed his forehead with the heel of his hand. "Damn."

McMahon forwarded the link to Frey's phone. Even if she was in a meeting with the CEO and others, she would want to see this.

Less than ten seconds later, she replied.

"My office. Now."

Chapter 12

CASSANDRA MORSE GLARED at her cell phone as she took another healthy swig from her oversized mug of dark, espresso grade coffee. Cassandra had learned there was nothing like industrial strength caffeine to keep the dreams away. "What the hell," she said to herself as she finished her drink and opened her desk drawer. She fumbled around for a few moments before she found what she was looking for. Picking up her mobile, she dialed the phone number on the card.

"Newman," the doctor answered crisply

"Hello Dr. Newman," she replied. "You may not remember me. This is Cassandra Morse."

"Yes, Lieutenant, what can I do for you?"

"It's just Cassandra now. I'm no longer in the Navy."

There was a short pause. "I see. What can I do for you?"

"I just have a few questions." She hesitated. "Do you remember my case?"

"Of course," Newman answered with a chuckle. "It is not every day we get an unconscious combat pilot delivered to our door."

"Other than the head injury, what kind of condition would you say I was in when I arrived at your hospital?"

Another pause. "I'm not sure I understand the question," Dr. Newman answered guardedly.

"Did you see the *Los Angeles Guardian* this morning?"

Newman glanced at the corner of his desk. "No, but I have a copy handy. Why?"

"Look at the front page." Cassandra heard the pages rustling then silence as Newman read the story.

"Oh, my," Newman said with sudden interest. "How long have you been having these dreams."

"Ever since the incident."

"I would like to see you again Lieutenant, sorry Ms. Morse."

"First, let me ask you some questions," she answered.

"Okay, but it would be easier if you would just…"

"Did they tell you I had been adrift at sea for twenty-two days before you saw me?" Cassandra asked.

"Funny you should ask that. It was going to be my first question for you."

"Excuse me?" Cassandra answered, suddenly off balance.

"When they told me that you had been at sea for that long, I didn't believe them."

"Really," Cassandra said as she leaned forward. "Why do you say that?"

"We get our fair share of people who have been transported here by the Coast Guard after their boats have capsized or become disabled," Newman answered. "You presented no indications of extreme dehydration or malnutrition. In fact, I don't even recall you having much more than a nasty sunburn on your face."

"I understand. I was still in my flight suit when I was found. Would that make a difference?"

"Some, but not nearly enough," Newman answered. "Have you ever heard of the rule of three?"

"I don't believe so."

"A person can go three minutes without air, three days without water and three weeks without food and survive." Newman paused again. "I told the investigator there was no way in hell you had been unconscious and adrift for over three weeks without water."

"You told them that?"

"I did, but they said they would need a second opinion from a Navy physician."

"What was the second opinion?"

"Unknown," Newman answered. "I never heard from them again after you were transferred."

"Interesting."

Cassandra's mind was now working at warp speed.

Why had the Navy withheld that information from me and, more importantly, from my lawyer? Was that the bomb they were going to drop on me if my case ever went to a court-martial? Damn. There would be no rational explanation to explain why I was still alive unless I had staged the entire event and stayed hidden for three weeks. No wonder they were so confident, they had me in a box.

"Are you still there?"

"Sorry," Cassandra answered. "Processing new information."

"I understand," Newman answered. "I would really like to get you in today if possible…"

Cassandra cut him off. "How difficult would it be to pull up my X-Rays?" Cassandra asked.

"Not difficult at all. Everything is digital these days," Newman answered. "Let me put you on speaker."

Dr. Newman pushed a button on his phone then pulled his keyboard closer. His fingers danced across the screen until an image of a skull X-Ray appeared on his oversized HD monitor.

"What am I looking for?"

"Check the area directly above my left ear, on the side of my head near the crown," Cassandra said.

Dr. Newman enlarged that area of the X-Ray. Leaned in, centered a spot then enlarged it even further.

"I'll be damned. I never would have seen that unless I knew exactly where to look," he said.

"What is it?" asked Cassandra.

"Someone… Someone very skilled, drilled a tiny hole in your skull."

"What! Why?"

"The hole is much smaller than the kind we drill to relieve pressure on the brain from an epidural hematoma, so it had nothing to do with your trauma. It looks like the kind used in deep brain stimulation to insert electrodes in Parkinson's patients," Dr. Newman said.

"You're saying someone inserted an electrode into my brain?"

"No. That would have shown up on your MRI. They may have injected something or given you an electrical charge. That would certainly go a long way toward explaining your unusual MRI results.

I've been a neurologist for twenty years and I've never seen anything like them before."

"What was so different?"

"There were sections of your brain firing that were usually mostly dormant and in patterns I had never seen before."

"What type of injection or stimulation would cause this?" asked Cassandra.

"Unknown, but I'd love to help you find out."

"Could this be what is causing my dreams?"

"Again, unknown," Dr. Newman answered. "But, possibly..." After a brief pause, while Dr. Newman continued studying the X-Ray, he muttered, "That's interesting."

"What?"

"Knowing what I know now, I would say someone gave you that blow to the head to cover their tracks. The impact was fairly superficial and never would have put you in an extended coma."

Cassandra heard the doctor shuffling paper. "That's unfortunate. We didn't run a tox screen."

"Is that relevant?"

"Based on this new information, definitely," Newman said. "You may not have been knocked unconscious when you arrived here. You might have been drugged."

"Are you saying someone held me captive and kept me drugged for over three weeks while they were messing with my brain?"

"I have no idea what I'm saying, but I would love to help you get to the bottom of this," Newman answered. "I'll clear my schedule and see you as soon as you can get here."

"Thank you, doctor," Cassandra answered with a shaky voice. "I need to process all of this. I'll make an appointment."

"Wait..." said Dr. Newman, but Cassandra, her hands quivering, pushed the end call button on her cell phone.

The phone rang a few seconds later. It was Dr. Newman. She hit the "ignore" button then turned off her phone.

Cassandra glanced at the ghost of her grandfather who was lounging in the chair nearby. "Did you know anything about this?"

The Admiral, who was dressed in cargo shorts, flip-flops and a Tommy Bahama shirt just shrugged and smiled.

"God!" Cassandra said with disgust. "Do you always have to be so damn enigmatic? Why can't I ever get a straight answer out of you?"

She tested her coffee, and it was now tepid; so she finished it in one gulp. She walked over to the coffee maker and tried to refill her mug from her thermal carafe. What came out was about two ounces of muck that looked closer to something you would use to repair a crack in a blacktop driveway rather than something to drink. Sighing she dumped the sludge down the kitchen drain, rinsed out the mug and carafe, and began another round of her coffee ritual. Before she had the grinder loaded with espresso beans, the front doorbell rang.

Cassandra rolled her eyes.

The odd little man had been a harbinger of things to come. Since his visit, a steady stream of reporters had been showing up unannounced and uninvited on her front stoop. Jacked up on caffeine, she had reached her limit.

"Cassandra," the admiral warned. "Don't do anything you'll regret."

She ignored him and strode purposely toward the front door. She picked up her Louisville slugger thirty-four-ounce bat in her right hand and jerked the door open with her left.

"What?" she demanded.

Instead of a reporter, her startled great-uncle, William Comstock, was standing on her front porch with a bouquet of lavender hydrangeas in his hand. He looked at the bat ready to strike and laughed.

"Did we come at a bad time?"

Cassandra leaned the bat by the front door and gave the old man a hug. "Sorry, Uncle Billy," she said. "Reporters have been driving me crazy."

"I can imagine," he answered as he extended the bouquet in her direction. "These are from my garden."

Other than growing older and a bit plumper, Cassandra's great-uncle hadn't changed much in the nearly thirty years she had known him. If Hollywood ever needed an aging college professor for a movie, he was a central casting dream. He would fit the part perfectly without the need of makeup or wardrobe. He still had a plentiful head of hair, which was now pure white and always askew. Cassandra could never remember seeing him when he wasn't wearing a tweed jacket with elbow patches and a floral bowtie.

She accepted the flowers, then looked at the man accompanying her uncle. He was around her age, rail thin and had a scruffy beard. He had a dark, serious expression on his face and looked like he hadn't smiled since Y2K.

"I'm sorry," Uncle Billy said. "This is Jeffery Nelson. He's a grad student and a true humanitarian," Comstock said with a laugh. "He selflessly protects the citizenry of Southern California from my diminishing driving skills." Comstock winked at Cassandra. "The fact that I'm his doctoral dissertation sponsor and he is a member of the inner-circle of my foundation may also contribute to his willingness to chauffeur me around."

"Pleased to meet you," Nelson said with a warm and engaging smile as he extended his hand. Cassandra found his grip to be both firm and confident, but something about him made her feel uneasy which was odd. She shrugged. She had a feeling if she had met him at Benny's near last call instead of when he was tagging along with her uncle, she might have had a much different reaction.

She motioned for them to step inside.

Comstock looked around the foyer with an odd expression on his face. "Your grandmother and I grew up in this house," he said with a wistful tone in his voice.

"As did my father," Cassandra added.

"I see you haven't changed much."

Cassandra smiled. Other than two burnt out light bulbs and fresh linen on her bed, she hadn't changed anything since she had moved in.

"Let's get these in some water," she said as they headed toward the kitchen. As they passed through the living room, the admiral, who was sitting in his usual chair, pressed his index finger to his lips. Since she was the only one who could see and hear him, she really didn't need to be reminded not to start a conversation when she had company.

"What brings you all the way out here?" Cassandra asked, even though she already knew the answer. He had seen the story in the *Guardian*.

"What? A man can't drop in on his niece without raising eyebrows?" he asked with a smile.

"You live in Santa Barbara, Uncle Billy," Cassandra said with a chuckle. "A two-hundred-mile round trip in California traffic hardly qualifies as 'dropping in'."

Then he motioned in Jeffery's direction. "We had to get our boat ready for this weekend's protest at Diablo Canyon."

"If I remember correctly, you dock your boat at the Morro Bay Marina which is in the opposite direction of Los Angeles from Santa Barbara."

"You got me," Comstock said with a mischievous grin. "We're down here trying to get some publicity for our next protest."

"You'll never give up, will you?" Cassandra said as she shook her head.

"No," Uncle Billy answered.

"I've never understood why a marine scientist like you has had such animosity towards Diablo Canyon."

"It draws in 2.5 billion gallons of seawater every day to cool its damn nuclear reactors. A few years ago, they had to shut down because a simple kelp infestation clogged their intake screens."

Cassandra pointed at Comstock. "I remember that," she said. "I also remember my grandfather convinced them to let you help fix the problem."

"I did feel a bit like I was sleeping with the enemy," Comstock said with a laugh. "I want it to shut down, not melt down."

"It's just a disaster just waiting to happen," Jeffery said with a hint of sadness in his voice.

"How so?" Cassandra asked.

"It's near three different earthquake fault lines," Jeffery answered. "If any one of them were to hit, it could make the Japanese nuclear accident look like a summer picnic."

Comstock patted Jeffery on the shoulder. "My young protégé here is a bit passionate about nuclear power. The good news is, they are already planning to decommission Diablo Canyon."

"Then spend decades and billions of dollars trying to clean up the site," Jeffery added bitterly. "It never ends when it comes to nuclear power."

"Now, now, Jeffery. Let's take our victories when we can," Comstock said and grinned at Cassandra. "Since they announced the decommission of Diablo Canyon, it has been tough to get anyone interested in shutting it down sooner, so our little weekend protest lacks the numbers we used to generate."

"Then why still do it?"

"I'll look for any excuse to get the Minnow out on the open sea, plus we need to run some tests."

"Tests on what?" Cassandra asked.

"I thought you'd never ask." He pulled a small plastic bag out of his pocket. "We've developed a revolutionary solution to cleaning up the oceans." Comstock was beaming. "Our foundation just got the patent on this."

"What is it?" Cassandra asked as she looked at the bag that had a dozen pea-sized white balls inside.

"Let me show you," Comstock said as he headed toward the kitchen. He pulled a bowl off the shelf and filled it half-full of water. Next, he dropped one of the balls in the water. Immediately the pebble began to expand. It absorbed most of the water in the dish and took the shape of a white rubber duckie.

Now it was Cassandra's turn to chuckle. "Boy, that's impressive. Do you have any sea monkeys?"

Comstock held up a finger. "Watch this." Comstock poured some cooking oil in the bowl and moved the rubber duckie around. The duckie began to absorb the oil and release the water back into the dish. The duckie also began to change color. In a few moments the sheen of oil on the top of the water in the saucer was gone. "The ducks absorb oil, and when they've reached capacity, they turn black. You just sweep them up and keep adding more ducks until all of the oil is absorbed."

"Amazing," Cassandra said.

"They'll absorb close to one hundred times their compressed weight in oil. A single fifty-five-gallon drum of these could soak up a nearly 5,000-gallon oil spill. Since they take up next to no space, we expect them to be mandatory on all ships in a few years."

"That should make you rich," Cassandra said.

"I'm already rich," Comstock answered. "All of the proceeds will go to my foundation." Comstock patted his assistant on the shoulder. "I couldn't have done it without Jeffery." Then he turned serious. "How are you doing?"

Cassandra shrugged but didn't answer as her mood darkened.

"We're all worried about you."

"All?" Cassandra asked as she bristled. "Have you been talking to my father?"

Comstock smiled and patted her on the arm. "He might have asked if I would look in on you," he said sweetly.

"Uncle Billy," Cassandra said firmly. "You really don't want to get in the middle of my father and I."

"Cassie," Comstock started to say, but Cassandra cut him off.

"You can tell my father I'm fine."

"He's very concerned about you, Cassie."

Cassandra began ushering her great-uncle and his wingman back toward the foyer.

"I'm sure he is," she said as she opened the front door for Comstock. "Thank you for the beautiful flowers." She extended her hand to Jeffery who quickly accepted it. "Nice meeting you."

William Comstock sighed and knew he was fighting a losing battle. He gave Cassandra a peck on the cheek as she stepped onto the porch. "If you need anything…"

"I know," Cassandra said. "And I appreciate your concern."

She closed the door and leaned her back against it and closed her eyes. "Shit," she muttered. Pushing off the door, she headed back to the kitchen.

As she passed through the living room to the kitchen, she glared at the admiral. Cassandra plucked one of the hydrangea blooms from the bowl and immediately returned to the porch and put the blossom on her mailbox.

As she returned to the living room, she pointed a warning finger at the admiral. "Not one word."

The admiral pretended he was locking his lips together then he tossed the imaginary key over his shoulder.

Chapter 13

THE CLOCK ON the wall was approaching 2 a.m. The crowd at Benny's Bar and Grill, on a side street just off of Venice Beach, had thinned to only a handful of the hardcore regulars. Cassandra was sitting at her usual spot on the last stool at the end of the heavy weathered-oak bar. She had her back to the wall and could see both the front door and the kitchen door. Old combat habits die hard. She knew pretty much everyone there by sight if not name. With marijuana now legal in California and many other states, the Great American Barfly was on the endangered species list. Cassandra was the youngest person in the room still bending an elbow. In another twenty years, when all of the regulars had either died off or moved to nursing homes, she doubted if there would be many corner dives like this place left.

Benny, a Vietnam era Gunnery Sergeant, had taken an immediate shine to Cassandra. He recognized her as ex-military before she had even reached a bar stool on her first visit. He, along with three of his Vietnam war buddies, had bought this place in 1974. Since the other partners had real jobs and Benny would be the one handling the day-to-day operations, they decided to call it Benny's. He had outlived all of his partners and now owned the business, the building and the land. He had a standing high-seven-figure offer for the place with a buyer willing to write him a check for cash whenever he was ready. Benny had lived in the second-floor apartment for nearly fifty years. With no wife, no kids and no place better to go, he figured he would leave feet first.

While in his early seventies, Benny was still a tough old bird. He could clear troublemakers out of his bar better and faster than most bouncers a third of his age. Benny's didn't make any efforts to appeal to the tourist crowd. He catered to his loyal, local crowd and made just enough to keep the doors open and the lights on.

Cassandra had five swizzle sticks next to her glass on the cocktail napkin under her drink. As her evenings progressed, she liked to hang on to them so she could keep track of how many drinks she had consumed. From experience, she had discovered, after the third or fourth round that her math skills would decline and she would start to lose count.

After the events of the day, simply getting pass out drunk wasn't enough. She was feeling the itch for a bit of male companionship. But, because it was late and a weeknight and not a weekend, there were limited prospects. First was a guy named Mel. He was older than Benny, needed a new liver and had a bad ticker. She figured an hour with her in the sack would probably send him off to that great distillery in the sky but at least he would have a smile on his face. The other was Donnie. He was forty-five but looked closer to eighty. He was at least double her weight, the only exercise he appeared to have gotten in the past few decades was by doing twelve-ounce arm curls with a can of Bud Light. Donnie had hit on Cassandra for the first month or so after she started showing up. After crashing and burning over fifty times, he had finally given up and left her alone.

Cassandra counted her stack of swizzle sticks. A girl has to know her limitations. Her goal tonight was pretty much the same as every other night. First, get so plastered here so that a single nightcap at home would be enough to assure she would pass out drunk in the clothes she was currently wearing. Second option, find herself a man, screw his brains out until she was so exhausted, she would pass out without any clothes on at all. From experience, she had discovered either option greatly minimized the potential for any new dreams. But, with option one, since she still had to navigate her way home, she had to walk a fine line. With option two, she had someone to lean on.

She knew six Scotches, okay, maybe seven, was her absolute limit if she didn't want to test her drunken swimming skills by falling into one of the canals on the walk home. Again. She rose to her feet and, while light-headed and listing to the left, she was confident she could make the trek home without assistance.

She reached for the wallet she kept attached to a biker chain and tucked in the rear pocket of her jeans. The biker chain was another added precaution. She had gotten tired of cancelling her credit cards whenever she woke up with her wallet MIA. Forcing her eyes to focus, she started to fish out some bills to settle her tab for the night. Before she got any cash out, Benny arrived with a fresh drink.

He pointed to a man at the other end of the bar she hadn't noticed come in. "Compliments of the gent over there."

Cassandra picked up the drink and smiled at the man. That was all the encouragement he needed, and he headed in her direction.

As he approached, Cassandra unbuttoned another button on her blouse.

It pays to advertise.

"Hello, there," said the man. He was a fit and trim specimen three or four years younger than her. His dark hair meshed perfectly with his dark, sunbaked complexion. He had on expensive well-cut casual clothing and sported a Rolex Stainless Steel Oyster watch that didn't look like a knock off. He had rich brown eyes with a mischievous twinkle, an easy smile and a five o-clock shadow.

He'd do just fine.

"Hello yourself," Cassandra answered. "I've never seen you in here before."

"I'm only in town for a few days," he answered.

Cassandra glanced at his left hand and saw the white line on his third finger where he had taken off his wedding ring. This guy kept getting better and better. With a wife at home, he would give her a phony name, be up and out before dawn and she would never see him again. If he proved to have youthful resilience combined with manly endurance, he would be perfect.

"Business or pleasure?" Cassandra asked.

"I'm hoping for a combination of the two," he said with a killer smile and leaned in closer. "But that will depend on you."

Cassandra, more than a bit tipsy, laughed and steadied herself by putting her hand on his bare arm. She felt a small jolt and immediately knew the guy had the same thing on his mind that she did.

A meaningless hook-up with no commitment.

A little fun tonight and by sunrise they would both be heading their separate ways, never to see each other again.

Perfect.

He pulled back and gave Cassandra an odd squint. "You look awfully familiar."

"If we had met," Cassandra purred, "I think I would have remembered."

He snapped his fingers then pointed in her direction.

"You're that woman in the newspaper this morning!" His voice got louder, and he looked around the room to see if anyone else had shared his epiphany. "Oh my God! You're the Dream Lady!" he said excitedly. "Can you tell me my future?"

"Sure," Cassandra answered. She picked up her glass and pressed it to her forehead. She closed her eyes then began softly muttering a nonsense mantra. After a few moments, her eyes flew open. "I've had a vision!"

"Yeah!" the guy said as he excitedly looked around the room for support. "What is it?"

Cassandra turned back and put her elbows on the bar, cradling her drink between her hands. "You're not getting laid tonight."

The man picked up his drink with one hand and patted Cassandra's hand with the other. As he started to leave, he glared at Cassandra. "That's okay, weirdo. You're a little too close to your expiration date for my taste anyway." He gulped down his drink and headed toward the door.

"Give your wife my best!" Cassandra shouted at his back.

Without turning around, he slammed his now empty glass on the bar and flipped her off with both hands before storming out.

"At least I got a free drink," she muttered to herself.

Cassandra sensed another person sliding onto the barstool next to her.

Chapter 14

CASSANDRA MORSE GLANCED to her right and saw Grant Olsen, the reporter who had written about her in the *Guardian*. She had talked to him briefly the day before while she was waiting to have her mugshot taken.

If she had to guess, Cassandra would have put Olsen at around thirty but, because he was such a slob, she could have been off by five years in either direction. He was about twenty pounds overweight, office soft and looked like he had slept in the clothes he was wearing. His hair was badly in need of a trim or at least some time with a comb or brush. There were food and coffee stains on the front of the wrinkled shirt he was wearing and the shirt resisted the concept of staying tucked into his pants. No Prince Charming on his best day and, after the article he had written about her, he was certainly no candidate to be invited back to her place for a nightcap.

"Haven't you done enough damage for one day?" she asked with a sneer.

"Reporters write the stories and editors write the headlines and select the pictures they use," Olsen answered.

Cassandra shrugged. He had a point. The article had pretty much stuck to the who, what, when, where, and why. It was the picture of her having her meltdown and the headline, not the spin of his writing which had set the tone.

"Where did you get the picture?"

"From one of the cops," Olsen answered as he motioned to Benny he would have one of whatever she was having. With only one other person still sitting at the bar, and only requiring Scotch, ice and a glass, the drink arrived almost immediately.

"Thanks," he said to the bartender. "I'm picking up her tab tonight."

Cassandra leaned back and gave Olsen an odd look. "Guilty conscious?"

"It's the least I can do."

"You got that right." Cassandra picked up her glass and used it to clink Olsen's.

Olsen leaned over and opened a battered briefcase that was leaning against his bar stool's leg, pulled out an inch-thick file and dropped it on the bar with a thud.

"What's that?" Cassandra asked as she took another sip of Scotch.

"I've spent the entire day researching you."

"That sounds more than a little creepy," Cassandra said.

"If you have any complaints send them to Google and LexisNexis."

Olsen opened the file and started reading the summary his research assistant had compiled. "You were top of your class at Annapolis and one of the few female combat pilots. You were on the fast track to be the next admiral in a family full of admirals. Then, without explanation, you're cashiered out of the Navy."

"Honorable discharge," Cassandra corrected.

Olsen turned and stared hard at Cassandra. "What the hell happened?"

Cassandra shrugged. "It was a medical issue."

"What kind of medical issue?"

"You ask a lot of questions."

"I'm a reporter. It kind of goes with the job description." Olsen tried again. "What kind of medical issue?"

"The latest theory is I was abducted by space invaders and given a brain probe that gave me my superpowers to make dreams come true," smirked Cassandra. If only Olsen knew how close that was to the truth.

"Right," Olsen said as he pushed the file aside and slid his drink in its place. "I heard a rumor you crashed a top-secret airplane."

Cassandra shrugged. "Sorry. Classified."

Grant snorted then continued, "I also discovered this wasn't the first time you had correctly predicted an event and the police had ignored you."

"Old news," she said with a shrug. "Why are you here bothering me?"

"I want to write a story about you. A real story, not some cheesy tabloid piece of crap."

"I'll let you interview me right after I volunteer to go to work for a Romanian sex trade trafficker who wants to have me make porn videos with deformed midgets and donkeys."

"Better the enemy you know," Olsen answered. "After my story hit the wire services, my phone lit up with queries from everyone from the supermarket tabloids to even one of the major networks. You're on everyone's radar screen now."

"I noticed," Cassandra said. "I had to turn off my phone and quit answering my doorbell."

"It's only going to get worse."

"Why?" Cassandra asked.

"It's the human-interest angle they all love. Like your mythological namesake, you accurately predicted an event, but no one believed you."

"And now you believe me?" she asked

"Oh, hell, no," Olsen said with a snort. "A half dozen times you've shown up at the police station with a vague notion of something you dreamed about and then something similar happens to happen." Olsen took another sip of his Scotch. "It sounds like a classic conman cold read to me. People believe because they want to believe."

Cassandra laughed. That was the exact same conclusion she had drawn about the odd little man earlier in the day.

"What's so funny?" he asked.

"Despite thinking I'm a charlatan, here you sit." Cassandra lifted her eyes toward the ceiling and began scratching her head. "What's different?" She snapped her fingers and pointed at Olsen. "I know! I've gotten better at interpreting my dreams. I predicted the exact time of a fire, plus the exact number of people who would die. And, I did it on the record, twelve hours before it happened."

"With that level of first-hand knowledge, I would put you at the top of my suspect list; not crown you queen of the psychic hotline."

"Apparently the LAPD agrees," Cassandra said as she took another sip of Scotch then grinned at Olsen. "But you're not so sure I'm a fake anymore, are you?"

Olsen clinked Cassandra's glass. "Don't mark me up as a true believer just yet." He noticed her glassy eyes and collection of swizzle sticks. "What's with the booze?"

"We're off the record, right?"

"Only if I have to be," Olsen answered.

Cassandra turned back to her drink and pretended Olsen was no longer there.

"Okay, Okay. We're off the record."

Cassandra shrugged then sighed. "If I get drunk enough, I don't dream."

"Wow, I hadn't thought of that. Are the dreams bad?" he asked with genuine concern in his voice.

"Sometimes," she answered. "The one about the fire was a living hell."

"Why?"

"In my dreams I'm not a spectator, I'm a participant."

"You dreamed you were burned alive in that fire?"

"Yup," she answered and took another pull of scotch.

Olsen shook his head and put his elbows on the bar. "That really sucks."

"It is pretty much why I live on caffeine during the day to stay awake and knock myself out with liquor at night, so I don't dream."

"Damn. How did the fire dream get through your defenses?"

Cassandra sighed. "I can only keep going like that for so long. A few days ago, exhausted, I fell asleep while I was stone cold sober."

"Huh," Olsen shook his head. "As crazy as all of this sounds, that makes some sense."

"Welcome to my world."

"Let me help you."

"How?"

"If you're working exclusively with me…" Olsen slid a stack of business cards in her direction. "When anyone asks you a question you don't want to answer, give them one of these and tell them to call me."

Cassandra eyed the business cards but didn't pick them up.

"I'll think about it."

"Don't think too long. The people on your doorstep today were just the harbingers of things to come," Olsen said as he took a sip of his drink. "Don't forget this is L.A. Some Hollywood bottom feeder is going to want to make a movie of your life story and those slime balls never let go. Then the real weirdos will start to come calling."

"Excuse me?" Cassandra asked.

"Psychics wanting to either recruit you or figure out your scam. Then there will be the damaged souls wanting you to dream something for them. They don't call this 'La La Land' for nothing." Olsen picked up his drink and downed it.

"Tell me one thing," Cassandra said with a slight slur in her voice.

"Sure, What?"

"Why should I trust you."

Olsen laughed. "I read your file. If you hadn't decided to be a pilot, you could have been a Navy SEAL or other special forces. Even drunk, you could probably kill me with those swizzle sticks. You think I'd risk pissing you off?"

"You've done a pretty good job of it so far," Cassandra said as she picked up one of the swizzle sticks then eyed Olsen.

Olsen chuckled. "Who else have you got?" Olsen asked as he tossed a handful of bills on the bar, picked up his briefcase and headed toward the door. Looking back over his shoulder he said, "I won't tell you to have sweet dreams."

Cassandra threw an ice cube at him and it hit the back of his head.

"Nice shot, Lieutenant," Benny said as he approached with a bottle of scotch in his hand. "Last call."

Cassandra slid her glass forward and he topped it off.

Benny glanced at the cash on the bar. "Your friend left a fat tip," he said. "This one is on the house."

"Thanks."

He counted the number of swizzle sticks, "Uber?"

"I only live seven blocks from here."

"Uber?" Benny repeated.

"Yeah," Cassandra answered dejectedly. "Thanks, Gunny."

As Benny walked away, her eyes fell on the stack of business cards which Grant Olsen had left on the bar. "Crap," she muttered as picked them up and shoved them into her pocket.

Chapter 15

IT WAS A bit after 5 a.m. on the East Coast. Carrie Finch was in her cubical, in a small office, surrounded by six other low-level security analysts in similar cubicles. The office of "Eastern European Affairs" was near the bottom of the barrel of the National Intelligence Agency. Finch, as usual, had finished her workload of reading every newspaper which was published in Bulgarian early. With over an hour left on her shift, she decided to check her "keywords" folder. To keep from going nuts from boredom, she had set up a subroutine on her computer that would search the internet for selected keywords and people. As usual, it was full of junk and she was about to delete the contents when she stopped and scrolled back. "No way," she muttered. "It can't be the same person."

She opened the link to the *Guardian*. Her fingers danced across the keyboard as she searched other databases, including the Los Angeles police department.

She checked again and even ran the fingerprints. They were a perfect match.

Glancing around the room, she saw her supervisor, Francis Donovan, chatting up the new female analyst. She caught his eye and motioned for him to come over. He held up a finger indicating he wasn't finished flirting and would be there shortly.

Finch put her two pinky fingers next to her mouth and sent out an ear-piercing whistle.

All activity in the room came to a halt and every eye turned first toward Carrie Finch and then toward Francis Donovan. With big eyes, Finch motioned Donovan over again.

This time, with his entire staff watching, he walked briskly to Finch's cubical.

"What?" he demanded as he tried to reassert his authority, but he could hear the snickers from the other cubicles. Everyone in the room had Donovan's number. Like so many in the Washington bureaucracy, he was a well-groomed and arrogant empty suit who only had a job because he had great political connections. In his case, his uncle sat on the House Ways and Means committee. Notorious for taking credit for anything and everything, and a relentless horndog, he had been assigned to a spot where he could do little harm. He was the night shift manager of a half dozen people whose only function was to read everything they could that was in print and look for something interesting.

"You need to see this," Carrie Finch said in a voice loud enough to carry to the adjoining cubicles.

Donovan glared at her then read the article. He read it again to see if he had missed anything. He was confident he hadn't.

"Jesus Christ, Finch," he said in a louder than necessary voice. "The last time I checked, Los Angeles wasn't in Eastern Europe. Plus, some weirdo psychic catches lightning in a bottle and I'm supposed to be impressed?"

Finch smiled. So predictable. "Apparently you missed the significance of the name of the woman arrested."

Donovan read it again. "Who the hell is Cassandra Morse?"

An audible gasp went up from the room and Francis Donovan felt his cheeks darkening as he heard every keyboard in the room begin typing.

"Other than being a former combat pilot, the test pilot for the SV-1 which was mysteriously knocked out of the sky seven months ago, the daughter of Admiral Hank Morse, and granddaughter of Admiral Henry Morse…"

"Okay, Okay," Donovan said bitterly. "She's well connected…."

Finch snorted. "She's a lot more than that. Since the SV-1 crashed, she has been eyes-only compartmentalized."

"And you know this how?" Donovan demanded.

"When I started my background check, everything about her was sealed and walled off, even from me. There has to be a reason for this. This is something the director will want to know about."

Donovan scratched his neck and shook his head. "We'll kick it upstairs and see if they want to add it to the DNI's morning briefing."

Finch made a cute face and batted her eyes at Donovan. "And I'm sure you'll put your name on it."

Donovan glanced at her screen and shook his head. "No Finch. Your name goes right on top of this little steaming pile."

As Donovan walked out of the bullpen and into his office, the analyst in the cube next to Finch, Nick Bergman, leaned back and said, "Nice catch." He leaned in closer. "He really is an idiot."

"Hardly world class analysis there," Finch answered.

Over the last six months, the two agents, who were roughly the same age, had formed a special bond. Her weaknesses were his strengths and vice versa. Finch had dreadful people skills while Bergman was a likeable guy who any woman would be delighted to take home to meet the parents. If you tried to describe Bergman in one word, it would be a toss-up between "cute" and "sweet".

They were also polar opposites when it came to their approach to work. Finch was always able to see the big picture and could quickly see how random pieces of a puzzle fit together. Bergman was a details guy and a certified genius when it came to computers, software and, most importantly, hacking. Both would usually complete their assigned tasks for the day with time to spare and devised other work to keep their sanity as they waited to be noticed and moved to a different department or before finally giving up and quitting.

They had become each other's sounding board whenever a weird notion would cross their minds. While Finch had been able to write a passable keyword search program, it was Bergman who had put her keyword search engine into super drive.

Finch smiled as she turned back to her keyboard and forwarded the report she had just written to Donovan. Checking the message tracking a few moments later, she saw Donovan had sent it upstairs so quickly he probably hadn't even bothered to read it.

Satisfied, she turned back to her work. While it was probably nothing, it was always nice to pull Francis Donovan's chain. She leaned in closer to her screen and began reread her report and, as she so often did, began to sink into her own world.

Checking his coffee cup, and seeing it was down to the dredges, Nick Bergman leaned around the partition and asked, "Coffee?"

Finch didn't hear him, but he wasn't offended. He knew that when she was focused hard on anything, the world around her no longer seemed to exist. Once, when she was on Planet Finch, Bergman had dropped a heavy book to the floor directly behind her chair. While the rest of the office reacted, she didn't even notice. He knew from experience that the only way to bring her back to this plane of reality was to touch her. But, since she sometimes reacted violently at the moment of contact, and since this was only an offer to refill her coffee cup, Bergman left her alone.

He didn't get very far.

Red in the face, Donovan burst out of his office and glared at Carrie Finch. "She wants you upstairs."

Finch didn't hear him and her eyes stayed locked on her screen.

Reluctantly, Bergman touched Finch gently on the shoulder then took a quick step back.

"What?" she demanded of Bergman.

Bergman pointed in the direction of Francis Donovan, who looked ready to explode.

"What?" she repeated, this time in Donovan's direction.

"She wants you upstairs."

"She?"

"The Assistant Director of National Intelligence."

Chapter 16

CASSANDRA STUMBLED OUT of the Uber after it had rolled to a stop in front of her house. Embarrassed by such a short trip, she gave the driver a five-dollar tip as a form of an apology. At this late hour, her street was deserted and quiet. Behind her she heard footsteps approaching and she quickened her pace and pulled her keys out of her front pocket. The keyring had a small can of mace attached to it. Before she released the safety on the deterrent, she relaxed as she heard the familiar voice of Detective Steve Foley.

"Morse. Hold up a second."

"Detective," Cassandra answered as she tucked her borderline legal can of mace back in her pocket before he saw it. It wasn't the stuff they sell to timid housewives online; it was military grade and could hit a charging grizzly between the eyes from thirty feet. "Did you come to arrest me?"

"Exactly the opposite," Foley answered. "I just wanted to let you know the owner of the building has confessed."

Cassandra grinned at Foley. "And?"

Foley looked down at his shoes then continued. "You were 100% correct on how and why he did it."

"And?"

Foley sighed. "And we were wrong to chalk you up as a person of interest."

"Ouch!" Cassandra said with a laugh. "That had to leave a mark."

"Yeah," Foley answered with a shrug. "Apparently -- as you suggested -- he thought the place was empty and didn't realize two squatters had broken in."

"Who was he?"

"Don't you know?" Foley asked.

"My dreams don't come with a line-up card or a program."

"He lives right around here," Foley answered as he pulled out his phone and showed Cassandra his mugshot.

"I'll be damned," she said. "I've seen him around. In fact, he was at Benny's Bar and Grill just the other night."

"Had he ever been there before?"

"Not that I remember," Morse answered then grinned at Foley. "While I appreciate the update, you could have just called or sent a text," Cassandra said.

"I know." Foley looked down at his shoes again.

"Detective Foley," she said seductively. "Now that I'm no longer a murder suspect are you flirting with me?"

"Maybe a little," he answered with a silly grin.

"Ah, that's sweet," she answered. "But it's never going to happen."

"Why not?" Foley asked.

"I've got some unbreakable rules. I would never date a pilot or a cop."

"Why not?"

"With a pilot, when you're alternating between competing with someone one day and putting your lives in each other's hands the next, you can't let emotions or hormones cloud your judgement."

"What's your problem with cops?" Foley asked.

"What happens the next time I have one of my dreams and I turn into a crazy bitch from hell and start trashing your precinct?" She laughed. "While handcuffs can be fun in the right situation, having your boyfriend toss you in a holding cell, or," Cassandra's eyes locked on Foley, "having you committed for a forty-eight-hour psych evaluation…"

Foley held up a finger in protest. "That was only one time and God knows I would have been justified more than once."

"Still," Cassandra said. "Tossing your girlfriend in the looney bin is the kind of thing that can really suck the romance out of a relationship."

Foley laughed. It was the kind of laugh that brings a smile to the face of everyone in the vicinity and makes others want to join in.

"You need to laugh more. You're really good at it."

"Thanks. But, not much to laugh at with my job."

Foley read her expression and knew he didn't have much of a chance of changing her mind about dating a cop.

Cassandra saw the look of resignation on Foley's face. Their conversation had reached that awkward moment. Unless Cassandra asked him in for a nightcap and possibly more, they had nothing else to say. "Goodnight, Detective," she said as she headed up the sidewalk leading to her front porch.

"Wait," Foley said urgently which cause her to stop walking and turn back to him. "There is something else," Foley answered with a serious expression on his face. "It's actually the reason I'm here."

"Okay," she said as she turned and took a few steps closer so they didn't need to speak loudly enough to wake the neighbors.

"Have you noticed most of the time when you've walked into our precinct you've ended up talking to me?"

Cassandra laughed. "I just figured your boss hates you."

"That's pretty much a given. But she tolerates me because I have a good close rate." Foley took a step closer and spoke even more softly, as if he was afraid someone might over hear him. "The reason you end up at my desk is because I've asked to be assigned to you."

Cassandra pulled back in disbelief. "Really? Why?" she asked.

"Detectives notice patterns. Over the past few months, you've wandered in with these crazy stories that have been hard to believe."

Cassandra sighed. "I'll have to give you that one."

"But so far," Det. Foley continued, "every one of them has turned out, more or less, to be true."

"Okay," said Cassandra. "What super-secret pattern has emerged from my insanity?"

"I've noticed that the things you're predicting have moved from misdemeanors to felonies to now, homicide."

"Huh." Cassandra's mouth opened slightly, and her eyes danced as she processed Foley's observation. "Now that you mention it, you're right."

Foley handed Cassandra one of his cards with an extra handwritten number on it. "If you ever need anything, I can be reached at this number 24/7."

"Are you flirting with me again, Detective?" Cassandra asked coyly as she lowered her voice a full octave.

"Not this time," he answered. "More of a head's up. Your latest dream, and the publicity it generated, embarrassed the daylights out of my lieutenant and by extension a whole lot of other people. If you walked into the precinct right now, someone might shoot you, put a throw down gun next to your body and a dozen cops would swear the shooting was justified."

"Good to know that even clearing a double homicide in record time for the LAPD doesn't carry much weight with our boys in blue."

"I'd be more worried about the girls in blue at the moment."

"Meaning?"

"I would definitely recommend giving Lt. Blanche Harrison a wide berth. She's been invited down to Headquarters for a chat with the Chief in the morning. If you have any more dreams it might be wise to call me directly."

Cassandra tucked the card in her bra. "I'll keep it close to my heart."

Foley shook his head, "Goodnight Morse."

"Goodnight Foley."

Chapter 17

WITH POWERFUL BINOCULARS, Tom McMahon watched the interaction between the unknown man and his target. He was deep in the shadows of the third-floor window of the house which was only one lot off from being directly across the street from Cassandra Morse's home. Behind him, a four-man surveillance team was setting up their equipment. Another team was currently setting up another observation platform on the canal side. In a few more minutes, and until they pulled out and headed home, everything that happened around the exterior of the building would be recorded and documented.

McMahon loved Vrbo and AirBnB.

With money no object, it had become fairly simple to rent a home or apartment wherever necessary on short notice and for any length of time needed. With limited paperwork and without raising any suspicion from nosy neighbors, he could set up an observation nest pretty much anywhere. Then, when the assignment was completed, he'd bring in one of his scrub teams to sanitize the place and no one was ever the wiser.

The man standing next to McMahon, also equipped with binoculars, was a very different specimen than the surveillance team. The tech guys were well-paid geeks. The closest they had ever come to combat was when they were playing "Call of Duty" or some other nonsense on one of their game consoles.

"He looks like a cop," Jack Logan said.

"Takes one to know one," McMahon answered.

Logan had spent six years in the Army's Criminal Investigation Division until he had been hired by Bathmann Aeronautics six months prior. Logan was compact, wiry and as tough as a two-dollar steak. He was a no-nonsense pro. He didn't ask a lot of questions, stayed focused on the task at hand and never bitched. With that combination, he had moved up the ranks quickly. He was now McMahon's number two.

Initially there had been some resistance to his rapid advancement but that went away early on. One night in a Navy bar in Nevada, three of the guys he had leapfrogged decided they wanted to tune him up. Big mistake. One ended up with a shattered nose and broken orbital bones from a massive head butt, the second guy was pissing red for a week after a single vicious kidney punch that had dropped him to his knees and taken all the fight out of him. After seeing his buddies, one a former Green Beret and the other a former Navy Seal, get completely dismantled in less than two seconds while Logan didn't even muss his hair, the third guy changed tactics and wisely bought Logan a beer. When word got around that there was a new alpha dog in the kennel, things calmed down and no one else wanted to try him on for size.

Both men lowered their binoculars when they saw Foley leaving.

"LAPD Detective Steven Foley," said a voice behind them. "Need a bio?"

McMahon grinned at Logan then shook his head.

"Are we going to do interior surveillance placement?" asked a second voice. "It might be tricky since she seldom leaves."

McMahon shook his head again. "Negative. Our target is Dr. Tanner Dawson."

Jack Logan leaned in closer. "If Tanner makes a fuss." He pointed at the older camera still aimed at the Morse house. "We don't need any extra eyes."

McMahon agreed and said over his shoulder, "Kill Mr. Black's feed."

Chapter 18

"FINCH," AN ARMED security guard said, not asked, as he approached her cubicle. "I'll escort you to Director Smith's office. Please follow me."

Bergman smiled and gave Finch's hand a squeeze. "Blow their socks off," he whispered as she got up from her chair.

Francis Donovan, who was standing in the doorway of his office, glared at her as she and her escort walked past him.

Carrie Finch's knees weren't exactly knocking when the elevator door opened on the seventh floor, but they were close. Compared to the office in the basement where she worked, this space was as different as the interior of a fifty-year-old fishing boat on its last legs and the bridge of the Starship Enterprise. There was a twenty-five-foot ceiling in the main bullpen area, and it had HD displays mounted on the walls large enough they would be at home at an NFL stadium.

The room had a vibe Finch loved. The people there were the ones who worked all night, every night, to craft the morning briefing for the Director of National Security and compiled the Daily Presidential Briefing.

She followed the guard as he weaved his way through a maze until all the commotion of the bullpen was no longer audible. They arrived at a door in a section of the building which was indistinguishable from the other dozen doors in the otherwise empty corridor. There were no markings of any kind on any of the doors to indicate whose office they may be. The guard tapped three times, waited for a click, then he opened the door for her before turning to leave. To Finch's surprise, the room was not the Assistant Director's office. Instead, it was a security center with four heavily armed men giving her the stink eye. In the corner of the room was a massive German Shepherd who appeared to be having difficulty deciding if she was large enough to be considered a full meal or just a snack.

As she stepped in, two of the men moved behind her and out of her line of sight. While they didn't exactly have the automatic weapons strapped over their shoulders pointed at her, she got the distinct impression that if she did anything unexpected or stupid, they wouldn't need much time to aim and empty their clips.

"Just like the airport, Ms. Finch," one of the guards said as he motioned toward a TSA style body scanner. "Cellphone and anything metallic in the tray."

"Shoes off?" Finch asked.

"No," answered the stone-faced guard. "Do you have any metal on your body other than your three piercings?"

Finch closed her eyes and shook her head. Granted, she worked for the National Intelligence agency, but she still didn't want to know how they knew about her body art.

Despite passing through the metal detector without any problems, she was given a pat down that bordered on sexual assault. Next, the big dog came over and gave her a thorough sniffing. He was not impressed. After he was satisfied, he backed up to his spot in the corner without ever taking his eyes off of her.

"Good to go," one of the guards said as he pushed a concealed button and part of the wall on the left-hand side of the room opened.

Finch smiled. She considered herself a good observer, but she never would have thought that the wall was actually a door.

"*Welcome to the big leagues,*" she thought.

As she entered the room, Finch saw the legendary Barbara Smith sitting at one end of a massive conference table that could comfortably seat twenty. Less than half of it was currently in use. While Finch had never seen her in person, she looked exactly like the picture she had managed to find on the web. Smith was notoriously camera shy and seldom spoke directly to the press. She left that kind of task to her boss, the Director of National Security. Smith was the one who made the place hum. Her boss was the one who chatted with the president every morning, and four or five times a year was grilled on Capitol Hill.

She was just under six feet tall in her stocking feet, had hair barely longer than a buzz cut, pale skin and piercing blue eyes. With

Smith, were eight of what everyone in the building called the "Twelve Apostles": the department heads of different divisions of the NIA.

"Ah, Finch," Smith said. "We're on a deadline here, so we'll dispense with introductions."

"I know who everyone is, ma'am," Finch answered.

"I see," Smith said as she put on a pair of reading glasses. "I also see you've been with us for ten months now."

Finch was not offered a seat, so she remained standing.

"Nine months and twenty-one days, ma'am," Finch answered.

"Are you always pedantic, Ms. Finch?"

"Yes ma'am," Finch answered unapologetically. "However, with the negative connotations associated with that word, I prefer to simply consider myself highly attentive to detail and precise."

"You're on the Bulgarian desk?"

"Yes, ma'am," Finch answered.

"Why did you choose that assignment?"

"I didn't," Finch answered. "Apparently there are only a few people on staff who are fluent in the primary language of Bulgarian and the secondary language of Turkish and are also conversant in the minor language of Romani."

"I see," Smith said. "What was the score of the Beroe versus Levski Sofia soccer match last night?"

Finch had been expecting a test question, but this one was particularly nasty. "Those two teams didn't play last night, ma'am," Finch answered. "Beroe beat Litex Lovech 4-3 on penalty kicks and Levski Sofia was idle."

"Are you sure?"

"*24 Chasa* is the largest daily newspaper in Bulgaria and you'll find the story of the Beroe Litex match on page fourteen, right hand column, of the print edition or by a quick search of the online edition at www.24chasa.bg."

Smith eyed Finch over the top of her reading glasses. "Are you a big soccer fan?"

"I think it is about as exciting as watching paint dry."

"Eidetic memory?"

Finch shrugged. "Possibly when I was a child, but now it is more mnemonic."

"I see," Smith said as she began reading again. "Fluent in sixteen languages. Georgetown BS, then MS in computer science from MIT, then a Ph.D. from the Harvard Kennedy School." Smith continued to read. "Your dissertation was on the forthcoming generational shift in foreign policy."

"Yes, ma'am."

"I would very much like to read it."

"I'll send you a copy."

"That won't be necessary. I'm sure we have it on file."

Finch was sure they did too.

Smith looked at Finch over her glasses again. "Why are you still working the Bulgarian desk?"

"You will have to ask my supervisor, Francis Donovan."

"I intend to," Smith said with snort. "When were you going to give your notice?"

Finch smiled. Barbara Smith was legendary for her analytical skills. "Two months and ten days, ma'am."

"Giving us a year?"

"Yes, ma'am."

"Understood," Smith replied. "Now to the matter at hand. How did you happen to notice the story about Cassandra Morse?"

Finch shifted her weight uncomfortably. She had no idea how much the A.D. knew about her and her extra-curricular activities with Nick Bergman which were done on company time and equipment. But since they knew the number and locations of her body art, she felt it would be a mistake to hedge or spin and decided to stick straight to the facts. "I, with the help of my associate Nick Bergman, wrote a keyword program which alerts me every time something on my interest list gets a new mention online."

Smith took her glasses off and tossed them on the table and smiled. "Really? Why were you interested in Lt. Morse?"

"She had the highest score ever at Top Gun. And, she was possibly the best combat pilot, male or female, the Navy had ever produced. She was the test pilot for the game changer SV-1. When it crashed, they called it pilot's error." Finch's eyes locked on Smith's. "With all due respect ma'am. That doesn't pass the smell test."

"Why not?" Smith asked.

"She was too damn good."

"What do you think actually happened?"

"I don't have enough information to form an answer to that question."

Smith stifled a smile and kept her poker face. "Without being held to your answer, what is your opinion based on the information you do have?"

Finch shrugged. "The Navy thought she was MIA and would never be seen again. That made her the perfect scapegoat since she would never be around to clear her name."

"And that offended you?"

"Yes, ma'am. Lt. Morse was, is, a patriot and a role model for other women. For some Beltway paper pusher to smear her for the sake of political expediency is offensive to me on multiple levels, ma'am."

A.D. Smith studied Finch closely and stifled another smile. "What prompted you to draw this preliminary conclusion?"

"I could understand the level of classification about the crash of the SV-1, but the wall that was built around her rescue, recovery and separation from the Navy, to have it be compartmentalized and eyes-only seemed like overkill to me."

"Is that all?"

"No, ma'am," Finch answered as she shifted uncomfortably again. She hated being the center of attention. "There are also the rumors."

"What rumors?" Smith demanded.

"There are reports on the dark web that the SV-1 was hit with a long dormant Star Wars weapon."

"You spend time on the dark web?"

"Yes, ma'am. My associate Nick Bergman is highly experienced with the dark web and he aided my search."

"Do you think someone was trying to kill Lt. Morse?"

"No, ma'am," Finch answered.

"Really?" Smith said with a hint of surprise in her voice.

Finch shifted uncomfortably again. "I think someone was trying to kill Admiral Morse and destroy the SV-1. She was just collateral damage."

Smith glanced around the table to gauge the reaction of her department heads. They were all leaning forward, giving Finch their full attention. "Why would anyone want to kill Admiral Morse?"

"Admiral Morse was trying to revolutionize military procurement," Finch answered in her usual monotone. "If he succeeded, the current contractors stood to lose hundreds of billions, if not trillions, of dollars. With the admiral out of the way, it was back to the status quo, good old boys' network."

"Anything else?"

"Yes, ma'am. I think Congressman Donald Warwick may have been murdered and didn't die of a massive coronary."

If she didn't have anyone in the room's full attention before, she sure as hell had it now.

"Do you have any proof?" Smith asked.

"No, ma'am, but the timing of his death coinciding with the crash of the SV-1 and the death of Admiral Morse is too much of a coincidence for my taste."

"Why would someone want to kill the congressman?"

"For the same reason they would want to kill Admiral Morse. Money. And a whole lot of it. My guess is he had outlived his usefulness, or he was shifting his loyalties. Either way, it was time for him to go."

"Who do you think would be capable of doing such a thing?"

"While capable, I would doubt any foreign governments were involved."

"Why?"

"A three-minute risk-benefit analysis would stop them."

"Explain," Smith said.

"Why risk a potential shooting war with the United States over arm's procurement minutia. Especially since the more money we pour down the rat hole on useless weaponry the better it is for them."

"Good answer," Smith said. "Who would be at the top of your short list?"

"To take out the SV-1, Admiral Morse and a powerful sitting congressman all in one fell swoop is a Machiavellian masterstroke of epic proportion." Finch's eyes locked on Smith's again. "If it were me, I'd follow the money and would be looking at whichever defense contractor would have had the most to lose because of the SV-1. Then I would see if they also built the weapon used to destroy the prototype."

Assistant Director Barbara Smith softly clapped her hands four times. She looked around the table and said, "I need a volunteer to add Carrie Finch to their senior staff, who is also willing to put someone her age and with her limited experience as the Lead All Source Analyst on this project."

All eight hands around the table went up.

Chapter 19

"I THINK DETECTIVE Foley is sweet on you," the ghost of Admiral Henry Morse said.

Cassandra, sitting in the chair facing her grandfather, still had three fingers of Scotch left in her highball glass.

"I'm more interested in that stranger who showed up today."

"Me too," the admiral answered. "With everything he knew, you have to wonder if he's the one feeding you those dreams."

"How could he possibly know about the fire, or any of the other things I've had dreams about?"

The admiral laughed. "The better question would be, how do you know about it?"

"Fair point," Cassandra said as she eyed her drink and yawned. "Clearly he knows more than I do since he knew about the hole in my head."

Cassandra took a long pull from her glass. She was struggling to keep her eyes open as she felt her blood alcohol level rising to the sweet tipping point of oblivion. "I'm wondering if our mystery man knew about the hole because he was the one holding the drill."

"Or at least if he had been in the operating room," the admiral speculated. "I wish you had taken him more seriously and gotten contact info."

Cassandra agreed. "I have a feeling we'll be seeing him again soon."

"The flower?"

"Of course."

"What are you going to do about Dr. Newman?" Henry asked.

"Part of me wants to go pound on his door right now and get some answers."

"And the other part?" Henry asked.

"The other part is scared to hear what he has to say."

"So, you're going to wait until you talk to the stranger before you see Newman?"

"You're reading my mind."

The admiral laughed. "I *am* your mind."

Cassandra took another sip of her drink. "I guess you're right about that."

"What are you going to do about the reporter?"

"He's a jerk."

"Just because he's not captivated by your charm, beauty, and ability to predict the future the way Detective Foley is, doesn't mean he wouldn't come in handy," the admiral said.

"How so?" asks Cassandra.

"If this dream thing continues…"

"Don't even say that," Cassandra said.

"Some people would consider what you have a gift."

"Well, let them sleep a night in my pajamas and see how they feel about it in the morning," she said with a slight slur.

"All I'm saying. If the dreams continue, having a journalist and a cop on your side would get you access to information you couldn't get otherwise," the admiral said.

"I don't remember you being this smart when you were still alive."

Henry laughed then yawned. "We ready?"

Exhausted, Cassandra glared at her bed. With a sigh, she finished her drink and on unsteady legs walked across the room and passed out face first onto her bed.

Chapter 20

*F*OR THE FIRST *time, Cassandra's dream was in black and white.*
She is dressed in a frilly skirt and she is moving around in an old-style kitchen like a 1950's housewife getting dinner ready for her husband. The house looks oddly familiar.

Then she recognizes it.

She has seen it before.

It is the house the DOD had built down range from an A-Bomb test. At the kitchen table are two child-sized mannequins.

The door opens and the admiral walks in dressed in an old-style train conductor's uniform.

"Honey! I'm home!"

Cassandra hands the admiral a martini.

"How was your day, darling?" she asks.

"It was swell!" the admiral answers. "The load was delivered exactly as planned. I brought you a memento. The Admiral hands Cassandra a postcard showing the famous "Hollywood" sign on Mount Lee overlooking Los Angeles.

"Remember you have that meeting tonight with your old friend," Cassandra says.

"How could I forget?"

Henry now looks like Bob Denver from "Gilligan's Island".

He has a yellow inflatable rubber duckie inner tube around his waist.

"Don't forget this!"

Cassandra hands the admiral a toilet plunger. Henry waves goodbye and steps out the door.

Cassandra turns to the window and in the distance a nuclear bomb goes off and the little house is blown away.

Cassandra awakened with a gasp.

"Ah, crap. Not again."

Chapter 21

CASSANDRA WAS PUTTING a tea kettle on the stove in her tiny kitchen and glaring at the admiral.

"Let me get this straight," he said, "It was the 1950s and I was in a train conductor's uniform. Then I was Gilligan with a rubber duckie inner tube around my waist and a toilet plunger. Then there was a nuclear blast."

"I have to lay off the scotch," said Cassandra.

"Right." Henry snorted. "If you joined AA, the Edinburgh economy would collapse."

The kettle started to whistle, and Cassandra poured herself a cup of hot water and inserted an herbal tea bag.

"What? No coffee?"

"The dreams only seem to come one at a time. Since the dream is already here there is no point in punishing myself," answered Cassandra with a sigh. "I can't un-dream it."

"What's the plan?" the admiral asked.

"I'm going to take your advice," Cassandra answered.

The admiral clutched his heart. "This is the big one Elizabeth!"

"Please stop it with the old television shows."

"Sorry," the admiral answered. "I wish I had lived long enough to have heard you were going to take my advice in person."

Cassandra flipped off her grandfather's ghost.

"Nice," he said. "What are you going to do?"

"I'm going to call Grant Olsen and, as you suggested, let him use his resources to see if any Cold War era nukes are being transported by rail through Hollywood," said Cassandra. "Then I'm going to take a five-mile beach run and then take a nap."

"I love this plan!" Henry answered enthusiastically.

She made her way upstairs to the spare bedroom she had converted into a makeshift office. As she reached for the stack of cards Grant Olsen had given her, she saw Detective Steve Foley's card on top. She drew in air then puffed out her cheeks as she released it.

"Should I call him and give him a heads up that I had had another dream?"

Shaking her head, she thought better of it and pushed his card aside. He would want the details of the dream and she had no desire to share her Ozzie and Harriet moment, much less her Gilligan with a toilet plunger imagery. She didn't want to burn through all of the credibility she had built up with her arson prediction with a single phone call.

Maybe later, when it was all in better focus.

Then another thought hit her.

"The hell with Foley. What was I going to tell Olsen?"

Cassandra leaned back and closed her eyes. She was right on the edge of falling asleep when she jerked herself forward, squared her shoulders and took a series of deep breaths.

She dialed the number on Grant Olsen's card and was surprised when a woman answered.

"Grant Olsen's desk," she said.

For a second she froze. Should she ask for Grant or Mr. Olsen?

"Is Grant there?" she asked sweetly. After all, he had bought her a drink the night before so that qualifies to be on a first name basis.

"I'm sorry," she answered, "but he's away from his desk at the moment."

"Tell him Cassandra called…"

"Cassandra? Cassandra Morse?" the voice asked, suddenly very interested.

"Yes."

"Hold on, hold on," she said with a sense of urgency. "He's in an editorial meeting right now but I know he will want to talk to you."

"I can call back later…"

"No, please wait," she said with a laugh. "He'll jump at any opportunity to get out of a meeting. He'll consider you a godsend. Hold the line."

The *Guardian* had dreadful "on hold" music. It appeared to be some kind of instrumental remake of a 60's rock song. She didn't have to suffer long.

"I can't believe you actually called," Olsen said, a bit out of breath.

"I can't believe it either," Cassandra answered. "I had another dream."

"No kidding," Olsen said. "Are you ready to share?"

"Not yet," she answered. "You need to understand my process."

"I have no idea what that means," Olsen said with a slightly annoyed tone in his voice.

"My dreams are fluid and are often open to different interpretations. They are almost like a riddle I have to solve."

"Okay," Olsen answered. "If you say so." He appeared to be losing interest fast.

"Right now, I need some facts to try and sort things out."

"All of the public library branches are currently open and Google is available 24/7."

Cassandra shook her head. "I should have expected this and normally, I'd blow you off, but this dream is too damn scary. And I can pretty much guarantee I won't find what I'm looking for online."

"Why?" Olsen said, only slightly more interested. "What do you need to know?"

"Is the U.S. Government planning on shipping any nuclear weapons by rail through Los Angeles anytime in the near future?"

Looking around, Olsen sat back down and cupped his hand over his mouth. "Are you fucking kidding me?" he hissed.

"No."

"Do you remember the dream?"

"More vividly than I would like."

"What was it?"

"Off the record."

"Seriously," Olsen said in a whisper as he was now leaning so far forward his mouth was below the level of his desktop. "You dreamed a nuke was going to go off in L.A. and you want it off the record?"

"I don't know what I dreamed yet," Cassandra answered. "That's why I want more facts."

"All right. All right. We're off the record for now. But," Olsen warned, "if it turns out millions of lives are in danger all bets are off."

"Fair enough," Cassandra answered.

"So, what was your dream?"

"I was a 1950s housewife in one of those houses the government used to level during A-Bomb tests. My grandfather, Admiral Henry Morse, dressed in a train conductor uniform, came in and handed me a postcard with the Hollywood sign on it and then he said, 'The load was delivered exactly as planned. I brought you a memento.' I answered, 'Remember you have that meeting tonight with your old friend.' Then he said, 'How could I forget?'"

Cassandra paused then reluctantly continued. "Right after that, an atomic bomb went off."

"Jesus," Olsen said. "Anything else?"

"Just some confusing stuff which I haven't figured out yet." For the moment, Cassandra saw no reason to mention Gilligan, rubber duckies or the toilet plunger.

Chapter 22

FTER A FEW more minutes of trying to pry more information out of Cassandra Morse with no luck, Grant Olsen returned his phone to its cradle and stared at it for a solid fifteen seconds. His face was ashen and his heart was racing.

"What did the Dream Lady want?" Holly Mullen asked as she approached Olsen's desk. When she saw his body language, she stopped cold in her tracks. "Whatever it was, it apparently wasn't good."

Mullen was a petite twenty-two-year-old with multiple tattoos visible on her arms. She also had multiple facial piercings, including her nose, eyebrow, and lip. The left side of her head was shaved to the scalp and the right side was bright purple. While she might get open-mouthed stares in Omaha or Peoria, she wouldn't turn a single head at Hollywood and Vine.

When she felt like working, which wasn't all that often, Mullen was a freelance researcher for a bunch of clients including lawyers and bail bondsmen and occasionally the *Guardian*. With her hourly rate, she only had to work a day or two a month to cover the rent and keep herself fed. When Grant Olsen approached her about doing research on Cassandra Morse, after a cursory search, she had given the *Guardian* the "friends and family discount" because she had been intrigued. In addition to compiling the dossier on Morse, she was the one who had answered the phone when Cassandra had called.

"What are you working on at the moment?" Grant Olsen asked.

"Limbo," she answered. "I've finished the Morse file you've requested and, since I'm here already, I was just about to see if Tony needs me for anything else." Tony being, Anthony LaRosa, Managing Editor.

Olsen picked up the receiver on his desk phone and hit an internal number as he motioned for her to take a seat. She listened to his side of the conversation with interest.

"There's been a development in the Morse case," Olsen said. "I'm going to need Mullen for another day." He paused. "I know what she charges," he said pausing again. "A few hours?" There was a final silence before he concluded. "Okay." Olsen turned to Mullen. "I have you for the rest of the day."

Holly Mullen gave him an awkward left-handed salute. "Your wish is my command."

Olsen looked around the newsroom and no one appeared to be paying them attention. He still leaned in and spoke softer. "This is hot stuff and we're going to need to keep it close to the chest."

"Okay," Mullen answered. "What do you need to know?"

Olsen leaned in closer and this time whispered. "How hard would it be to get confirmation that the U.S. government was shipping nuclear weapons via rail through Los Angeles?"

Mullen's eyes grew large. "What?" she said loudly enough to turn a few heads in the newsroom.

Olsen motioned for her to lower the volume.

"And find out if Admiral Henry Morse, deceased, had any friends in the L.A. area."

This time Mullen was the one leaning in closer. "Did Dream Lady say a nuke was going to go off in LA?"

"She wasn't sure."

For the first time since she had graduated from St. Catherine's High School, Mullen made the sign of the cross and muttered, "Forgive me father, for I have sinned."

"Amen," Olsen added. "How hard would it be to find out?"

"Somewhere between highly unlikely and impossible," she answered.

"Can you do it?"

"All I can do is try." Holly Mullen looked down at Olsen. "We need to be really careful here. Some of the dark net people are real conspiracy nuts. If I even whisper a word about nuclear bombs and L.A., they're going to start coming out of the woodwork and the research would be contaminated and useless."

"Okay, okay," Olsen repeated. "Frame this like you're seeking information on the safe transportation of nuclear material and make it as general as possible and try to read between the lines."

"You got it."

"What do you need from me?" Olsen asked.

"A helicopter on the roof, gassed and ready to get me out of the blast zone would be nice."

"I'll save you a seat."

Chapter 23

CARRIE FINCH LOOKED at her new ID, which was on a lanyard around her neck, for the third time and still didn't believe it. Across the top of her badge, it read, "National Counterintelligence and Security Center". Under her name and picture, it read, "Senior Lead All Source Analyst" then printed below her name, in block letters was "(TS/SCI)", which meant "Top Secret/Sensitive Compartmented Information".

She still couldn't believe it.

She looked up when she heard a tap on her closed door and said, "Come in."

Standing in the doorway was the same guard who had escorted her to the conference room earlier. His body language toward her had changed dramatically in the hour since he had last seen her. Previously, while being completely professional, he had been borderline dismissive. Now, he had the demeanor of a military second lieutenant speaking to an officer with multiple stars on their shoulder. Apparently, someone moving from a crappy cubicle in the sub-basement to their own office on the seventh floor in one day was not an everyday occurrence at the NIA.

"Nick Bergman, ma'am," he said briskly.

Carrie Finch smiled, *"Ma'am."* She liked that.

Bergman walked in with a small cardboard box in his hands and a stunned expression on his face. "What the hell did you do, Finch?" he asked.

"Close the door," Finch said.

"Yes," Bergman said with a silly grin on his face, "ma'am."

That was one of the many things she liked about Nick Bergman. He didn't miss much, and he was about the only person on the planet who could regularly make her laugh.

"Can you believe this shit?" she said as she motioned around her private office.

"You even have a window," Bergman said.

"It's fake," Finch answered. "The walls here are eighteen inches thick and would stop an artillery shell." Finch indicated Bergman should take a seat. He put his box in the corner then sat down.

"About a half hour after you left, a crew came in and sanitized your workspace. Bergman was beaming. "They did the same to Francis Donovan's office."

"Since we were tight on time, I wanted the computer and monitor I was used to, so I had them brought up here."

"Oh, right. You just snap your fingers and…" Bergman stopped when he saw where she was pointing. Stacked in the back corner was everything that had previously been on her desk in the sub-basement.

"Damn!" Bergman said.

Finch grinned, then held up her new ID.

Bergman read it, leaned in, blinked twice, then read it again. "Jesus, Finch," Bergman said in disbelief. "Senior Lead and TS/SCI." Bergman fanned himself with both hands. "Do you have any idea how turned on I am right now?" Bergman tested the strength of her desk then asked, "You want to break in the new office? I think the desk would hold us."

Finch shook her head and chuckled. "Maybe later." She opened her middle desk drawer, pulled out another lanyard ID combination and tossed it to Bergman.

"What's this?"

"You are now officially an All-Source Analyst. And," Finch's eyes twinkled when she added, "my number two."

"Sweet!" Bergman said as he removed his old ID and replaced it with his new one. "Seriously if we lock the door." Then Bergman tried to turn serious. "You're not a screamer, are you?"

Finch held up her hand to stop him. "I'm already regretting moving you upstairs."

Bergman looked at his now obsolete ID and asked, "What do I do with this?"

Finch pushed a button on her phone, which was also the only thing currently on her desk, and almost immediately the door opened and a thin man in his mid-twenties, named Kevin Meyer, came into the office. "Yes, ma'am."

Finch motioned first to Bergman, then Meyer. "Give him your old ID."

"Yes, ma'am," Bergman answered with a hint of sarcasm in his voice and extra emphasis on the "ma'am", which earned him a nasty glare from Meyer, as he handed over the old ID.

"Is there anything else?"

"When are the movers going to get here?"

"On their way upstairs now."

"Thank you."

Meyer closed the door.

"What do you need movers for?" Bergman asked. "You've only been here five minutes."

"It's not for me," Finch answered. "It's for you."

There was another tap on the door and Meyer stuck his head in. "The movers are here," he said.

"Excellent," Finch said as she got to her feet. Half a beat later, Bergman did the same. "You know the configuration I want?"

"Yes, ma'am," he answered.

"Come on, Nick," Finch said as she headed to the door. "Let's give them the room."

Back in the main lobby area, Nick saw his old desk and chair from the sub-basement on a push cart. A team of four people were carrying boxes containing his files, phone and various other electronics and personal items from his cubicle.

"You have five minutes," Finch said to the team, which didn't protest or make excuses. Finch nodded to Bergman that he should follow her.

"Where are we going?"

"The Deputy Director wants to meet you."

Reflectively, Bergman ran his fingers through his hair. "Seriously?"

"Relax," Finch said with a laugh. "It is just a quick meet and greet. You'll get one minute tops which dramatically diminishes the chances of you doing anything galactically stupid and making me look like an idiot."

"I appreciate the vote of confidence," Bergman said as he took another swipe at his hair.

They arrived at a desk outside the office of the Deputy Director, John Thomas. A male secretary in his mid-thirties, without introductions said, "The Director is on a call, Ms. Finch. It shouldn't be long." Then he typed, "Finch and Bergman" on his keyboard which would instantly pop up on the Deputy Directors screen so he would know they were there.

"What exactly am I going to be doing?" Bergman asked as they waited.

"Nothing much," Finch said with a laugh. "We're just going to track down the person or persons who killed a sitting congressman and an admiral, blew up a fighter jet prototype and tried to sink the USS Ronald Reagan. And, with any luck, in the process we'll bankrupt a major defense contractor."

"Oh. Okay," Bergman said brightly. "That takes care of this morning. What are we going to be doing the rest of the day?"

The secretary gave them a look then shook his head. "The Director will see you now."

"After you," Bergman said, as he motioned for Finch to take point.

D.D. Thomas was an old school, Cold War veteran. He had been the Station Chief in Berlin the night the Wall fell, in the Pentagon when the 9-11 jet hit and helped in the hunt for Bin Laden. He had the perfect temperament and appearance for a spy master. He was so plain vanilla no one would pick him out of a police lineup and he could walk into any room without being noticed. Most importantly, he was a serious man doing a serious job. Unlike the elected buffoons on Capitol Hill, he could be trusted to keep the nation's secrets secret.

Now in his mid-sixties, John Thomas was thin and fit with no extra poundage on his six-foot three-inch frame. His face was heavily creased with wrinkles and what little hair he had left was snow white. His close-set deep brown eyes didn't miss much and his mouth never said much.

As usual, Finch had been correct. The meeting was short and to the point. Less than a minute after they had entered the office, they had made their exit. Less than ten seconds later, the phone on the desk of the secretary for the Deputy Director beeped.

"Get my car," Thomas said.

"Yes, sir," the secretary answered, and then made the call.

The Deputy Director came out of his office while still pulling on his overcoat. "I'll be at the Pentagon for the next two hours. Go ahead and take your lunch break."

"Yes, sir," the secretary answered. "Do you want me to pick anything up for you?"

Thomas shook his head and left.

Ten minutes later, in line for his usual coffee, the secretary handed the barista a twenty-dollar bill for his order but didn't let go of the bill until the barista looked up. Just before putting the twenty-dollar bill in the drawer, the barista turned it over. Written on the back of the note were two words.

Three hours and six dead drops to burner phones in four different countries later, the two-word message arrived at the desk of the CEO of Bathmann Aeronautics.

"They know."

Chapter 24

"YOU DON'T THINK she's just getting even with you for that article you wrote, do you?" Holly Mullen asked.

Grant Olsen sighed as he started to read the report which had been compiled by Mullen for a second time. "The thought had crossed my mind."

"How confident are you about your research?"

"As far as I can tell there are no decommissioned nukes being put on trains anywhere in North America, much less in the greater Los Angeles area," Holly Mullen answered.

"She said her grandfather was meeting a friend," Grant said. "Did that turn up anything?"

"Yeah, I looked into that angle too and didn't get anywhere," Mullen answered. "While Admiral Morse's wife raised his family in the house where Cassandra Morse is currently living, he never spent much time there. He had a place in Northern Virginia and you can count on one hand the number of times he'd been to Los Angeles in the past twenty years. With that being said, he ran with an interesting crowd. He was one of the big players in the acquisition of high-tech military weaponry for the Pentagon but he had a lot of academia contacts."

"Any of his old buddies active in nuclear weapons?" Grant asked.

"The only thing that came up when I did a search with the admiral and nuclear was his brother-in-law, William Comstock."

"That name sounds familiar."

"He should," Mullen said with a laugh. "His picture is in your paper at least once a month." Mullen's fingers danced on her keyboard and Comstock's picture came up.

"That old looney tune gasbag with the bowtie?"

"I'll admit he's colorful," Mullen answered, "but, he is also the Professor Emeritus of Marine Biogeochemistry at the University of California Santa Barbara and happens to be the driving force behind the Diablo Canyon protests."

"Those are still going on?" asked Grant.

"Seriously?" Mullen said with a snort. "Since the Fukushima Daiichi disaster in Japan, Diablo Canyon has moved to the top of the list of nuclear plants most likely to fall into the ocean," answered Mullen.

"I work the crime desk, okay, cut me some slack. What kind of damage would that plant do if there was a major accident?"

Holly Mullen shrugged. "Oceanfront property values from Monterey to Malibu would go to zero and California, at least the parts that were still inhabitable, would become Third World," answered Holly with a smirk. "Other than that, not much."

"Okay," Olsen said. "I get it. It's a big deal."

"Professor Comstock has been trying to shut the place down since it opened nearly 40 years ago. He conducts a regular protest that has had a longer Saturday run than the *Rocky Horror Picture Show*."

"And this is still active?"

"Currently he's fighting Diablo Canyon's renewal request."

"Any luck?" Grant asked.

"So far, they are not renewed and have a shutdown date around 2025, but they're still fighting for an extension."

"What are the chances of them getting the extension?"

"Diablo Canyon has a lot of money and a lot of powerful friends, but Comstock, despite his clownish appearance, is one tough customer."

Grant looked at his screen and the image of the grinning Comstock and his bowtie. "Yeah. Right."

"He was able to get the San Onofre nuclear facility near San Clemente shut down in 2012," Holly said.

Grant asked, "Isn't that Diablo place as old as dirt and rocks?"

"It was a state-of-the-art design for the 1960s but the guys who built it were the engineering dregs that weren't good enough to either work for the NASA space program or the aerospace industry at the time. It was a nightmare from the first day. At one point, they installed a 420-ton nuclear-reactor vessel backwards," said Holly.

"Geez. Does this Comstock have any ties to terrorists?" asked Grant.

"Not that I could find. He's an aging hippie who has been in mourning ever since Jerry Garcia died. He's done some seriously good environmental work, but he loves being on camera."

Grant grunted.

"What's the plan?" Holly asked.

"Go back on the dark net and shake the trees harder and see if anything falls out," Grant said. "If nothing happens in a few hours, then we mark this up as half a day spent getting jerked around by a nut job and move on."

"Can I use your computer?" Mullen asked.

Olsen shrugged. "Sure? Why?"

"Despite my best efforts, I think I had a lurker."

"Do I want to know what that means?" Olsen asked.

"Probably not."

Olsen picked up his battered briefcase from under the knee hole of the desk and let Mullen have his seat. "I need to get down to LAPD Headquarters and see if I can get a minute with the Chief."

"I bet you're real popular there right now."

After Olsen left, Mullen rolled up to his keyboard and logged in to a different VPN than the one she had used earlier. It was never a good idea to be a stationary target. You couldn't be too careful. There were too many people smarter and better than her on the dark net, some with evil intent. She started bouncing her request for admission to the dark net off of a series of different servers. As she waited, she put the palm of her left hand on her chin and her right hand on the back of her head and gave her neck a twist to work out a kink. After a few second delay, she was in.

***

"Charon, AKA Holly Mullen, is back," Nick Bergman said as he activated the search program to identify her location.

Carrie Finch was sitting opposite Bergman and the wall created by their monitors kept them from making eye contact. "Any more Cassandra Morse information requests?"

"No," Olsen answered as his fingers danced over his keyboard. "Now, apparently she's interested in a shipment of nuclear weapons by rail through the City of Los Angeles."

"Seriously," Finch said with a chuckle. "The only bombs in L.A. come out of Hollywood."

"Look at this." Bergman whistled softly. "She's kicked over the hornet's nest and a couple of the sites are going nuts. Half of them have their hair on fire, the other half are reaching for their tin foil hats." Bergman chuckled. "This is kinda fun to watch."

"Show me," Finch said and instantly the same information on Bergman's monitor was mirrored onto hers.

That little outpost of the dark web was having a meltdown. Words such as "Train", "Nuclear Weapons", "Terrorist", "Los Angeles", began flying around the site at warp speed and the story was gaining traction fast.

Bergman shook his head. "Within an hour, every conspiracy theory nut job in the world is going to be talking about a terrorist attack on L.A."

Finch pushed a button on her phone and instantly Kevin Meyer appeared at the door. "Yes, ma'am."

"If I have credible data relating to a rumor that is getting ready to go viral about a possible nuclear attack by terrorists on Los Angeles, who should I notify?"

Meyer didn't even blink at the question and reacted as calmly as if Finch had asked him for directions to the cafeteria. "The chain of command says you should give it to the Director of Counter-Terrorism at Homeland Security. But if it is time sensitive, you should take it straight to the Deputy Director and let him decide what to do with it."

"Is the Deputy Director still at the Pentagon?" Finch asked.

"He just got back," Meyer answered.

Finch grinned at Bergman, who was completely oblivious of the two people in the room. "Nice try, Rookie," Bergman said to his screen. "You can run but you can't hide." His monitor beeped. "The IP address traces to the offices of the *Los Angeles Guardian*." Bergan muttered an obscenity under his breath. "From the desk of none other than Grant Olsen."

"The guy who wrote the article about Cassandra Morse yesterday," Finch and Bergman said in unison.

Finch bolted out of her chair, brushed past Meyer, and sprinted toward the office of the Deputy Director. Without waiting to be announced or admitted, she burst into the D.D.'s office with Bergman and Meyer each a half step behind.

"What the hell!" D.D. Thomas shouted.

"Sorry, Director," Finch said. "The internet is about an hour away from having a meltdown on, what I pray, is a bogus rumor. Do we have any nuclear material going through the city of Los Angeles by rail soon?"

"How the fuck did you..." He stopped and waved his startled staff away. "Come in and close the door."

Chapter 25

CASSANDRA MORSE HAD just finished chugging down her fourth large glass of water when the doorbell rang. Now that her latest dream had arrived, she wanted to flush any residual caffeine and alcohol out of her system. Other than the expected craving from a cold-turkey coffee withdrawal, her mind felt clearer and more focused than it had in months.

As she reached for the doorknob, she glanced at the Louisville Slugger bat leaning nearby. For the moment at least, she didn't feel the need for it. If it was another pesky reporter, from what she had seen of them so far, she was pretty sure she could toss them back to the sidewalk without any armament.

Instead of a reporter, she saw an express delivery driver dashing back to his van. Looking down, she saw a small 4 x 4 x 2 box on the threshold. Examining it, the package had her name printed in block letters on the front and no return address. The box was completely generic and looked like something you could pick up in any office supply store.

Looking around again to be sure there were no other surprises, she suddenly felt a cold tingle go up her spine.

It wasn't fear exactly, but more of a warning sign.

She felt all of her senses go on high alert, the way they would if she had heard an unexplained twig snap while walking in the woods.

Her reaction was primal and visceral.

Stepping out on her porch, her eyes started doing a grid search. She took her time and focused her full attention. She didn't want to miss anything.

Her eyes stopped when she saw them.

About twenty feet up on the streetlight pole across the street was a small box that she was 100% sure had not been there a few days ago and another one that also seemed out of place but with the dust and dirt on it had been there for a while.

Cassandra Finch, for the first time since she had been blown out of the sky, felt her old warrior instincts starting to kick in. She immediately retreated through her front door. The last thing she wanted to do was be in the open and stationary, making her an easy sniper target. Once inside, she engaged the lock and deadbolt.

As she entered the living room, she saw her grandfather standing erect in his full-dress blues. Above his left breast pocket were a row of full-size medals. He had on white gloves and the sword his father, her great-grandfather, had given him the day he had made Vice Admiral, was attached at the waist.

"Welcome back, Lieutenant."

"Thank you, sir," she answered as she pulled the blinds closed.

"We've missed you."

Cassandra smiled then headed to the kitchen in the rear of the house. She tossed the package on the kitchen table, then, standing in the shadows, she began a modified grid search. This time she started with the light pole and that was as far as she needed to go. It also had a new small box which had not been there before attached about twenty feet above ground level and an older one next to it.

The admiral joined her and looked out the window. "It would appear you've been under surveillance for some time, Lieutenant."

"They've upgraded since my appearance in the newspaper and the visit by the stranger yesterday."

"Clearly, you're making someone nervous," the admiral said.

Cassandra turned and carefully opened the box. Inside there was a burner phone and what appeared to be a small tactical flashlight but she knew better. It was a military grade laser that could knock out any unshielded video equipment in short order. She powered up the phone and called the only number in the contact. It was answered on the third ring.

"You really need to speak to Dr. Newman."

"My next stop," Cassandra said.

"Have you found them yet?"

"Front and rear light poles. Small boxes which were not there a few days ago and one that was."

"Excellent. The more you detox, the better your instincts will be."

"We need to meet," Cassandra said.

"Too risky for me at the moment," the male voice said.

"Ah," Cassandra said. "They're looking for you and think you may return here."

"Excellent and spot on," the voice said. "Meet the doctor then we'll chat again."

"Do you have a solution for me?"

"I do, but you won't like it."

The line went dead.

Cassandra dashed upstairs and changed into cargo shorts, a loose t-shirt and slipped on her most comfortable running shoes. While she wasn't in anywhere near the physical condition she had been in during her military days, she had not allowed herself to completely go to seed. A few days a week, when she needed to blow off some energy, she would take late night beach runs which were measured in miles not blocks.

She pulled her underwear drawer out of the dresser and dumped everything on her bed. Next, she pried up the false bottom of the drawer which exposed a thousand dollars in small, used bills. She grabbed about half of her stash and tucked it in her bra and then tucked the other half in her right front pocket. She turned off her cellphone and the burner phone the odd little man had sent her. Next, she put both in a small waterproof Faraday bag that would block any RF signals and make her impossible to track her via either. She crammed the Faraday bag in her right back pocket. It was a tight fit, but she was sure they would not impede her. She pulled her hair back into a ponytail and tucked it through her Dodger's cap.

Checking the mirror, she was ready.

Cassandra, as she headed back downstairs, picked up the tactical laser and opened the back door.

Across the canal, the geek monitoring Cassandra Morse's activity leaned forward when the rear door opened. It was the first action his side of the house had seen since the surveillance equipment had been installed. "Shit," he muttered as he watched her stare straight at his camera. Then she raised the middle finger of her left hand and aimed the military grade laser at his lens. His screen instantly went blank.

He immediately reached for his phone. "Sir, we have a problem."

Chapter 26

AFTER TAKING OUT the front cameras the same way she had the ones in back, Cassandra Morse was sure whoever was watching her was scrambling to get human assets in place. Hopefully, they would be too late. She took off running in the direction of the Grand Canal footbridge. Even if they were in pursuit, because of the famous Venice Beach canals, they would have to abandon any vehicles and follow her on foot. Unless they had a massive team on standby, in position and ready to jump into action, which was unlikely, she had, for the moment at least, the advantage of surprise.

Plus, she knew where she was going and they didn't.

The man picked her up before she had even gone half a block.

"Damn," Cassandra muttered. In addition to the surveillance cameras, they had a manned observation nest near her house.

Cassandra took a quick glance over her shoulder. While she was dressed for a run, the same could not be said for her pursuer. In shorts and running shoes, Cassandra wouldn't turn a head as she blew past any pedestrians. A man in long pants and a windbreaker in eighty-five-degree weather was odd. Seeing him sprinting at full speed was weird, even for California.

The man chasing her was faster than she was. He had the body and smooth effortless stride of a middle-distance runner. Despite her wardrobe advantage, he was closing the gap.

Not good.

Grabbing another quick glance, things got worse. The man was talking into his wrist. She had already lost the element of surprise and he was in contact with his team.

They knew her exact location.

She needed something to change the game.

She felt a primal tingle, as if she'd caught the smell of a predator drifting down wind. Running next to her was a much younger version of the admiral. "Listen to your instincts, Lieutenant."

She did. For no logical reason, even though she wanted to get to Pacific Avenue, instead of going straight, she took a hard right onto Strongs Drive.

As she turned the corner, she nearly ran into four oversized specimens. They were talking loudly and reeking of a combination of liniment and sunscreen and walking in the direction of Muscle Beach.

That was what she had sensed.

Help.

The smallest had to weigh in at one ninety and the largest closer to three hundred than two fifty. She knew show muscle looked impressive, but in a street fight it was a liability instead of an asset. There was a reason almost every Navy SEAL was under six feet tall and lean. In combat, speed and agility will beat muscle mass every time.

The four heads turned in her direction.

Cassandra immediately made herself burst into tears.

"My boyfriend is chasing me and he's going to kill me!" She shrieked.

The four heads looked past her when they heard her pursuer round the corner and skid to a stop.

"Please! Please!" Cassandra shouted as her body shook in terror. "That's him! Don't let him get me!"

The four men exchanged glances and immediately came to an agreement to help the nice lady. After all, it was four to one. Shoulder to shoulder, they build about a thousand-pound wall of beef between Cassandra and the man chasing her. Seeing the unexpected development, her pursuer grinned in Cassandra's direction. He was confident he could make short work of the four men, but he knew it would take some time. He also knew, from what he had just seen, that if he ever lost sight of his target, his chances of reacquiring it approached nil.

With the four men's eyes now all on her pursuer and not her, Cassandra morphed back to herself. She blew the man a kiss and waved goodbye. She took the next right and headed for water.

To avoid drawing attention to herself, she slowed to a walk as she headed down Pacific Avenue. It didn't take long before she saw what she was looking for. A late model Camry sedan was at the curb in front of a coffee shop. On the right front corner of the windshield, there were Uber and Lyft decals.

She walked up to a man of around thirty who appeared to be of Middle Eastern descent sitting at an outdoor table sipping an espresso.

The smell of the coffee made Cassandra's mouth water but she ignored it. She had business to conduct.

"Is that your car?" Cassandra asked politely.

The man, his tiny cup about halfway to his lips, stopped and sized up Cassandra. While perspiring profusely, she didn't look like she was having drug withdrawal and she certainly didn't look like a hooker.

His head went and down maybe a half inch.

Cassandra glanced around and saw he was the center of focus for all the other outdoor tables.

"*Hal tatahadath al arabiya*?" Cassandra asked which roughly translated to, "Do you speak Arabic?"

The man nodded.

"*Ahtaj tawseela*" which translated to, "I need a ride."

The man shrugged and started to take another sip of his coffee. He stopped when Cassandra laid ten twenty-dollar bills on his table. The man raised an eyebrow, finished his drink, dabbed a napkin on his lips, swept the bills into his pocket and motioned in the direction of his car.

With Cassandra in the rear and the driver behind the wheel, they pulled away from the curb.

"Your Arabic is dreadful," the driver said with a slight British accent.

Cassandra laughed. "I don't get the opportunity to use it often."

"Where can I take you?"

"I would like to be dropped off two blocks from the University of Southern California Medical Center."

"Do you need to gain entrance without being seen?"

"Yes," she answered.

"What would it be worth to you?"

Cassandra passed another two hundred dollars over the seat.

"That will be enough for me," he said softly. "But we will need to stop and make a purchase."

Cassandra dropped the last of her back pocket wad of cash over the seat and showed the man her empty hand.

Satisfied he had milked her dry, the driver turned his attention back towards the road. After a quick stop and wardrobe change, the Uber pulled into the main parking lot of the USC Medical Center.

"Stay a step behind me, avoid eye contact and for Allah's sake do not speak."

Cassandra, now dressed in a black burka with only her eyes showing, stepped out of the Uber and submissively followed the driver into the hospital.

At the door to Dr. Newman's office, they parted ways. The door was unlocked and Cassandra, still in the burka, entered. The lobby area was empty; apparently the doctor did not have any patients scheduled.

"Damn," Cassandra muttered. Not confident in either her phone or Dr. Newman's, she hadn't felt safe calling for an appointment. "I go through all this trouble and he's probably on the back nine."

She was still considering her options when she heard a male voice deep in the bowels of the office laughing. As she got closer, she realized it was a pair of men's voices. As she walked into Dr. Newman's office, it begged the question of who was more surprised.

Dr. Newman seeing Cassandra in a burka or, Cassandra seeing the odd little man in the chair across from Dr. Newman's desk.

Chapter 27

TOM MCMAHON WAS mad at himself. He had not done his due diligence properly on Cassandra Morse. He had noted she was a pilot but had missed that she was a combat pilot. That is a whole different breed of cat than somebody flying cargo planes until they get in enough air hours, on the military's dime, to land a job with a major airline.

Jack Logan, patted McMahon on the shoulder. He knew what his boss was thinking.

"You wouldn't have done anything any differently if you had known," Logan said. "She wasn't the primary, Tommy. Besides," he said with a laugh, "it wasn't your ass she kicked, it was mine."

McMahon shook his head. "Doesn't help."

"Come on," Logan said, "that was righteous what she did." Logan smiled. "I wonder if she's seeing anybody. Is her phone number in the file?"

"Look for yourself," McMahon answered as he threw the folder in Logan's direction.

Logan ducked and the file hit the wall behind him and scattered across the floor. "Have you called the boss yet?"

McMahon shook his head. "I was holding out in hopes that the Alpha Team might have reacquired."

"In your dreams," Logan said, and he intertwined his finger behind his head and leaned back on in his chair. "That lady's got game."

On cue, the door opened and the pair that made up the Alpha Team strolled in.

"In the wind," the older of the two said as he eyed Logan and grinned. "We were thinking about going out for a beer at a dive called Benny's." He turned his full attention to Logan. "It would be perfect for you. I hear they have a great Shirley Temple and women who don't run very fast."

"I earned that one," Logan said. "You want to talk about Seattle?"

"No. No. No," the guy answered.

"Do we sit on her house and try to reacquire?" Logan asked.

"I'll tell you in a minute," McMahon said as he reached for his phone.

"The Wicked Witch doesn't know yet?" Alpha leader asked.

Logan shook his head.

"Ouch. I need to hit the litter box."

"Same here," Alpha Leader's partner said as they both left the room.

McMahon put his phone on speaker so Logan could hear.

Much to McMahon's surprise, neither Rachel Frey nor her secretary answered the phone. Instead, it was a man.

"Who is this?" he asked cautiously as he reached for the button to disconnect the call.

"This is Gabriel Ashton, McMahon."

McMahon and Logan exchanged startled looks. Instead of Rachel Frey, the call to her phone had been diverted. McMahon was on the line with his boss's boss. The Senior VP of Security for Bathmann Aeronautics.

"Report."

"We lost her, sir."

"Forget about her," Ashton said. "We have bigger problems and I have a new assignment for you. Sanitize the L.A. operation and get your entire crew over to LAX. I have a jet waiting for you."

McMahon said, "Yes, sir," to a line which was already dead.

Chapter 28

"I'LL BE DAMNED," Dr. Daniel Newman said as he tossed a hundred-dollar bill in the general direction of the odd little man but missed badly. "I should know better than to ever bet with you."

The man picked up the bill off the floor and tucked it in his pocket. "Always a pleasure doing business with you."

"What the hell is going on here?" Cassandra demanded as she shimmied her way out of the burka.

"Sorry," Newman said. "Cassandra Morse, Dr. Tanner Dawson."

"Who the hell is Dr. Tanner Dawson?" Cassandra asked as she felt her blood pressure starting to rise.

"Dr. Dawson is the one who drilled the hole in your head."

"What?" Cassandra shouted as she took two quick steps and closed the distance between her and the surgeon. "What the hell did you do to me?"

"I plan to tell you everything," he answered calmly. "It will take a while so you may want to sit down."

"You really need to listen to what he has to say," added Newman with concern in his voice.

"At the moment what I want to do is listen to him screaming and then hearing him begging me to put him out of his misery." Cassandra turned her attention to Dr. Newman. "Do you know if this hospital has a crematorium? If not, maybe a blast furnace?"

"Wonderful!" Dawson said. "Your warrior side has completely re-emerged! This is excellent news."

Cassandra poked Dawson hard in the chest with her index finger. "You don't seem to realize how close I am to ripping your lungs out, shoving them down your throat then doing it again."

Dawson laughed again while rubbing his chest. "I'm perfectly safe for the moment."

"Don't bet on it," Cassandra snarled.

"In a few seconds your anger is going to vanish and your intellect and instincts are going to kick in."

"How do you know that?"

"You're about to realize, I'm no threat to you. Instead, you're going to see me as the person with answers to all of your questions." Dawson's eyes twinkled. "That makes me much more valuable to you alive and talking than dead."

Cassandra blinked twice, took a step back and glared at Dr. Dawson. She wouldn't admit it, but he was right. She felt her anger flowing away and her curiosity starting to build. Cassandra fell heavily in the other office chair and glared at both doctors. "What was the deal with the hundred-dollar bill?"

"Tanner bet me you would show up within two hours of receiving his phone call," Newman said with a laugh. "He had twenty-one minutes to spare which is pretty amazing since you had to take the I-10."

"You were expecting me…ah," Cassandra said. "That's why the office door was unlocked."

"Precisely," Newman said as he got up from his desk. "Which reminds me, I should probably relock it."

"Your disguise was brilliant," Dawson said.

"Flattery will get you nowhere. All I want to know is who the hell you are, what you did to me and how you're going to fix it."

"Dr. Dawson," Newman said as he reclaimed his desk. "is the head of neurosurgery at George Washington University Hospital in Washington DC. He has been making great strides in PTSD research at Walter Reed and various VA Hospitals around the country including here in Los Angeles," Newman continued. "Tanner has been helping a lot of injured veterans get their lives back in order. He's doing really important work."

"Okay," Cassandra said, her voice softer. "What did you do to me?"

"We had been doing research with microsurgery similar to what they do to relieve the symptoms of Parkinson's Disease. We drill a microscopic hole in a patient's skull then simulate a section of the brain."

"Okay," Cassandra said.

Dr. Dawson hesitated.

"You have to tell her, Tanner," Newman said.

"I was flown into a private research facility where they had brought you after the crash." For the first time the smile vanished from Dr. Tanner Dawson's face. "They told me you had been injured in a training exercise. They had all of the proper paperwork and you were in no condition to give me a verbal confirmation."

"So, you drilled a hole in my head and," Cassandra said with a sneer, "without my consent, ran your little experiment on me."

"In our efforts to improve brain function for disabled vets we discovered a section of the brain, if stimulated, dramatically increases sensory perception. You were presented as an ideal test candidate. We could try the procedure on someone recently injured instead of sometime after the damage had started to heal and scar tissue had formed. I understand…" Dr. Dawson started to say but Cassandra cut him off.

"You don't understand anything." Her eyes flashed with anger. "You ended my military career and you've made the past six months of my life a living hell."

"He's not the one you should be angry with, Ms. Morse," Newman said. "They lied to him every step of the way and he operated on you in good faith. If he had known you had survived…"

"What do you mean if he had known I survived? My rescue was in all of the papers."

"The medical records they gave him were completely fabricated," Newman answered.

"Right down to using a false name for you."

Cassandra blinked a few times then grunted. "Damn."

"You came through the surgery with flying colors," Dawson added. "but you were still in an induced coma for your other injuries. Two days after I had gotten back to DC, they told me you had died from complications of your other injuries."

"Ironically," Newman added. "I consulted with Dr. Dawson about your case during the brief time you were in this facility. With the additional recent head trauma they had inflicted upon you just before your rescue, and a different name and medical history, there was no reason Dr. Dawson would have thought you were his previous patient."

"Damn," Cassandra repeated. "Why would someone want to do something like that to me?"

Dr. Dawson hesitated.

"In for a penny, in for a pound," Dr. Newman said with a knowing look on his face.

"You were not the first person to have this procedure," Dawson said. "We knew the potential side effects and apparently so did the people manipulating you."

"What side effects?"

"My procedure is fairly simple and not very invasive. We stimulate neural pathways that have been blocked or damaged which heightens sensory perceptions. In your case," Dawson said, "since there were no blockages, I'm afraid I kicked your sensory perceptions into overdrive." Dawson shook his head. "The mind is a complicated piece of machinery. Since I inadvertently stimulated a section of your brain that was already functioning at an extremely high level, I gave your brain more information to process than it was capable of handling." Dr. Dawson stared hard at Cassandra. "When you were under Dr. Newman's care, you claimed to be having conversations with your deceased grandfather."

Cassandra shifted uncomfortably in her chair. She knew what question was coming and she wasn't sure if she was ready to answer it.

"Are you still seeing your grandfather?"

Dr. Dawson reached over and patted her hand. Cassandra felt a mild electrical jolt and assumed it came from static electricity in the carpet. "Relax," he said warmly as he gave her hand a squeeze. "You're having a perfectly natural response to the stimulus I gave you and you're not losing your mind."

For some reason and on some level, Cassandra knew even if what the doctor was saying was not true, he believed it and was not trying to fool her.

Cassandra looked up over Dr. Dawson's shoulder and saw her grandfather leaning against the file cabinet and smiling. "Trust them, Cassie," the admiral said.

Both Newman and Dawson followed her eyes.

"Is he here now?" Dr. Newman asked.

The admiral gave her a thumbs up.

"Yes," she answered meekly as she felt tears welling up in her eyes.

"This is important," Dr. Dawson said as he leaned closer to Cassandra. "Is he serving as a mentor and guide and offering you advice?"

Cassandra chuckled. With the genie out of the bottle on her conversations with her grandfather, she felt her body relaxing. "A bit more advice than necessary from time to time."

The admiral stuck his tongue out at her and blew a raspberry in her direction.

"How often do you see him?"

Cassandra rolled her eyes. "A couple of times a day."

"Is it during stressful moments or when you need to make a decision?"

When Dr. Dawson pulled his hand away, she felt her skepticism instantly start to rebuild.

Cassandra straightened up. "Where is all this headed?" she asked.

"The brain does not like things it can't understand or logically explain," Dr. Newman said.

"By manifesting your grandfather," Dr. Dawson continued, "you're using him to make sense of the information overload."

"He just told you to trust us, didn't he?" Dr. Newman asked.

"How did you know that?"

Newman laughed. "While I can't read body language at your level, the way you relaxed meant you had dropped some of your defenses."

"I'll be damned," Cassandra said. "What about the dreams?"

"Like your grandfather, your dreams are just another vehicle to process the input which is overwhelming your brain," Newman answered.

"Your dreams didn't just arrive from the heavens, Ms. Morse," Dawson added. "They are not divine intervention or the voice of God. Right now, without consciously knowing it, you are soaking up information from anyone and everything around you."

"Were you near the man who set the fire that killed those people?" Dr. Newman asked.

"How in the world did you know that?" Cassandra demanded.

"It's the proximity factor," Dr. Newman answered. "You only pick-up signals from people and things that are near you."

"Where did you see this man?" Dawson asked.

"He was sitting a few bar stools away from me the night before the fire."

"Did you speak to him?"

"I don't think so," she answered.

"Was he agitated or behaving irrationally?"

"Not that I noticed," Cassandra answered. "He seemed sad and deeply depressed, like he had the weight of the world on his shoulders."

Newman glanced at Dawson.

"What?" Cassandra demanded.

"Did you ever get near the two victims?" Dawson asked.

"I seriously doubt it…" Cassandra stopped, and her eyes grew larger. "I'll have to check if they are the same people, but there was a pair of homeless guys I used to walk past all the time. One of them had been sick for a while…" Cassandra closed her eyes and shook her head, "which was why they wanted to get off of the street at night." Cassandra rubbed her forehead. "My subconscious knew all of that and sent me a dream."

Cassandra looked up to the smiling face of her grandfather who, like when they played charades, double tapped the end of his nose twice then pointed in her direction.

"This brings me back to my original question," Cassandra said, "Who did this to me and why?"

Chapter 29

DR. TANNER DAWSON shook his head. "There are several possible scenarios about what happened to you and none of them are good."

"Let's hear them."

"For the past year or so, the military has been pestering me to use my procedure on healthy military personnel, particularly combat pilots."

"Why?"

"They felt it might enhance reaction time and make the pilots more intuitive." Dawson shook his head again. "I had no desire to produce super soldiers and I refused. The first scenario is that they were trying to trick me into using my procedure on a combat pilot without my knowledge and then see what happened."

"I take it you don't think much of that scenario," Cassandra said.

"I doubt the Pentagon would have had many problems finding volunteers," Dawson answered. "I've refined the procedure to the point where it could be done in less than an hour and on an outpatient basis. While the results can be initially disorienting, once a candidate for the procedure understands their new reality, they're fine. Better than fine actually." Dawson grabbed Cassandra's hand. "With a bit of therapy, we're confident you will be able to regain control over your life."

"Whoever did this, obviously had me at their mercy. Why not just kill me and toss me overboard? Why go through all that trouble and expense when they're probably already using your procedure without telling you?"

"It's like you can read my mind," Dawson answered with a chuckle.

"What is your best guess?" Cassandra asked.

"Somebody really wanted to discredit you," Dr. Tanner said. "They knew, post-surgery, many of the patients were terrified and confused. Like you, some hallucinated a mentor they had regular conversations with and swore they were with them in the room. For most, the mere knowledge of what was happening to them was enough for them to stabilize."

"It was like a light switch was flipped on," Cassandra said.

"My thought exactly," Dawson said. "I think that's the case with you. For others it might take weeks if not months of therapy and counseling before they are able to understand their new reality."

Cassandra shook her head. "Since no one knew I had gone through your procedure and I received no counseling, I would come off as a delusional nut job."

"Reading my mind again," Dawson answered with a laugh.

"Who hired you to work on me?"

"That's where it gets interesting," Dawson said as he gave her hand a gentle pat.

"Let me guess," Cassandra said. "It was a division of the DOD you had worked with previously and trusted. Everything was fine until you saw my picture in the paper about my dream and recognized me. When you went back to investigate, they had no record of you ever being at the mystery facility. No record of the procedure you performed on me and no record of a Lt. Jane Kelly ever being a pilot in any branch of the military."

"You're getting really good at this," Dawson said as he continued to hold Cassandra's hand.

"Too good," Dr. Newman said with a startled expression on his face. "We never told you the fake name they had given you."

Dr. Dawson fell heavily back in his chair, releasing his grip on her hand. His mouth was open wide in disbelief. "You're right," he said softly.

"It's about to get even more interesting," Dr. Newman said as he turned his full attention to Cassandra. "What was the name of that project that created such a stir when you mentioned it?"

"Icarus?" Cassandra answered with no idea where this conversation was headed.

"You told me your grandfather had told you about Icarus for the first time in the hospital room."

"Correct."

Newman jumped out of his chair and started pacing. "Is it possible?"

"What?" Cassandra demanded.

"It could have been in her short-term memory," Dr. Newman offered.

"What?" Cassandra demanded more loudly.

"When you were able to come up with the alias they used for you with me sitting next to you while holding…GOOD GOD!" Dawson shouted as he looked at his hand then Cassandra's.

"What?" Cassandra demanded.

"Mental activity is just a series of weak electrical charges," Newman answered.

"With your heightened sensitivity, while making flesh to flesh contact, you may be able to sense them and…" Dawson said as he grabbed Cassandra's hand again.

"And actually be able to read people's minds," Cassandra finished.

"Yes," Newman said as he shook his head in disbelief.

"There is one major issue," Dawson said grimly as he tightened his grip on Cassandra's hand.

Cassandra's face turned ashen. "The procedure happened days after the crash," she muttered. "At that point, my grandfather was already dead."

Dr. Daniel Newman said, "How the hell did you read the mind of a dead man?"

Chapter 30

A HEAVY SILENCE fell over the office as Dr. Newman and his two guests, Dr. Tanner Dawson and Cassandra Morse, were all lost in their own thoughts.

Finally, Newman said, "Have you ever seen anything like this before, Tanner?"

"Nothing even close," Dawson answered.

"What about Roland Turner?" Cassandra offered. "He was always chatting with his dead wife and he had a similar dream issue as mine."

"When you do that," Newman asked, "do you hear it in your mind first or does it just appear?"

"Oh," Cassandra answered sheepishly as she looked down at her hand which was still being held by Dr. Dawson. "I was the first one to mention Roland Turner, wasn't I?"

Both doctors nodded their heads.

"It was just there when I needed it," Cassandra answered.

"This opens up an entirely new possibility," Newman said with a far-off expression on his face. "Maybe the psychic gene is real."

"Excuse me?" Cassandra said. "Ah!" she said as she read Dr. Dawson's thoughts. "Since psychic ability tends to run in families…"

"Especially on the female side," Newman added.

Cassandra's mouth flew open and she stared at Dr. Dawson. "Do you think it's possible?"

"Would you two mind keeping me in the loop here?" Dr. Newman protested.

Cassandra motioned to Dawson. "You speak his language better than me."

"What if the psychic gene does exist? What if my procedure stimulated a latent ability in Ms. Morse? Then amplified it to measurable levels."

Newman made a face. "Are you saying, some of those psychics really do have a sixth sense?"

Dawson shook his head. "One thing for sure…"

"We can't let any of this out of this room," Cassandra finished for him.

"And, when you are outside of this room," Newman said with a chuckle, "you really need to stop finishing people's thoughts for them."

Cassandra shook her head. "Imagine if any government got wind of this?" Cassandra shivered as she glanced at Dawson. "You're right. They would lock me up and dissect me."

Dr. Daniel Newman furrowed his brow. "Try me," he said. He held out his hand and Cassandra released her grip on Dawson's hand and grabbed Newman's.

"What am I thinking right now?"

Cassandra shook her head. "No idea. Why, what were you thinking?"

"I was thinking you've got a great pair of legs and are probably a terror in the sack."

"Really?" Cassandra said."

"I wanted a primal thought to see if it triggered you." Newman looked at Dawson. "You try it, Tanner. And make it primal."

Dawson grabbed her hand and an instant later, Cassandra's eye and mouth flew open and she slapped Dawson on the arm with her other hand. "Oh my, doctor! Such a naughty boy!" Cassandra said with a wicked grin. "I know a shop in Hollywood where we can get everything we need."

Dawson pulled his hand away. "Interesting. What am I thinking now?"

"Not a clue," Cassandra answered.

"Physical contact," Dr. Newman said as he extended his hand across the desk and Cassandra shook it. "Try me again."

Cassandra took his hand then shook her head.

"Damn," Dr. Newman said. "So, it doesn't work on everyone."

"Hold on," Dr. Dawson said as he grabbed Cassandra's hand again. "Can you sense anything from my memory?"

Cassandra closed her eyes and concentrated then shook her head. "No," she answered.

"Try recalling a memory," Newman said to Dawson.

"Ah," Cassandra said with a smile. "I don't know which is prettier. The cherry blossoms or your daughter."

"Amazing," Dr. Dawson said as he reclaimed his hand. "Try touching my arm."

Cassandra touched the sleeve of the doctor's jacket then shook her head.

"So we agree," Newman said. "A connection can only be made with certain other subjects, requires physical, flesh to flesh contact and she can only read current brain activity and nothing stored."

"Thank God," Cassandra said as she let out a sigh of relief. When she saw the puzzled expressions on both doctors' faces, she continued. "If that's the case, that would greatly diminish my value to the military."

With the connection broken, Dawson and Cassandra were no longer on the same page and he was confused. "I'm not sure I follow."

"It would be very easy to create countermeasures for this skill. Once it became public knowledge, everyone from diplomats to spies would wear long sleeves and gloves and never let anyone get close enough for physical contact. This skill might be good for civilian interrogation for people who didn't know better. Once the word got out, the first thing they'll teach to anyone in the military or any of the alphabet spy agencies would be techniques for how to clear your mind."

"Fascinating," Newman said.

"Countermeasures are always easier and cheaper to create than weapons. A five hundred-thousand-dollar stealth cruise missile can sink an eight-billion-dollar aircraft carrier with another five-billion-dollars' worth of aircraft on the flight deck."

Dawson smiled at Newman. "I think we can safely forgo extensive therapy with Ms. Morse."

"Indeed," Dawson answered. "I'd be willing to wager she has completely reverted back to her old persona."

"What about him?" Cassandra said as she pointed to the admiral who was grinning at her from across the room.

"You may need to get used to him being around," Newman said.

"You might even consider him a blessing," Dawson added.

Cassandra rolled her eyes when the admiral blew Dawson a kiss.

"Some blessing," Cassandra muttered.

"Cassandra," Newman said gently. "Tanner is right. Your grandfather will allow you to be in touch with your better angels and help you process the information overload you're going to be constantly hit with."

"Will this fade over time?" she asked.

"Unknown," Newman answered.

"What about my dreams?"

"Again, unknown," Newman answered. "You could use the countermeasures you discussed earlier as a two-way street. If you don't touch anyone, then you'll not make the connection and probably not have the dreams."

"Speaking of dreams. Did you touch the arsonist?" Dawson asked.

Cassandra thought about it for a moment as she did a mental rewind. "Yes. The arsonist was deep in thought and bumped into me when we were both coming out of the bathroom at the bar at the same time. I had on short sleeves and he touched my arm." Cassandra's head swiveled back and forth between the two doctors. "The contact was only for a moment."

Newman thought about that for a second. "You say he was lost in thought?"

"Yes."

"He was probably considering the arson option at the time."

"The homeless guys?" Newman asked.

Cassandra closed her eyes. "Yes," she answered. "I put some change in one of the guy's cups and he shook my hand and blessed me." Her eyes flew open. "That was the night before the fire and the very night I had the dream."

Suddenly Cassandra was on her feet doing a happy dance.

Newman and Dawson exchanged worried looks.

"Relax, I'm not crazy. My grandfather knew exactly what was coming and just before Icarus hit us, we held hands." She finished her dance and bowed. "That's how I knew about the Icarus Project. We were connected when he died, and the procedure Dr. Dawson performed a few days later allowed me to move Icarus from my subconscious where my grandfather had left it to my conscious mind."

"That is a workable hypothesis…" Newman said but stopped when he saw Cassandra was heading toward the door. "Where are you going?" he demanded.

"I'll be back, but I have a bigger problem to deal with at the moment."

"What could possibly be bigger than this," Newman asked.

She told them about her dream.

"What are you going to do?" Newman asked.

"Find the man of my dreams," Cassandra answered.

"And who might that be?" Dawson asked.

"A semi-cute twenty-five-year-old guy who tried to pick me up a bar."

"Why?" Newman asked.

"He was the last person to touch me before the dream."

Chapter 31

CASSANDRA SPENT THE first fifteen minutes of her ride home in the back of an Uber deciding exactly what to say to Det. Steve Foley. How could she convince him to search for a random guy who claimed he was just in town for a few days? She could describe him, but other than that, she had nothing else for Foley to go on. While gridlocked on the I-10, she decided on a strategy. Tell him pretty much the truth about the dream but not tell him how the guy fit in.

Like she had learned at Annapolis, no battle plan ever survives the first contact with the enemy.

Using her phone instead of the burner, she hoped he had her in his contacts and would pick up when he saw her name on the caller ID. She dialed the number she had memorized that Foley had given her.

He answered on the fourth or fifth ring. "No."

"No? I haven't asked you anything yet."

"The answer is still no."

"Too bad," Cassandra said. "I was going to invite you over for a night you'd never forget."

"Tempting but still no."

"Why?"

"I have a seriously pissed Lieutenant who has instructed our entire precinct that anyone who works with you in any way, shape or form can either put in their retirement paper or request a transfer. Failure to comply with this request will result in severe and immediate disciplinary action for ignoring a direct and unambiguous order."

"I take it her meeting with the chief did not go well."

"It was about as bad as it gets," Foley answered with a laugh. "No one knew it, but she was on the short list for Captain at the Hollywood

Division. Apparently, this arson case, and the publicity it has generated, has moved her from the top of the list to so far down they have to pump daylight to her to keep her from getting a vitamin D deficiency."

"Ouch."

"Yeah, ouch."

"I'm just guessing here, but this is probably not a good time to ask for a favor," Cassandra stated.

"I've always found smart women attractive," Foley answered.

Cassandra chuckled. "I had another dream."

"Good lord," Foley said with an exasperated tone in his voice.

"Bad timing, I know," Cassandra said.

"Ya think?"

"Look," Cassandra said with a sigh. "What I really want to do, instead of counting the body bags on the sidewalk after the event, is stop this before it happens."

There was about ten seconds of silence, but Cassandra knew she had to wait him out. The next one to speak lost. "If," Foley said guardedly. "If I were able to help you, what would you need?"

"I need you to find somebody."

"Who?"

Cassandra thought about it for a few seconds but couldn't think of any way to make it sound better. "I need to find a guy who was hitting on me at Benny's the other night."

"Why?" Foley snapped angrily.

"I can't tell you."

"Then I can't help you."

The line went dead.

"That went well," Cassandra muttered as she put her phone back in her pocket. When they turned the corner onto her street, she saw Grant Olsen pacing in a tight circle on the sidewalk in front of her house. "This can't be good."

The moment she was out of the Uber, he was on her.

"Very funny. Ha Ha. Now we're even."

"What are you talking about?" asked Cassandra.

"You jerking me around to get even with me for the story I wrote," Olsen shouted.

Cassandra saw several of her neighbors on their porches trying to see what all of the commotion was about. "Let's take this inside," she said.

After Grant Olsen was safely in her foyer, she closed the door. She smiled when she noticed the surveillance boxes had been removed.

In the living room, Olsen wheeled on her again. "Are you aware that there is a seven-hundred-man nuclear courier squad based in Oak Ridge, Tennessee?" asked Grant.

"No," answered Cassandra.

"Are you aware they're responsible for the safe movement of all weapons grade nuclear material in the USA?"

"This is fascinating but…" Cassandra said.

"Do you know they exclusively use special trucks and airplanes to ferry this material around and they haven't used a damn train in over fifty years?" asked Grant, now red in the face with anger.

"Oh."

"Oh? OH? That's all you've got?" asked Grant.

"Sometimes my dreams are difficult to translate."

"When my research associate, who spent an entire day banging her head against the wall, searched for anything nuclear attached to you and your family, all she came up with was Professor William Comstock."

"Uncle Billy? You can't be serious."

"He's the only one we could find from your grandfather's old circle of friends that was even in the same time zone with anything nuclear related. Could he be a terrorist?"

"Uncle Billy's a vegan. He won't even eat animals, so he certainly isn't going to hurt any people."

"Look lady. I don't know what kind of game you're running here but I don't like being played for a fool."

Olsen headed toward the door.

"I have something else for you."

"Sell it to somebody else. I'm not buying."

He slammed the door hard as he made his exit.

The admiral came up behind her, giving her a start. "You need to follow him," the admiral said

"Why?" she asked.

"I'm your subconscious, remember?" the admiral said. "You already know why."

Cassandra was out the door and nearly at the bottom of the front steps when she saw Grant Olsen heading to where he had parked his car.

Out of nowhere, two men dressed in black grabbed Olsen and put a cloth bag over his head.

A black windowless van squealed to a stop and the reporter was roughly shoved inside.

Cassandra broke into a full sprint, but by the time she arrived at the spot where Olsen had been taken, all she could see was the van disappearing around the corner.

Chapter 32

CASSANDRA WAS SITTING on the bottom step of the stairs leading to her front door. She was rocking back and forth, with her eyes only partially open, fighting a losing battle to stay awake. The adrenalin rush from her meeting with Newman and Dawson then Olsen being kidnapped had worn off and anything that might have been left in her reserve tank of caffeine was now fully depleted. At the moment, all she wanted to do was sleep.

The street was alive with the flashing lights of police cars and, with L.A. being L.A., there were multiple news helicopters hovering overhead.

Detective Steve Foley ducked under the crime scene tape and approached another detective, Frank Richard, who was grinning from ear to ear. Richard was in his mid-fifties and was in the butter zone of the LAPD. He was one of the best and most experienced investigators the department still had on the street. Over the years he had built up a lot of goodwill by solving numerous high-profile cases and not trying to hog the glory. He also had enough years in to be fully vested in his pension and if anyone decided to give him too large a ration of crap, they knew he would turn in his papers and retire. That would put his abuser uncomfortably in the spotlight of having to explain why they had run off one of the department's best detectives. Because of that, everyone pretty much left him alone and let him do his job.

"You're not going to believe this shit," Richard said as he pointed his pencil in Cassandra Morse's direction. "She's an eyewitness."

"Of course she is," Foley answered with a sigh. "She give you anything worthwhile?"

"Actually, she did," Richard answered, trying to keep the surprise out of his voice. "Make, model, color and was only a year off on the age of the van, plus the first four digits of the license plate. Not that it helped much."

Foley nodded. "Stolen?"

"Yup," Richard answered. "A black and white found it abandoned less than six blocks from here. They made no attempt to hide it so they had a switch vehicle ready and waiting and left in a hurry."

"What else you got?"

"Pros. It happened in broad daylight on a busy street. Took less than five seconds from bag over the head to bye-bye." Richard pointed in the direction of two men in suits and a small army of people in Homeland Security windbreakers. "Notice anything interesting?"

"Hmm," Foley said. "Homeland usually takes their sweet time to get to a potential crime scene."

"I've never seen them respond to anything this fast before," Richard added. "They were only ten minutes behind the first on the scene and if I had missed two more lights, they would have beat me here."

"Almost as if they were standing by and waiting for the 9-1-1 call to come in."

"My thought exactly," Richard answered then added, "I'd love to stick it to those assholes."

"Same here." Foley motioned toward the CCTV camera on a nearby pole. "Was there anything on the traffic intersection cameras?"

"You're going to really love this," Richard said with a laugh. "Every traffic cam in L.A. County went offline just before the snatch and the system didn't reboot until 10 minutes after it was over."

"That's a heck of a coincidence," said Det. Foley.

"If I were a suspicious man," Richard answered. "I'd be looking hard at our brothers in arms at Homeland Security."

"Who was snatched?" Foley asked.

The detective made a sound closer to a cackle than a laugh. "You don't know?"

"Would I be asking if I did?"

"It was that *Guardian* reporter who wrote the story about your girlfriend over there that got Lou's panties in such a bunch." The detective pointed his pencil in Cassandra's direction again. "Apparently he had just left her house when they tagged him."

"Did she say why the reporter was here?"

"She claims they only chatted briefly, but a couple of the neighbors said our missing boy and your lady friend were going at it pretty loud on the sidewalk a few minutes before the snatch."

"How loud?"

"Loud enough to bring everyone in a five-house radius out on their porch."

"Crap," Foley muttered and shook his head. "This just keeps getting better and better."

"Oh, goodie," Richard said. "It looks like round two is about to start." The detective motioned in the direction of a pair of black Suburban SUVs with government license plates as they pulled up to the crime scene tape and parked in the middle of the street. The doors opened and six people in "FBI" windbreakers poured out of the cars.

Instantly a shouting match broke out between the rival federal agencies.

"This is a kidnapping which makes it our jurisdiction," said the FBI agent.

"This is a possible national security issue..." the Homeland Security agent replied.

"I hate it when mommy and daddy fight," Richard said.

"Can I talk to her?" Foley asked.

Richard shrugged. "It's your gold shield at risk not mine."

"Thanks."

"I would get straight to the point and not waste a lot of time on idle chit-chat," Richard said. "Once the Feds finish their pissing contest, LAPD is likely going to be off this case and they're going to want to have a nice long chat with your lady friend. Probably downtown."

"Agreed," Foley said as he headed in Cassandra's direction.

Foley," Cassandra said with limited enthusiasm as she motioned for him to have a seat next to her on the step.

When his hand brushed against her bare leg there was no reaction. She wasn't sure if that was a good or bad thing.

Morse," he answered as he sat down. "You understand your legal rights?"

"Right to remain silent, blah, blah, blah."

"The Feds are going to want to take you downtown for questioning."

"Good luck with that," Cassandra said as she pointed to the edge of the crime scene tape where a near riot appeared to be on the verge of breaking out. At the tape line, Foley could see a man with a headful of unruly white hair, a tweed jacket with patches on the elbows and a floral bowtie waving his arms frantically.

"Is that…"

"William Comstock, AKA 'Uncle Billy', he's my great uncle on my grandmother's side." Next to Comstock, with his publicist and videographer was Kyle Briner, one of the most flamboyant and powerful attorneys in Los Angeles. Lurking in the background was the ever-present Jeffery Nelson, Comstock's grad student and personal aide.

Foley whistled to get Det. Richard's attention then pointed to the tape line. "You want to let Ms. Morse's attorney speak to her?"

Richard craned his neck and when he saw Kyle Briner, he smiled broadly. Richard and Briner had a history and normally when one of the best celebrity defense attorneys showed up at one of Richard's crime scenes, sparks would fly. This time Richard was delighted to see his nemesis since in a few minutes Briner was going to be the FBI's or Homeland Security's problem and not his. Richard turned back to Cassandra. He put both of his hands over his heart and mouthed silently, "I love you." He trotted away and let the attorney and his posse through the barricade.

Comstock gave Cassandra a hug and a quick peck on the cheek. Since she now knew exactly what to be looking for, she felt an unmistakable tingle. She was glad the contact was brief. His brain was working so fast it was making her dizzy. The only thing she was sure of; Uncle Billy was having the time of his life.

"Let me introduce my great-niece," Comstock said more to the camera than to Cassandra. "Cassandra Morse, this is Kyle Briner."

Cassandra shook the attorney's hand but there was no connection.

From behind them a gruff voice said, "Please turn off your camera."

Kyle Briner's eyes lit up and he winked at Det. Richard as he turned to confront the voice. "You are?"

"Special Agent James Rose of the FBI," he said as he quickly flashed his ID. As he started to put it away, Kyle Briner extended his hand.

"Whoa, cowboy," Briner said. "Not so fast. May I see that please?"

The agent who looked young enough that he had possibly been out of Quantico for less than a week and probably hadn't needed to shave since leaving Virginia, hesitated.

"Don't be bashful," Briner said. As the attorney read the credentials and motioned for his videographer to capture it for the record. Briner smiled then asked, "Are we standing on a public sidewalk, Special Agent Rose?"

"No Kyle," said another approaching voice. "You're standing in the middle of an active crime scene and we're requesting you turn your camera off."

"Hello Donald," Briner said brightly. He introduced him to the others. "This is the special agent in Charge of the Los Angeles office of the Federal Bureau of Investigation, Donald Whitmore."

"Counselor," the S.A.G said coldly, "turn off the camera."

Briner turned to Cassandra. "Is this your residence?"

"Yes."

"Do we have your permission to record from your front porch?"

"Yes," Cassandra answered firmly.

"Thank you."

The videographer bounded up the steps and kept recording.

"Who let you into our crime scene?" Whitmore asked.

Det. Frank Richard cleared his throat and raised his hand then waved to the cameraman. "At the time it was, and as far as I know, still is an LAPD crime scene."

Briner turned to the camera. "This is senior Detective Frank Richard of the Los Angeles Police Department." Richard waved to the camera again.

Whitmore glared at Richard who just smiled back at him with a "why don't you go screw yourself" expression on his face.

"You should be notified shortly that the FBI is taking charge of this investigation," Whitmore said.

"Be still my heart," Richard answered sarcastically. "Until officially relieved, this is my crime scene and I'll let whoever I damn well feel like in."

Whitmore turned to Cassandra. "Ms. Morse, you need to come with me."

"As counsel for Ms. Morse, may I see your warrant."

"We just want to ask her a few questions, counselor."

Briner pulled Richard closer and they both faced the camera. "Detective, have you interviewed Ms. Morse?"

"Why yes I have," he said as he beamed into the camera. "She has been a cooperative witness who has provided highly useful information to our investigation."

"Do you consider her a suspect?"

"Absolutely not," Richard answered. "I have multiple witnesses who saw her in foot pursuit after the kidnapping and she was the first call to 9-1-1."

Would you be willing to provide a copy of your interview notes to Special Agent in Charge, Whitmore?"

"Notarized and in triplicate."

"Thank you, detective," Briner said warmly.

"No," Richard said as he glared at S.A.G. Whitmore then smiled into the camera. "Thank you, Mr. Briner."

Briner turned to Whitmore. "My client has fully complied with the Los Angeles Police Department. So, unless you have a warrant, I will be happy to schedule a time for you to interview Ms. Morse in my office at her convenience. Until then she is invoking her right to remain silent." Briner smiled at Whitmore. "I believe you've met my publicist, Judi Monroe."

Whitmore frowned at Briner, Monroe and then the camera. To his credit, he knew when he was licked. "We'll be in touch," Whitmore said, then stormed away.

"We're not normally on the same side, Detective," Kyle Briner said with a toothy smile.

Richard patted Briner on the back. "You're still a horse's ass, Briner; but that was fun."

"Any suspects?"

"Off the record?" Richard asked as he glanced at the camera. Briner made a slashing sign across his throat and the videographer turned off his camera.

"No proof, but my money is on Homeland Security or someone who has them in their hip pocket."

"Really?" Briner asked as he looked at Foley for confirmation.

"Who snatches a local crime beat reporter off the streets?" Foley asked.

"All of the traffic cameras in L.A. County go down moments before the snatch and DHS almost got here before I did," Richard added. "They knew it was coming."

Kyle Briner rubbed his hands together and flashed his famous smile. "Lovely."

Chapter 33

"MULLEN!" BARKED MANAGING editor Anthony LaRosa. When she looked up, he said, "My office."

From the grim expression on his face and the sudden flurry of activity in the office, she knew this couldn't be good.

"Shut the door," he said. "Grant Olsen has been kidnapped."

Holly Mullen shrugged.

"You don't seem surprised."

She shrugged again.

"What were you two working on?"

"Didn't Grant tell you?" she asked.

"He said it was a follow up story on the Dream Lady. Something about another dream she had. Then he gets snatched right in front of her house! What do you know about that?"

Holly Mullen wanted to make this conversation as brief as possible. Time was not on her side.

"I'll send you the complete file."

"Do that," the editor answered tersely. "We're meeting with the publisher in fifteen minutes. Until then, don't leave the building."

"Okay."

Mullen turned and headed straight to the temporary desk they had assigned to her instead of Olsen's where she had been working. She pulled a Ralphs Grocery paper sack containing her "Go Bag" out from the knee hole. Then, after stopping at Olsen's desk to reclaim her laptop, headed straight to the ladies' room. After starting her research and seeing how tight the lid was on Cassandra Morse, she was afraid something like this might happen. And that was even before the idea of nukes and terrorists had become a part of the equation. There had been too many roadblocks and too many dead ends. Too many strangers wanting to chat with her on the dark web.

She put her "Go Bag" on the sink and looked at herself in the mirror. Earlier, at home, she had used pliers to loosen the stud caps on all of her facial piercings and now they were only on finger tight. She had all of them out in less than thirty seconds. Picking up her bag, she stepped into one of the stalls and locked the door. She stripped down to just her panties then opened the brown paper sack. First out was a padded push up bra that added two letters to her cup size. Next, she pulled out a girly, short-sleeved bright yellow sundress, shook the wrinkles out of it and then pulled it over her head. Next, she reached into the bag and came out with a sassy pageboy blond wig. Tucking her brightly colored hair inside, she adjusted the wig until it felt right. Sitting on the toilet, she slipped on a pair of flat sandals.

Next came the most important part. The tattoo sleeves. Normally the sleeves were worn by people who wanted the look of body art without the pain or the lifetime commitment. These sleeves were very different. They were opaque and designed to hide her ink. She slipped them on and, while they would not stand up to close scrutiny, they were near enough to her natural skin tone that they would be easy to miss unless you were looking specifically for them.

Stepping outside the stall, she shoved her old clothes and boots into the trash can. Lastly, she pulled out a ridiculous pink purse large enough to hold her computer. Inside were a pair of oversized dark sunglasses, three burner phones, over a thousand dollars in cash, a tube of cheap bright red lipstick and Faraday bag large enough to hold all of her electronics.

Looking in the mirror she adjusted the wig and then pushed her breasts up and adjusted them for maximum cleavage. Next, she applied the ghastly red color to her lips. She hadn't worn makeup in years, so she took her time to be sure the color was on correctly. Satisfied, she checked to be sure she had powered down all of her electronics and dropped them in her RF signal blocking bag. Finally, she put on the oversize dark sunglasses which hide most of her face.

As she was getting ready to leave the bathroom, a frantic female reporter on the city beat brushed past her without even a second glance. Mullen watched as the reporter began pushing each stall door open before stepping back into the newsroom. The bullpen was in turmoil. Reporters and editors were running around and shouting.

Apparently, her absence had been noticed.

Holly Mullen, with an extra sway in her hips, headed for the stairwell unnoticed and unrecognized by the people she had worked with off and on for years. As she stepped out the main entrance of the building and into the bright sunlight, she looked more like a perky struggling actress on her way to a casting call than a brooding punk rocker eluding the Feds.

She walked down the sidewalk, stopping occasionally to look in the shop windows when in reality she was checking to see if she was being followed. After about ten blocks, she was satisfied. She had scouted the area previously and knew it had limited CCTVs and she had already figured out all of the blind spots. She ducked into a doorway and pulled one of her burner phones out of her purse. She typed a text message, sent it, then pulled out the SIM card, crushed it under her heel, and then flipped it out into the middle of the street where it was almost immediately run over by a car and pulverized. A half block later she stomped on the burner phone and dropped the pieces down a storm drain.

Less than a minute after the text was sent, the message started hitting the dark net message boards.

They kidnapped
a reporter.
DEFCON 1
fuckufeds.ru

On the webpage, safely on a Russian hacker's private server that would be difficult if not impossible to find, were all of the files she had been working on. She speculated that within an hour the website would be viral. Within two hours, the site have over a million hits and a similar number of file views and downloads.

"You screwed with the wrong girl," she muttered as she started walking in the direction of a cheap hotel with hourly rates that only took cash and didn't ask for ID.

Chapter 34

NICK BERGMAN SAW the link go on up on the message board immediately and muttered, "Oh man." He opened the link, scanned it briefly then panicked. Carrie Finch was in the office of Assistant Director Barbara Smith but she needed to see this now. He bolted out of the office and saw Kevin Meyer at his desk.

"I have to get a message to Carrie…Ms. Finch, and she is with the Assistant Director."

"Urgent?"

"Extremely."

Faster than he would have thought possible, Meyer was out of his chair and headed toward the A.D.'s office. Nick Bergman had to trot just to keep up. Blowing past the A.D.'s secretary's desk, he tapped twice on the door then opened it before being given permission to enter.

Nick Bergman froze in the doorway.

Meyer motioned to him. "Come on."

Drawing in a deep breath he stepped across the threshold. Inside with the A.D, and Finch were D.D. John Thomas and about a half dozen other men and women he didn't recognize. Assistant Director Barbara Smith looked up at him and calmly asked, "Yes?"

"You need to open 'fuckufeds.ru'." In less than two seconds, the site was on an eighty-inch screen on the wall.

"When did this go up?" Smith asked calmly.

"Less than two minutes ago," Bergman answered.

"Can we get it down?" Smith asked one of the men in the room who was already reaching for his phone.

"I doubt it," he answered "Even if we do, by the time we get it down the damage will already be done. The files will be copied and on a hundred servers in the next ten minutes." He got up from his chair, stuck a finger in the ear that didn't have the phone in it and headed toward a quiet corner.

"John," Smith said to the Deputy Director Thomas. "Start damage control." The D.D. was already in motion.

Smith rose to her feet and motioned to Finch and Bergman. "You're with me."

"Yes, ma'am," Finch answered. "Where are we going?"

"Los Angeles," Smith answered as she glanced at Meyer.

"Your car and security detail are downstairs and your jet is standing by at Andrews."

"Efficient as always," Smith said as she headed for the door.

Finch saw the puzzled look on Bergman's face. "Kevin Meyer has been her personal aide for years," Finch said. "She'd been using him to keep an eye on me."

Bergman chuckled. "Why am I not surprised you knew that?" he muttered to himself then had to double time his steps to keep up with the long strides of A.D. Smith.

"How's our little lady doing?" Smith asked Meyer who was half a step behind.

"Younger version of you."

Chapter 35

I T HADN'T TAKEN Grant Olsen long to realize he was in no
danger. He doubted terrorists or murderers would be so polite and
apologetic. While clearly detained, the room he was being held
in had comfortable chairs, a private bathroom and a small refrigerator
stocked with a variety of soft drinks and designer bottles of water.

Olsen looked up when the door opened and a man in a well-
cut suit came into the room. The visitor was around forty and carried
himself with confidence, bordering on distain, which often came from
having an Ivy League diploma hanging on your office wall. If Olsen
had to guess, he would peg the guy as either a Fed or a lawyer, or most
likely, both.

"My apologies," the man said in a deep baritone, "for the dramatic
way we brought you here."

"No problem," Olsen answered with a snort. "Thankfully, it
occurred in front of witnesses which should add a couple of zeros
to my settlement and really help my chances with the Pulitzer Prize
committee."

The man smiled. "I wouldn't spend any of that settlement money
just yet. When someone is surfing the net and talking about nuclear
weapons in Los Angeles, the first word that springs to mind is terrorist
not Pulitzer."

"How long should I expect you to hold me here?" Olsen asked.

"We have a federal warrant which allows us to keep you as our
guest for up to seventy-two hours," the man answered.

"Are you going to tell me who you are and why you decided to
make me your guest?"

"In due course," the man said calmly. "First we have a few
questions."

"You don't really expect me to answer any of them, do you?"

The man ignored Olsen's response. "Who told you about the shipment?"

Olsen scratched his chin. "I don't remember if it was FedEx or UPS."

The man's smile vanished, and Olsen suspected someone was talking to him in an earpiece.

"I don't think you appreciate the seriousness of your situation, Mr. Olsen," the man said coldly. "You've proven to be in possession of top-secret information and you've shared it on the internet. At this point we haven't decided whether to charge you with espionage or treason."

Olsen yawned.

"I understand it is quite muggy at Guantanamo Bay this time of year."

"Does that ever work?" Olsen asked.

"You'd be surprised," the man answered as his smile returned. "We know your information about the shipment came from Cassandra Morse. Do you know where she got the information?"

"No comment."

"Mr. Olsen, we're prepared to hold you for the full three days of our warrant which means you'll miss the story of the year and someone else will get your Pulitzer."

A concerned expression covered Olsen's face, but he did not answer.

They had found his weak spot.

"In case you're wondering how we know about Morse, after we picked you up, your assistant, Holly Mullen, posted all of your files on the internet."

"I don't believe you."

On cue, the door opened and a young woman came in with a laptop which was logged into fuckufeds.ru. She placed the computer on the table in front of Olsen and left just as quickly as she had arrived. Olsen leaned forward and started scrolling through the site. There was no doubt about it, they were his files. Either Holly had posted them as they claimed, or they had hacked his computer. They knew everything he knew. They even had his notes about Morse telling him about her dream.

He had no bargaining chips, and he could tell by the smug expression on his interrogator's face that he knew it too.

"At this moment the feeding frenzy is just starting. For now, you have a head start and the inside track to Cassandra Morse." The man grinned at Olsen. "While you're sitting in here, the clock is ticking." The man folded his arms across his chest and leaned back like he had nothing but time to kill. "Answer our questions about where Morse got the information and you'll be back at your desk within the hour. Otherwise, make yourself comfortable."

"You wouldn't believe me if I told you," Olsen said.

"Try me."

"Did you read my piece about the arson fire."

"I did."

"You've read my notes," Olsen protested. "She claims she dreamed a train was going to be heading through Los Angeles with nuclear material and it was going to blow up."

"Everything you know about this is in your notes?"

"Yes."

"You have nothing to add? Nothing which was off the record."

"No."

"You're right Mr. Olsen. I don't believe you." The man gathered up the laptop and headed toward the door.

"What's for dinner?" Olsen asked.

The man smiled and left the room.

A few minutes later two men entered the room. One had a black bag for Olsen to put over his head.

"Is that really necessary?"

"Only if you want to get out of here," one of the men answered.

Chapter 36

CASSANDRA DIDN'T LIKE nor particularly trust Kyle Briner so, after they moved inside her home, she kept any information except her contacts with Olsen and the kidnapping to herself. Uncle Billy was sitting in the admiral's normal chair and was letting Briner do most of the talking.

Once the FBI officially took over the kidnapping, the LAPD pulled down their crime scene tape and moved on. A few minutes later, the knocks on the door started. After the second reporter arrived, Foley began answering the door with his badge in his hand and shoving it in the pushy reporters' faces. It didn't slow down the number of knocks, but it certainly shortened the time each reporter spent on Cassandra's stoop.

Cassandra's phone was easier to deal with.

She just turned it off.

Briner was just about to pack up and leave when Foley's cell phone rang. He looked at the caller ID.

"National Intelligence Agency? Nice try," Foley said as he hit the reject button.

Less than a minute later, his phone rang again. This time the caller ID said, "Lt B Harrison."

"Crap," Foley muttered as he hit the "accept" button.

"Foley."

"You're at her house?"

"Yes."

There were a few seconds of silence as the Lieutenant counted to ten. "We'll deal with that later. For now, answer your damn phone."

Foley was confused. "I just did."

"Not when I call, when the NIA calls." The line went dead.

Almost immediately, Foley's phone rang again. It had the same caller ID he had previously rejected. This time he accepted it.

"Foley."

"Detective Foley," a male voice said. "Are you with Cassandra Morse?"

"Yes."

"Please put her on the line."

Foley handed his phone to Cassandra. "It's for you."

Cassandra accepted the phone then said, "Hello."

"Is this Cassandra Morse?" Kevin Meyer asked.

"Yes."

"Please hold for the Assistant Director Barbara Smith of the National Intelligence Agency."

Cassandra's jaw dropped. She held up a finger for Briner to indicate he should stay.

"Ms. Morse," Smith said. "I'm Barbara Smith with the NIA…"

Cassandra cut her off. "Before you say anything else, I'm going to put you on speaker."

"Why?" Smith asked.

"I would like to have witnesses to our conversation." Cassandra's eyes locked on Foley then she nodded in the direction of Briner's videographer. Foley understood immediately and whispered "National Intelligence Agency" in Briner's ear. Briner's eyes lit up and he immediately motioned for the videographer to start recording.

Cassandra hit the speaker button and sat the phone on the table so everyone could hear.

"Every phone call I make is recorded," Smith said with no emotion in her voice.

"If something goes sideways, and it comes down to my word versus yours, what would be the chances I would be able to get an unaltered copy of this conversation from the NIA?" Cassandra asked.

"Fair point. Who are your witnesses?"

"My attorney, Kyle Briner, his videographer and public relations liaison. Also present are my Uncle, Professor William Comstock and his research assistant Jeffery Nelson and Los Angeles Police Department Detective Frank Foley."

***

Without being asked, Finch and Bergman, who were monitoring the call on their headsets, were typing furiously on their keyboards then data began to appear on the screen in front of A.D. Smith.

Comstock, William Allen. 74. Retired professor. Environmental activist. Gadfly.
Briner, Kyle Emmett. 46. High-powered Lawyer, publicity hound.
Foley, Michael Matthew. 34. Vet, sniper school. 11 years LAPD.
Nelson, Jeffery Sherman. 29. Trust fund brat, environmental activist, multiple minor arrests.

"Quite the eclectic gathering," Smith said as she pushed the speaker icon on her phone. "Can you hear me?" Her voice sounded like she was in a barrel and there was a great deal of ambient background noise.

"Where are you?" Cassandra asked.

Smith glanced out the window of the G-650 Gulfstream. "I guess we're over Memphis, Tennessee. For the record, I am Barbara Smith, Assistant Director of the National Intelligence Agency. With me are Paul Rogers, the Director of the Department of Homeland Security and two of my senior analysts, Carrie Finch and Nicholas Bergman."

***

Briner leaned in closer to the phone. "Director, this is Kyle Briner, attorney of record for Cassandra Morse. Please be advised that this conversation is being recorded. Do you have any objections?"

"The National Intelligence Agency has no objections to the recording of this conversation," Smith stated.

"And," Briner continued, "this conversation is neither privileged nor confidential and my client would be in no jeopardy if she were to make any or all of this conversation public."

"Considering the gravity of this conversation, the NIA would expect discretion would prevail, but it is not mandatory."

Briner nodded.

"Okay," Cassandra said. "What can I do for you?"

"You can tell me where you learned about a train containing nuclear material."

"I had a dream about it."

"So you've said," Smith replied. "We've read Grant Olsen's notes."

Cassandra pulled back in disbelief. "You admit hacking a reporter for a major newspaper's files? Unbelievable!"

"We hardly needed to hack him, Ms. Morse," Smith answered calmly. "They are available on the internet."

"What?" Cassandra shouted.

"Soon you're going to be quite popular."

"Is this your doing?"

"I suppose by extension, yes," Smith answered. "An over-eager person in the Los Angeles Office of Homeland Security, without authority from Washington, ordered the kidnapping of Grant Olsen."

Det. Steve Foley gave Kyle Briner an "I told you so" look.

"I," Barbara Smith continued, "along with the Director of Homeland Security are on our way to Los Angeles to take charge of the situation."

"Where is Grant Olsen?" Cassandra asked.

"He has been released."

"How did his notes get online?" Cassandra asked.

"Apparently he had a doomsday scenario in place which would release them if anything happened to him."

"Right," Cassandra said.

"You sound skeptical, Ms. Morse."

"Reporters don't release their notes. Ever. Even under threat of going to jail."

"I suppose," Smith said. "But what possible reason would the NIA have for releasing information which would embarrass us?"

"I have no idea, but I don't know you and I certainly don't trust you."

"Indeed," Smith answered. "Let me try to earn your trust. Your dream is accurate. There is shipment, by rail, of nuclear material scheduled to come through the City of Los Angeles. However, it is not weapon grade but spent nuclear fuel rods from the Diablo Canyon nuclear power plant near Avila Beach in San Luis Obispo County, California. Diablo Canyon is the only operating nuclear facility in California, but it has started to approach its waste storage limit. The San Onofre Nuclear Generating Station, south of San Clemente, was shut down in 2012 after a replacement steam generator failed and is currently in the process of being decommissioned. San Onofre is on more stable ground than Diablo Canyon and since San Onofre is no longer operational, it has excess storage capacity. The decision has been made to transfer the excess waste from Diablo Canyon to San Onofre."

"By God!" Jeffery exclaimed. "They've admitted it on the record."

"Who is speaking," Smith asked calmly.

"My assistant, Jeffery Nelson," Comstock answered.

"Rein him in Bill," Smith answered.

"You know my Uncle?" Cassandra asked with a dumbfounded expression her face.

"Yes," Smith answered. "We've known each other for years."

"I was not the source of the leak about the shipment," Comstock stated. "And I never mentioned it to my niece."

"I never thought for one moment you were the source of the leak," Smith said. "But, that ship has already sailed."

"Is it dangerous?" Cassandra asked as her mind flashed back to the A-Bomb that went off in her dream.

"Obviously any nuclear material is dangerous, but what we're looking at here are spent rods with no capacity to be converted to a nuclear weapon. While in transport, they are stored in massive containers that can survive a full train derailment undamaged. In fact, over the last 60 years, more than 2,500 cask shipments of used fuel have been transported across the United States without any radiological releases to the environment or harm to the public."

"I'm surprised you're being so candid," Cassandra said.

"We're surprised this information was not leaked to the public sooner," Smith answered. "While we've put a tight lid on the transfer, multiple people at both Diablo Canyon and San Onofre have direct knowledge of the transfer. Plus, the railroad people, the National Guard and local law enforcement, while given a fake cover story, we assumed someone would eventually connect the dots."

"If this is not some big state secret," Cassandra asked, "aren't you overreacting a bit?"

"We consider this transfer to be completely safe and routine. Unfortunately, your dream has created a firestorm. Our concern would be protesters trying to block the tracks."

"You can count on that!" Jeffery Nelson blurted.

"Which is rather short-sighted on your part, Mr. Nelson," Smith said. "If you are the least bit serious about the environment, you would be celebrating this."

"Right," Jeffery huffed. "And if you were serious about the environment you never would have built the damn things in the first place!"

Cassandra was a bit stunned by the overt passion of Jeffery Nelson when it came to nuclear energy. It was almost like he had a Dr. Jekyll and Mr. Hyde split personality. One moment he was sweet and handsome. The next, he bordered on being a frothing-at-the-mouth, raving lunatic.

The sound of A.D. Smith's voice broke Cassandra's chain of thought.

"Anyone who is not blinded by dogma and living in the real world realizes San Onofre is a much better long-term storage solution than Diablo Canyon," Smith said. "The storage facilities are newer, and the geography is much more stable than Diablo Canyon."

"I would respectfully disagree," Comstock answered defiantly.

"You're entitled to your opinion, Bill, which throughout the years has proven to be impervious to logic or reason," Smith said. "What we would very much like to know, Ms. Morse, is how you learned of this shipment?"

"Don't answer that," Briner warned, "she could be setting a perjury trap."

"Nonsense," Smith answered. "I'm only concerned about the safety of the shipment, not wasting my time in court."

"What is the risk level?" Cassandra asked with a cool professional tone.

"While the transportation of these materials is safe and routine," Smith hesitated for effect, "in the wrong hands they could make a devastating dirty bomb."

"Terrorism?" Cassandra asked.

"Yes," Smith answered. "The kind of attack that could make any major city in America uninhabitable for the next few thousand years. So, I ask you again. How did you learn about this shipment?"

"Don't answer that," Kyle Briner said as he leaned forward. "I will advise my client to not answer any of your questions unless she is given witness immunity."

"Granted," Smith answered.

Cassandra started to speak but Briner put a hand on her arm to stop her. "Remember you are being recorded. Please give a more detailed response."

"We will grant witness immunity from federal prosecution to Ms. Cassandra Morse for any and all information she gives to the National Intelligence Agency with regards to a shipment of nuclear material through the City of Los Angeles," Smith said. "Is that sufficient?"

"I would like to see this agreement in writing before I allow my client to answer any more of your questions."

"It's okay," Cassandra said. "This is too important to get bogged down in silly legalese." Cassandra cleared her throat. "I'm not sure how, but I believe I received the information from a man in Benny's Bar and Grill at around 2 a.m. two nights ago."

"Believe or you actually received the information?" Smith asked.

"Believe only," Cassandra answered.

"Why do you believe this man is responsible?"

Cassandra knew she couldn't say he had touched her, and she had read his mind without sounding like a complete whack job. "I have no idea," Cassandra lied. "Possibly the same way I was able to identify the arsonist who I had also met at Benny's."

"Okay," Smith said with more than a small dose of skepticism in her voice. "Can you describe this man?"

"Twenty-five to twenty-eight years old. Five feet ten inches tall and around one hundred and seventy pounds. Dark hair, dark skin with a five o'clock shadow. If I were guessing, he is of Southern Mediterranean or Greek descent but was born and raised in America."

"How do you know that?" Smith asked casually.

"He used idioms when speaking which would have confused someone who was not a native speaker."

"I see," Smith said. "Anything else?"

"He claimed he was in town only for a few days and he was married…"

"How do you know he was married?"

"Tan line on his left ring finger," Cassandra answered. "He left the bar a bit after two and he would have turned right in the direction of the beach."

"Did you see him turn right," Smith asked.

"No," Cassandra answered as she was starting to get annoyed. "I concluded it since if he had turned left, he would have been heading into a residential area. If he were a local, I would have recognized him. If he were visiting someone, it would be unlikely he would have come into the bar alone."

"She's good," Bergman whispered in Finch's ear. Finch nodded her agreement.

"I see," Smith said. "Anything else?"

"He had a Rolex Stainless Steel Oyster watch on his left wrist. He was wearing a dark blue two button golf shirt, chinos and slip-on loafers with no socks. There are traffic cams at every intersection of Pacific Avenue and many of the local businesses also have closed circuit cameras. He did not appear to be attempting to elude observation so in all likelihood, he is on video somewhere."

"Got him," Cassandra heard Nick Bergman say in the background. "Her description was spot on."

"That was quick," Cassandra said.

"We're going to send you a camera grab of the man you described. Please confirm we're talking about the same person."

When Foley's phone beeped, being unfamiliar with it, she let Foley open the jpeg file. She glanced at the picture and instantly confirmed they had the right man. "That's him."

"Excellent," Smith said. "If we need to speak with you again, is there a better phone number than this one?"

"Please do not contact my client directly," Kyle Briner said flatly.

"That's okay," Cassandra answered as she fished the phone Dr. Dawson had given her out of her pocket. "For routine contacts please call Mr. Briner. If it is an emergency call this number." Cassandra gave Smith the number.

After a brief pause, Smith asked, "Why do you have a burner phone?"

"Don't answer that," Kyle Briner said. "My client has told you everything she knows about the person you're looking for. Are we done here?"

"For the moment," said Smith.

"While my client may have given you her phone number, all future contact should be through me. Are we clear?"

"Of course," Smith answered as the line went dead.

***

Barbara Smith turned to see Nick Bergman and Carrie Finch both typing frantically on their keyboards. Nick Bergman won.

"Got him," Bergman said. When he saw the look on both Smith's and Finch's face he continued. "Since Morse was so accurate in her description, I used the details she provided to filter the facial recognition database."

"Who is he?" Smith asked.

"Joseph Santino from Cincinnati, Ohio." Bergman shook his head. "Morse is good. He's twenty-six years old and married, with a daughter and another child on the way. His grandfather immigrated to the US fifty years ago from Sicily. His father married Maria DeAngelo. He is an only child."

"He's currently staying in room 204 of the Erwin Hotel on Pacific Avenue," Finch added.

The Director of Homeland Security reached for his phone. "I'll have him picked up."

"You will not!" Smith's voice cracked like a whip. "The FBI will pick him up."

"Why?" he demanded. "This is possible terrorism."

"Your L.A. office so far has completely screwed this up," Smith said. "I'm not going to let them try to save face and end up making everything worse."

"You don't have that authority," the Director of Homeland snarled.

Kevin Meyer handed Barbara Smith a telephone.

"No," she answered, "but I know someone who does." She held up her finger and a heavy silence settled over the interior of the G-650. Finally, she said, "Thank you for taking my call, Mr. President."

Chapter 37

BETWEEN DEALING WITH L.A. traffic and LAX, it took longer to get out of Los Angeles than it did to fly to the Bathmann Aeronautics testing facility in Texas. Apparently the word had gotten out that Los Angeles might start glowing in the dark at any moment now. With that in mind, every celebrity, Hollywood mogul and anyone rich enough to own their own private jet had decided it was an excellent time to visit that second home in Aspen, or Jackson Hole or Martha's Vineyard. From the time the Bathmann jet was in the queue for take-off, it was a bit over an hour before it was finally airborne.

Tom McMahon glanced over at Jack Logan who had claimed his own row of seats and was sound asleep. He chuckled. Logan was military through and through. He lived by the creed of "Sleep when you can. Eat when you can. You never know when you'll get another chance." McMahon, on the other hand, was a man of action. While in the military, the "hurry up and wait" attitude always drove him crazy.

The primary testing facility where they landed was a sprawling complex located about halfway between Austin and San Antonio. With dual 12,000 ft. runways, anything and everything with wings had plenty of room to land and take off. While the suits all worked in the downtown glass and steel monstrosity, the testing facility was the home base for his team and the rest of the elite security details employed by Bathmann Aeronautics.

As they taxied to the hangar, Jack Logan gave McMahon a nudge and pointed out the window. "The Batmobile is here."

"This can't be good," McMahon answered.

Parked inside the hangar, and bracketed by a pair of Cadillac Escalades, was a black, heavily armored limousine. It was not quite as formidable as the "Beast" the President of the United States rode around in, but it was close. One of the newer team members, who had never seen the limo before, whistled, "That's some ride."

"Louis Bathmann the Fourth is in the house," Logan said with a laugh as he patted the rookie on the shoulder. "Be on your best behavior."

"And, if you happened to run into him in the building," McMahon said, "for God's sake don't make eye contact or speak to him."

"Seriously?" the rookie asked.

McMahon and Logan, along with the rest of the team, started to laugh.

Logan patted the rookie on the shoulder again. "Mr. Bathmann is a nice man…"

"Unless you cross him," McMahon added.

Logan shook his head and continued, "Or screw up."

"Then he's hell on wheels," McMahon finished.

This time no one laughed.

After the steps of the commuter jet were extended, McMahon was first off, followed by Logan. They were greeted on the tarmac by Gabriel Ashton, VP of Security for Bathmann Aeronautics. Ashton was a West Point grad whose career had topped out at full bird colonel. Seeing no stars in his future, and with his twenty in, when Bathmann Aeronautics came calling, he listened. Long and lean, Ashton was one of the elite few who had run a full 26.2-mile marathon in all fifty states. In the past year, since he had turned sixty, he often had the fastest time in his age group. His hair was still cut high and tight. With his weathered face, perfect posture and no-nonsense demeanor, he was the poster boy for "retired military".

"McMahon," Ashton said. "You're with me."

"Yes, sir," McMahon answered.

"You too, Logan," Ashton added.

"Sir?" Logan asked, a bit confused.

"You were CID, correct?" Ashton asked.

"Yes, sir."

"For this, we need someone with Criminal Investigation Division knowledge."

"Yes, sir."

Ashton turned his attention to the rest of McMahon's team that was now on the tarmac looking a bit confused. "You gentlemen have the next three days off. Report back on Monday at oh eight hundred for your new assignment. Dismissed."

Ashton motioned in the direction of one of the Cadillac Escalade SUVs that was idling nearby. Ashton took the front passenger seat with McMahon and Logan got comfortable in the middle row as the driver pulled out of the hangar.

It was a bit over a mile to the business office. Rebuilt after nine-eleven, the two-story building was now closer to being a Medieval castle than modern office space and had cost a king's ransom to renovate. No one at Bathmann had cared about the cost since the Department of Defense was the one picking up the tab. The exterior walls and roof were twenty-one inches thick and layered with titanium, Kevlar, and concrete. Surrounding the complex, about ten feet apart, were twenty-inch-thick poles that extended well above the roof line. Each had a flag of a NATO nation or other American allies flapping in the breeze. While they appeared decorative, the custom built "flagpoles" were designed to slow down any airplanes or missiles aimed at the building.

When terrorists started flying passenger aircrafts into commercial real estate, the appeal of a corner office on a top floor had faded. The premium office space in this building was in the middle where it would have a greater likelihood of surviving an attack. That was where the trio of Ashton, McMahon and Logan found Louis Bathmann IV. The door to his satellite office was open, and since the entire reason he was here was to talk McMahon, and now Logan, they all walked straight in without knocking.

"Close the door," Bathmann said softly as he pulled his girth out of his chair and extended his hand to first McMahon than Logan. "Sit down, sit down," he said with a warm smile. As his name would indicate, Louis Bathmann IV, was the fourth generation to head the company which was notorious for building weapons to fight the last war and not future ones. Louis the First, at the beginning of WWII was lobbying for the government to buy more biplanes. Louis the Second spent the 1950s trying to convince the Pentagon that jets were just a passing fancy. Louis the Third did everything he could to discredit stealth technology. Louis the Fourth hated cheap and easy to build drones. Despite a near one-hundred-year record of never delivering anything on time or on budget, Bathmann Aeronautics was considered a pillar of the Military Industrial Complex.

And there was a good reason.

Bathmann Aeronautics had one of the largest lobbying offices in Washington which was littered with retired senior military officers and former members of congress. A wag once noted, if Bathmann had been half as good at making airplanes as it was at getting government contracts, they would be the only manufacturer of military aircraft in the world. America's allies were less than impressed. The British refused to deal with Bathmann. Their Defence Secretary once told Louis the Fourth to his face that "he would rather flush money down the loo than down the Louis".

Bathmann IV didn't care what anyone said or thought. He had several billion dollars in the bank he couldn't hide and an even larger amount in off-shore banks which he could. At sixty-eight he was approaching being a perfect sphere. At five-foot-five, he was sixty-five inches tall and had a sixty-four-inch waist. When he stood next to the thin and ramrod straight Ashton, they looked like the number 10.

"Gentlemen," Bathmann said softly. He often spoke at barely above a whisper, the classic passive aggressive move of rich and powerful men. It forced people to lean in closer and listen intently when he spoke. "We have a problem." Bathmann's eyes danced back and forth between McMahon and Logan. "Have you heard about the congressman who died of a heart attack on the USS Ronald Reagan seven months ago?"

McMahon and Logan nodded.

"We have discovered some disturbing information. The congressman may have been murdered by Rachel Frey." Bathmann paused to let his little bombshell go off, but, from the impassive reaction he got from both McMahon and Logan, apparently it was a dud.

"Neither of you seem surprised," Bathmann said.

"Permission to speak freely, sir," McMahon said.

"Of course," Bathmann answered.

"I've had the occasion to do work for Ms. Frey," McMahon said. "Frankly, sir, nothing she would do would surprise me."

"In that case," Bathmann said, "I see no need to sugarcoat this." He motioned in Ashton's direction who started a video on a large screen on the wall.

"What we have here is a video taken in the USS Ronald Reagan just moments before Congressman Duke Warwick died."

The video was muted but appeared to be an interview with one of the Bathmann customer reps that both McMahon and Logan had seen before but couldn't put a name to. In the background they could clearly see Rachel Frey carefully handling the glass and flask that Bradley Doorman used to pour the congressman his drink.

"Note how careful she is that her fingerprints are not on either the glass or the flask," Ashton said. He hit the fast forward to the place where the congressman collapsed. There was some confusion on the tape, then the camera settled back to where Frey was visible. "Note," Ashton said, "her first concern was not for the man who had collapsed only inches away from her. All she was interested in was getting the glass and flask carefully wrapped and back in her purse."

"What other evidence do you have?" Logan asked cautiously.

"The sudden resignation of Bradley Doorman," Ashton answered. "We think she threatened him."

"Was an autopsy performed on the congressman?"

"Of course," Ashton answered. "Warwick was a walking time bomb. They found no trace of poison in his system, but they really weren't looking for it."

Logan shook his head. "No offense, Sir, but this can be explained away…"

"How?" Bathmann demanded.

"Warwick was a neat freak or he could have been a germaphobe," Logan answered.

"Why was she being so secretive," Ashton asked softly.

Logan looked at Ashton in disbelief. "Really?"

"I hadn't thought of that," Ashton said to McMahon before turning his attention to Bathmann. "The Navy has hard and fast rules that nothing glass can be brought on one of their warships. The last thing they need in battle are glass fragments flying around the ship. Frey knew she was breaking a rule and tried her best to cover it up and not embarrass her boss."

"The defense rests," Logan said.

"What if you locate the flask and glass?" Bathmann asked.

"It would be inadmissible."

"Why?"

"No chain of custody," Logan answered. "Even if I could find those items, there is no way they could ever be presented to a jury."

"Again," Bathmann asked, "why?"

Logan shrugged. "Where to begin. How do you prove they are the same items from the video? Even if there were traces of poison, it could have been added later. Plus," Logan said as he measured his words carefully. "The entire video is BS."

"Why do you say that?" Ashton asked.

"Are we still speaking freely here?" Logan asked.

"Yes," Bathmann answered.

"You just happened to have a video crew filming at that exact moment? The video crew just happens to catch Frey in the act? Plus, your cameraman was an idiot." Logan got up and pointed to the frozen image on the screen. "When you're interviewing someone, they are always in the center of the frame. In this case the person being interviewed is slightly off-center. Clearly the cameraman was more concerned about capturing Frey in the act in the background than recording the interview." Logan's eyes locked on Bathmann. "If anything, this video does more damage to you than to her. It shows that you knew what she was doing and wanted leverage over her."

Ashton smiled. "I told you they were good."

"Indeed," Bathmann answered. "How difficult would it be to find the flask and glass?"

McMahon snorted. "Even if they weren't at the bottom of the Pacific or destroyed, after seven months, I would say maybe a million to one."

Bathmann turned to Logan. "Are you equally pessimistic?"

"I think a million to one is a best-case scenario. You can send an army of investigators looking for these items and they'll never find them."

"What if I told you we've already had an army of investigators looking and had her under constant surveillance since she left the USS Ronald Reagan?" Ashton asked.

"Has she ever eluded her tail?"

Ashton shook his head. "We've had eyes on her constantly. She hasn't visited a bank to put them in a safe deposit box. She uses the gym in the home office and we've searched every locker." Ashton sighed. "I think she is aware she is under surveillance and is toying with us."

"She thinks they're safe." Logan leaned forward. "Are you 100% sure she had them when she left the Reagan?"

"Yes."

"You knew what she was doing," Logan stated. "Why didn't you take the items from her the moment she stepped off the Reagan?"

Ashton shifted uncomfortably in his seat and cleared his throat. "We thought we did," he answered as he tried to avoid Bathmann's eyes.

Logan chuckled. "She had a second set and that's what she gave to you?"

"Yes," Ashton answered as he looked in Bathmann's direction for permission to continue. Bathmann nodded his head. "She showed the real items to Bradley Doorman which is what convinced him to resign."

"She showed them to him in this building?" Logan asked.

"Yes," Ashton answered

A puzzled expression covered McMahon's face. "Why resign? He's an attorney and has to know the same rules of evidence we know. He would never be convicted."

Logan laughed "He wasn't worried about being convicted."

"What?" McMahon demanded.

"What is the first thing required to work in this industry at Doorman's level."

Now it was McMahon's turn to laugh at not seeing the obvious. "While it never would have been enough to send him to prison, it certainly would be enough to get his top-secret clearance pulled."

"Which would make him unemployable," Ashton added. "And, he had a 'morals' clause in his contract. If he ever lost his clearance for any reason, he would also lose his pension and his stock options."

"I've worked with Doorman," McMahon said. "He doesn't seem like the type to go quietly."

"Doorman was point on the E-38 and Congressman Warwick was about to pull the plug in favor of the SV-1," Ashton answered. "If we lose the contract, he loses his job. His days with Bathmann Aeronautics were numbered and he knew it."

"He made the smart play," McMahon said. "He kept the money and his clearance and if he ever gets the itch to come back and work for another defense contractor, he could."

"The items were verified to have been in this building seven months ago?" Logan asked.

"Affirmative," Ashton answered. "Before you ask. The entire building has been searched from top to bottom by people who had unlimited time and unlimited resources and they didn't find the items."

"You're confident Frey never removed the items from the building?"

"Yes," Ashton answered. They are either still here or she destroyed them after Doorman was out of the way."

"Knowing Frey," Bathmann added, "she wouldn't trust anyone to remove the items. We've had her mail and trash intercepted and searched."

"Why do you want to find them so badly?" McMahon asked.

"You've worked with Frey," Logan answered. "She is ambitious and ruthless. Combined with the video, if they can get their hands on the flask and glass, they would have the same leverage over Frey she had over Doorman."

Neither Bathmann nor Ashton protested.

"Do you think you can find them?" Ashton asked.

Logan shrugged. "Unlikely but now I'd put the odds at only a thousand to one."

"So, you think you have a chance of finding them?" Bathmann asked.

Logan shrugged. "The trail is ice cold and has been trampled over. Frey knows she's being investigated." Logan's eyes locked on Bathmann. "But she has a weakness."

"Really?" Bathmann said. "What would that be?"

"Hubris," Logan answered. "With an ego like hers, if challenged properly, she may want to prove she's the smartest person in the room and make a mistake."

"You plan to take her head on?" Ashton asked.

"Nibbling around the edges hasn't accomplished much," Logan answered. "But I'm going to need your full backing and support."

"You've got it," Bathmann answered.

"In writing," Logan added. "I want a letter from both of you giving me full access to all files and facilities. Then, I want you to send out a companywide email warning employees that whoever fails to cooperate with my investigation will be terminated with cause immediately."

"I'll get with legal and the email will go out within the hour," Bathmann said.

"We'll want all of the files sent to my office," Tom McMahon said.

Logan pointed to the screen. "I'll want to see the full video."

Ashton checked his watch. "Let's circle back on this in four hours."

McMahon and Logan rose to their feet and left. Ashton closed the door behind them.

"You were right about Logan," Bathmann said.

"He's very good," Ashton agreed.

"How long before he notices the section of the video you fast forwarded through?"

"Within the hour," Ashton answered. "Then fire and brimstone will start falling on the head of Rachel Frey."

Chapter 38

JOE SANTINO STROLLED into the lobby of the Erwin Hotel with a spring in his step and a signed contract in his pocket. He glanced in the direction of the bar and considered going in for a drink. Instead, he decided to go upstairs and change into his "hunting" clothes and see if he could find some female companionship to help celebrate his big sale.

He didn't get that far.

Oblivious to the world around him, Santino was about to push the button for the elevator when he felt a firm hand on his shoulder.

"Joseph Santino, you need to come with us."

"Who the hell…" He stopped when he saw four stone-faced men in suits and with ear coms.

The one with his hand on his shoulder had his FBI identification out in his other hand and showed it to Santino. "Please put your hands behind your back."

"What's this all about?" Santino asked.

"There is no need to make this any more difficult than necessary," the FBI agent said softly. "We just need to ask you a few questions."

With his heart pounding and beads of sweat starting to form on his forehead, Santino slowly put his hands behind his back. As soon as the cuffs were in place, he was given a quick pat down by one of the other agents. "He's clean."

All eyes were on Santino as he was escorted out of the Erwin Hotel.

***

Four FBI agents, including Donald Whitmore were standing in the darkened room glaring through the glass at Joseph Santino. Santino, shackled to the floor, had his head resting on the table and was softly sobbing.

Stanley Doyle, the senior interview officer shook his head. "If that guy's a terrorist, then so is my grandmother."

Donald Whitmore closed his eyes and shook his head before turning to his aide. "Give me that picture of Cassandra Morse." Once he had it in his hand, he entered the interrogation room and sat down across from Santino. He put the picture of Morse face down in front of him.

Santino, looking ten years older than when he had arrived at the FBI L.A. office, lifted his head but didn't speak.

"Mr. Santino. I'm Donald Whitmore, the Special Agent in Charge of this office."

"Can you please tell me why I'm here?" Santino pleaded.

"We were given information that you might have been involved in a terrorist plot."

"What?" Santino demanded. "I sell machine tools for God's sake! I play golf every Saturday!"

Whitmore sighed, then turned over the picture of Cassandra Morse and slid it across the table in front of Santino. "Do you know this woman?"

"No…wait," Santino said as he straightened up a bit. "That's the Dream Lady who has been all over the news."

"So, you know her?"

"I met her briefly a few nights ago."

Whitmore glared across the table. "This is not the time to be coy, Mr. Santino."

"Okay. Okay," Santino answered. "I tried to pick her up in a bar."

"Exactly what happened?" Whitmore asked calmly.

"I had the bartender send over a drink and things were looking good," Santino answered as he started to relax. "Then I recognized her from the newspaper story. She got all offended when I asked her to predict something for me. Then, she predicted I wasn't getting laid."

"And?"

"And I told her she was past her expiration date anyway and I left. I talked to her for less than five minutes." Santino straightened up and the color started to return to his face. "Is this what this is all about? Did that bitch report me to the FBI as a terrorist?" Santino slammed his fist down on the table. "I'll sue her ass! And you too for false arrest!" Santino folded his arms across his chest. "I want a fucking lawyer! NOW!"

Donald Whitmore had a great poker face. While he was seething on the inside it never showed on the outside. Without another word, he picked up the photo of Cassandra Morse. Once he was back in the observation room he said, "Cut him loose and get A.D. Barbara Smith on the phone."

Chapter 39

DET. STEVE FOLEY pulled the curtain aside, looked out the window and shook his head. "This is getting out of control." Outside on the sidewalk in front of Cassandra's house reporters were jockeying for position. Overhead, multiple news helicopters were circling like buzzards. Along the street, news vans, with their anchor team's smiling pictures painted on the side, were extending their antennas to broadcast live back to their stations.

When Foley saw a TV reporter starting up the sidewalk in the direction of the porch, he had had enough.

As Foley headed toward the door, Kyle Briner grabbed his arm. "Let me talk to them."

"Why?" he demanded.

Briner's chemically enhanced smile had gone from a mere 100 watts to stadium light level. "These are my people."

Foley stepped out on the porch first with his badge in his left hand and his right hand resting on his highly visible gun holstered on his belt.

With Cassandra watching from the shadows from her front window, she could see and hear questions being shouted at Foley as he headed down the steps. A smarmy paparazzi stepped off the public sidewalk and started to head up the flagstone path toward Cassandra's porch. Foley grabbed him roughly by the scruff of the neck and pushed him back on the sidewalk. That got the reporter's attention and in the brief calm, Foley shouted loudly enough that everyone could hear him. "You all know how this works. The next person to step off of the sidewalk and into this yard will be arrested for trespassing and will be held in the county jail overnight!" Foley's eyes slowly scanned the throng. "Am I clear?"

"Who the hell are you?" Shouted a voice from somewhere in the peanut gallery.

"Det. Steven Foley, LAPD."

A microphone was shoved in his face by an attractive young blonde. "Det. Foley?" she asked sweetly. "Madison Street from Channel Four. Is Cassandra Morse inside?"

"I have no comment," Foley answered then pointed toward Cassandra's house. "But he does."

Seeing the flamboyant attorney and his PR person on the porch promoted a cascade of shouted questions. He motioned for quiet but it had no effect. "I'll come back later." As he turned to leave the shouted questions stopped. "That's better," Briner said as he turned around and smiled. "Please give your stations a ten-minute warning that I'll be making a statement and if you behave yourselves, we may take some questions."

"Do we have permission to set up microphones?" one of the tech guys asked Foley.

"Yes," Briner said before Foley could say "no."

Briner, with Foley two steps behind, retreated back inside Cassandra's house.

Checking to be sure the door was locked, Foley reached for his phone. "Lieutenant, I could use some back up at Cassandra Morse's house." He paused. "Turn on your television." Pause. "Any channel you like." Pause. "Thank you. I look forward to that conversation."

Foley put his phone back in his pocket. "Reinforcements are on the way."

Before Cassandra could thank Foley, her burner phone began to ring.

"Don't answer that," Briner warned.

"Only two people know this number," Cassandra answered. "I'll take a call from either one of them."

"At least put it on speaker," Briner requested.

"Dr. Dawson, my attorney has requested I put you on speaker." She pushed a button and laid the phone on the tabletop. "You should also know the National Intelligence Agency has this number and is likely listening."

Dr. Dawson immediately caught up. "I saw you on the news," Dawson said, "and I just wanted to be sure you're okay."

"I'm fine doctor," Cassandra answered. "I appreciate your concern."

"If you need me for anything, you know where to reach me."

"I do doctor. Thank you."

The line disconnected.

While the exchange came across innocent enough for Briner and his crew, the same could not be said for Foley. His eyes locked on Cassandra's then he looked down at the phone then back at her as if silently asking why she and her doctor were communicating via a burner. Cassandra glanced at Briner then back at Foley and shook her head maybe a half inch. "Later," she silently mouthed.

He nodded in agreement.

Cassandra turned her attention to Briner. "What are you going to tell the media?"

"As little as possible," Briner answered with a laugh. "Just stand beside me and no matter what happens, don't say anything." Briner glanced at his publicist and videographer and they both headed toward the door. "Give them a two-minute warning," Briner said. The PR lady headed outside.

Briner, standing in front of the mirror by the front door, ran his tongue across his teeth, checked his hair and adjusted his tie.

"Do you mind if we join you?" Uncle Billy asked sheepishly.

Briner smiled. "Only if you let me get my spiel in before you hijack the press conference."

"Deal," Comstock said. "Are you going to mention the conversation with the NIA?"

Briner's smile got even bigger. "I thought I would leave that to you."

"Bless you my son," Comstock said with a chuckle.

Briner opened the door and Cassandra, Briner and Comstock stepped out, with Foley and Jeffery a half step behind. The five barely fit on the small porch.

To Cassandra's surprise, the press didn't immediately begin shouting questions. Briner saw the look on Cassandra's face and leaned in and whispered. "Molly has given them my stock warning. Anyone who shouts a question before I finish my opening remarks moves to the bottom of the list of reporters I will ever call on in a press conference. They also know, Madison Street always gets the first question."

"You have them well-trained," Cassandra said with a smile.

Briner cleared his throat as he stepped up to the hastily assembled collection of microphones. "Good afternoon. I'm attorney Kyle Briner and with me today are Cassandra Morse and her great-uncle Professor William Comstock." Briner looked around the crowd of reporters who were hanging on his every word. "As I'm sure you're all well aware, a few days ago Cassandra Morse made a startling prediction which proved to be 100% accurate based on a dream. This was covered by reporter Grant Olsen of the *Los Angeles Guardian.* When Ms. Morse contacted Mr. Olsen earlier today to inform him that she had another dream, he began to do some research which apparently triggered some alarm bells." Briner paused for effect. "A few hours ago, Cassandra Morse witnessed the kidnapping of Mr. Olsen by the Department of Homeland Security." This news sent a ripple through the reporters. Briner pointed to Madison Street who was waving her hand frantically. "Yes, Madison," he said.

"Are you claiming the Department of Homeland Security snatched a reporter off the street simply for following up on a lead?"

"I am," Briner answered brimming with confidence.

"Do you have any proof?" asked the reporter next to Street with an incredulous tone in his voice.

Briner gave Comstock an apologetic look for stealing his thunder. Comstock shrugged to indicate he understood. Briner continued. "Would a recording of a phone call which occurred just moments ago from Barbara Smith, Assistant Director of the National Intelligence Agency and Paul Rogers, the Director of Homeland Security, admitting what had happened be sufficient proof?" Briner smiled. "Smith, and Rogers are currently in transit to Los Angeles."

Every hand in the gaggle of reporters was now waving. Briner pointed back to Madison Street.

"Ms. Morse, since you seemed to have started this circus, would you like to share what your dream was about?"

Briner glanced at Professor Comstock who stepped forward. "The Atomic Energy Commission is planning on shipping a large quantity of nuclear waste by rail through the City of Los Angeles. My niece dreamed that it would result in a disaster."

At that point, all discipline among the reporters vanished and they all began shouting questions. Cassandra shook her head and stepped to the microphone and waited. It took about ten seconds but finally the shouted questions ceased. "My uncle, who is a well-known anti-nuclear activist, has put his own spin on my dream." Cassandra sighed, gathered herself then continued. "My dream had a train conductor, who said, 'The load was delivered exactly as planned. I brought you a memento.' Then he gave me a postcard showing the famous 'Hollywood' sign."

Cassandra pointed to Madison Street. If she were good enough for Briner, she was good enough for her.

"So, you did not dream there would be a train disaster and a nuclear spill?"

"My dreams are never specific," Cassandra answered. "It often takes a few days to sort them out and make sense of them."

"We'll take one more question then I'll leave you with Professor Comstock." Briner started to point to a reporter in the middle of the pack, but Cassandra grabbed his hand and stopped him. "I'll take his question," Cassandra Morse said with a smile as she pointed to a man working his way to the front of the pack. When the other reporters recognized him, the pack parted like the red sea had for Moses.

"Grant Olsen, *Los Angeles Guardian*."

The scene turned into total chaos as Cassandra waved Grant Olsen forward and he joined them on the porch, and she gave him a hug.

"You okay?" she asked.

"Yeah," he answered. "I'll have something to tell my grandkids." Olsen turned back to the mob and motioned for quiet. "I'm sure you all have a thousand questions." His eyes twinkled as he winked at Cassandra. "They will all be answered in tomorrow morning's edition of the *Los Angeles Guardian*."

A female voice shouted above the din. "Will Holly Mullen be included in the byline?"

A huge smile broke across Grant Olsen's face as he recognized the voice but scanning the crowd, he couldn't find the face. A petite blonde in a frilly sundress elbowed her way to the front of the pack but was stopped at the gate by two police officers.

"I'll be damned," Olsen muttered then leaned toward Cassandra. "That's my research assistant Holly Mullen. You've talked to her on the phone."

Cassandra waved Holly through.

As Holly started to climb up the steps, there were angry shouts behind her.

"Who is she?"

"Why is she being allowed in?"

Cassandra did a quick head to toe threat analysis of Mullen and noted the wig and tattoo sleeves and smiled. "Why don't you show them?" Cassandra said.

Like Gypsy Rose Lee, Holly peeled off the sleeves revealing her ink. Then with a dramatic flourish, pulled off her wig exposing her purple hair.

Cassandra, all of her senses on high alert, saw a pair of young men working their way through the crowd. She nudged Holly Mullen and pointed in their direction.

Mullen shook her head. "Just what we need, more feds."

"FBI," Cassandra Morse said, then added, "not DHS."

Holly Mullen leaned back and glanced over her shoulder at the taller Morse. "Another one of your dreams?"

Cassandra shrugged. "I caught a glimpse of one of their sidearms and it was a Glock 19M. DHS uses the Sig Sauer P229."

"The Secret Service also uses the Glock," Mullen answered.

"Since I didn't see the president or any counterfeit currency, my money is on the FBI." Cassandra grinned at Mullen. "Odds are available."

Mullen shook her head and was a bit surprised when the two men stopped briefly then headed straight for her instead of Cassandra Morse.

Chapter 40

SITTING NEXT TO Bergman was Smith's assistant, Kevin Meyer. They were both watching the satellite feed of Cassandra's press conference. "Oh God," Meyer muttered. "I was afraid of that when I saw her name in the report."

"Morse?" Bergman asked.

"No, Holly Mullen," Meyer answered as he shook his head. "She has a history with the A.D."

"Really?" Bergman said with a smile as he turned to his keyboard. Twenty seconds into his search he laughed. "You never told me you had an evil twin," Nick Bergman teased Carrie Finch.

Finch was so focused on her own laptop, she hadn't noticed Holly Mullen's striptease. She glanced up at the HD screen and glared at Bergman. "Right."

"Around the same age, height and weight. Computer whiz slash world-class hacker. Fluent in multiple languages. The resemblance is startling."

Finch sighed then her finger danced across her keyboard. "Yeah. High school dropout; Harvard PhD. Dark web princess; NIA senior lead analyst." Carrie Finch gasped when Mullen pulled off her wig. "Good lord," Finch muttered. "Look at that hair."

"Holly Mullen," A.D. Barbara Smith said as she came back from the galley with an extra-large coffee in her hand. "That name sounds familiar."

"You want the highlights?" Bergman asked.

"Yes," Smith answered as she tried a sip of coffee, but it was too hot for her, so she set the to-go mug on the table. She sat down next to Finch and across from Bergman at the conference table the analysts had commandeered. "I heard what you told Finch. Pick it up from there."

"At sixteen she was offered a full ride to MIT, Stanford and Cal Poly. There is a gap where she fell off the grid, then she started doing research work for the *Guardian* and several ultra-high end private investigation companies." Bergman chuckled. "I think I'm in love. The L.A. office of Homeland Security, figured she was smarter than the reporter they snatched. They sent their B team after Olsen and their A team after her. Despite knowing her exact location and having every entrance of the building covered, she walked right past them. Whoa," Bergman said as he looked up from his screen. "Six years ago, she was flown to the Washington headquarters of the NIA on the orders of Senior Lead Analyst Barbara Smith."

"Ah," Smith said. "I thought her name sounded familiar. I tried to recruit her."

"What happened," Finch asked.

"She recommended...how did she phrase it?" Smith shook her head and smiled. "I should attempt a rectal cranial inversion."

"If she felt that way, why did she get on the plane?" Bergman asked.

"I thought she had gotten tired of me pestering her and wanted to tell me in person she would never work for me," Smith said.

"Her real reason was that she wanted a ride from the West Coast to get to some underground music venue in New York City," Meyer added.

"She used an NIA jet as her personal Uber?" Bergman asked with a grin on his face.

"Pretty much," Meyer answered. "We lost her in the airport, and she went to ground. Despite our best efforts we could never find her again."

Finch's eyes danced back and forth between Smith and Meyer. Bergman had seen that look before and made a mental note the next time they were alone to ask what she saw that he didn't. Finch scanned the file on Bergman's screen, then pointed to the monitor while shaking her head. "She's a decent hacker but hardly world-class," Finch said with a dismissive snort. "You would actually hire someone like her?"

"In a heartbeat," Smith answered, then she looked at Bergman. "Your evil twin analogy is not that far off the mark. She is fluent in every major hacker native tongue, Russian, Mandarin, Romanian, Korean and a few dozen others. Her memory also rivals our own Little Mary Sunshine here."

Carrie Finch let out a dramatic sigh, rolled her eyes and went back to her screen.

Bergman chuckled then pointed to the screen. "The delivery has arrived." Two grim men in dark suits and wearing sunglasses were working their way through the scrum.

"Are we in contact with them?" Smith asked.

"We can be," Finch answered and less than two second later said, "You're online with Special Agent Kyle Ryder."

"Special Agent Ryder, this is Barbara Smith, Assistant Director of the National Intelligence Agency."

On the screen they could see Ryder come to a dead stop and put his hand over his left ear. "Yes ma'am."

"Instead of handing your delivery to Cassandra Morse, please give the package to the young lady with the purple hair. And tell her compliments of Barbara Smith at the NIA."

"Yes, ma'am."

"Keep the com line open."

"Yes, ma'am."

On the screen they watched as the agent approached the porch. "I'm Special Agent Ryder from the FBI." S.A. Ryder stopped when he saw Morse give Mullen a nudge and a smug grin. Shaking his head, he extended the package in Mullen's direction. "Compliments of Assistant Director Barbara Smith of the National Intelligence Agency."

They watched as Mullen smiled broadly then over the com, they heard Mullen ask Cassandra, "Okay, Miss Smarty britches. Which one is the NIA live feed?"

Without a moment's hesitation, Morse answered, "Third from the left. Dressed wrong and the equipment looks like it just came out of the box."

"Nice," Mullen answered. Then she leaned in closer to Agent Ryder's earpiece and said, "Thanks, Babs! You shouldn't have."

"Tell her she looks nice in a dress," Smith said with a smirk.

"Ma'am?"

"You heard me."

The agent gathered himself then said, "Assistant Director Smith told me to tell you, you look nice in a dress."

They watched as Mullen handed Cassandra the box, then whispered in the com, "Sit on it and rotate, bitch." Then she swiftly raised her left arm and crossed it with her right in the classic "up yours" hand gesture.

"Oh. My. God!" Bergman roared as tears streamed down his cheeks. "Can we keep her?"

Chapter 41

CASSANDRA MORSE AND Holly Mullen left the others on the porch to continue dealing with the press. Det. Steve Foley had had his fill of the Fourth Estate for the day and tagged along behind the women. After stepping back into the house, Cassandra offered the package back to Mullen. Mullen eyed Morse. "What do you think is in the box?"

"Three burner phones."

"Why three?"

"The box rattles so it's an odd number."

Mullen took the box and gave it a shake. "Right. If it were an even number, they would stack up better and not move around as much. How did you come up with three and not one or five?"

"Too heavy for one." Cassandra shrugged. "Plus, why go to all the trouble of turning an FBI agent into a delivery boy for one phone and why would we need five? That seems like overkill to me."

"Huh," Mullen said as she nodded her approval. "You're getting back to your old form, aren't you?"

"What are you talking about?" Cassandra asked.

"I've spent the past two days researching you. Since you put the SV-1 in the drink you've been a drunken slut and an emotional basket case. Now you're back to being Wonder Woman's more talented kid sister again. What changed?"

Cassandra shrugged but didn't answer.

Mullen waved it off and yawned, making no effort to cover her mouth. "It doesn't matter. I'll figure it out for myself." Mullen looked down at her dress. "You got anything that would fit me? I'd love to get out of this clown costume."

Cassandra pointed to the stairs. "First door on the left."

Det. Foley watched Mullen head up the stairs and when he was sure she was out of earshot, he turned to Cassandra. "Be careful with that one."

Morse shrugged. "I've got bigger problems than her."

"I'm just saying. Anyone who'll go out of their way to piss off the A.D. of the National Intelligence Agency is someone to keep an eye on."

"Or someone you want as an ally and not an enemy."

"Talking about me?" Mullen asked as she thundered down the stairs in a faded blue "Navy" sweatshirt and yoga pants. The sweatshirt was at least one size too big but the yoga pants, which were too tight for Cassandra and she seldom wore, were about right for Mullen. "Garbage can?" she asked as she held up the crumpled yellow dress and push up bra she had in her hand.

"Kitchen. Under the sink," Cassandra answered.

"What's the over and under on the call?" Mullen asked over her shoulder as she headed out of the room.

"I'll take under thirty seconds," Cassandra answered.

"I bet you would," Mullen answered from the kitchen. "I'll take under fifteen."

"What are you two talking about?" Foley asked.

"She and I are in agreement that there are phones in the box," Cassandra said. "The bet will be how soon we'll get a call from the NIA after we power one of them up."

"You haven't even opened the box yet," Foley said.

Mullen returned to the room and ignored Foley. "Fifteen seconds. Do we have a bet or not?"

"What are the stakes?" Cassandra asked.

"Make it easy on yourself," Mullen answered.

"You sound pretty confident."

"As you can probably tell, Barbara Smith and I have a history. I bet she's already teed-up."

"No bet," Cassandra said as she ripped the box open, looked inside then held up three fingers.

"Hold on," Mullen said as she fished her laptop out of her oversized bag and then removed the secondary bag it was wrapped in.

"Faraday cage?" Cassandra asked.

"What's a Faraday cage?" Foley asked.

"A Faraday cage blocks RF signals from both being sent and received to an electronic device," Cassandra answered.

"That way my old friends at the NIA can't track me," Mullen added as she booted up her computer. "That should wake them up."

"That was why you were so confident they would call so quickly." Cassandra chuckled. "Do you need my WIFI password?"

"No," Mullen said as she logged in. "I got it yesterday when I hacked your laptop."

If Cassandra was shocked or offended, it didn't show. She pulled one of the cell phones out of the box and hit the power button. It wasn't password protected.

At eleven seconds the phone rang. Cassandra tossed it to Mullen who pushed the "accept" button. "How's it hangin' Babs?"

A.D. Smith ignored the question. "Is Cassandra Morse with you?"

"My new BFF? Of course she is."

"Anyone else?" Smith asked.

Mullen eyed Det. Foley. "Just a local LEO."

"Put me on speaker."

"Your wish is my command," Mullen answered as she pushed the speaker button.

"The guy at the bar has been eliminated as a suspect."

"Really?" Cassandra answered.

"Yes," Barbara Smith answered. "I wouldn't be expecting a Christmas card this year from either the FBI or the Department of Homeland Security."

"I'll add them to the growing list," Cassandra answered.

"Do you have any other candidates?" Smith asked.

Cassandra shook her head. "I'm afraid not," she answered.

"That's unfortunate," Smith said. "So why don't you give me everything which was in the dream and not the edited version you gave to the always gullible Ms. Mullen and the reporter."

Holly Mullen was about to respond but Cassandra put her hand on her arm and mouthed "don't let her in your head".

Mullen smiled and silently mouthed "I like you".

"I'm not sure what you're asking," Cassandra said to Smith.

"Ms. Morse," Barbara Smith said bluntly. "I'm more than happy to run interference for you with the FBI, DHS and LAPD. Don't piss me off. I'm an enemy you don't want to make. Besides, I'm on your side."

"Right."

"I want to prevent your dream from coming true as much as you do, and I want to hunt down the bastards that blew you out of the sky and killed one of the finest men I've ever met."

"You knew my grandfather?"

"Yes," Smith answered and left it at that.

Mullen put her hand over the cell phone's mouthpiece. "She's one tough bitch but you can trust her."

Cassandra shook her head and sighed. "I left out some of the details of my dream because they sounded so weird, I was afraid no one would believe me."

"Try me," Smith said.

Cassandra gave Smith all of the details of her dream, holding back nothing.

"Give me the last part again."

"I said, 'Remember you have that meeting tonight with your old friend.' Then the admiral, now dressed like Bob Denver from Gillian's Island with an inflatable inner tube in the shape of an oversized rubber duckie around his waist, answered, 'How could I forget?' Then I said, 'Don't forget these!' as I handed the admiral a toilet plunger. Then the admiral stepped out the door and an atomic blast flattened the house I was in."

"I can see why you didn't share that part," Smith said then sighed.

Carrie Finch tapped Smith on the shoulder and whispered. "I have a thought."

"Don't be bashful," Smith said as she pulled Finch closer to the speaker on the phone. "This is one of my top new analysts Carrie Finch. Who, by the way, was the one who poured life back into the investigation of your grandfather's murder."

Mullen began a web search for Carrie Finch.

Smith chuckled. "I hear you typing Holly. Check your email." Instantly a file from the NIA popped up in Mullen's inbox. "That's more than you'd get in a week on Carrie Finch and we really don't have time to dick around."

"Thanks, Babs," Mullen said as she opened the file. She speed read the summary and made a dismissive snort. "Typical NIA gnome."

"She would eat you for lunch," Smith said.

Mullen started to respond, but Cassandra's hand on her arm and shake of the head stopped her. Instead of something snippy, she said, "Let's hear what she has to say."

Carrie Finch cleared her throat. "Let me be sure I'm correct," Finch said. "When you dreamed about the arson fire you were in close proximity with both the arsonist and his victims."

"Correct."

Holly Mullen's eyes and mouth both flew open as she saw where this was going before anyone else. "You've got a keeper there, Babs!" Mullen exclaimed.

"May I finish?" Carrie Finch snapped.

"Sorry, Princess," Mullen answered. "I wasn't trying to steal any of your glory."

Finch snorted then continued. "In your arson dream, you received information from two different sources, the arsonist and his victims."

"Oh! Oh!" Bergman said excitedly. "That is brilliant!"

"Right!" Mullen concurred.

"Will you two please shut up and let me finish!" Carrie Finch shouted.

"Yes. Please let her finish," Smith added with an authoritative tone.

"Thank you," Finch said. "You received information from two sources, but you only had one dream…"

"Oh my God!" Cassandra said as it was her turn to interrupt.

"I give up," Finch said.

Smith laughed and patted Finch on the back. "I think we all see where this is heading."

For the first time Det. Foley spoke. "You all may see it, but I certainly don't."

"My new dream was in two parts just like the arson one and my subconscious lumped it together into one dream."

Foley gasped. "We're looking for two different people with very different agendas."

Chapter 42

SMITH GLANCED AT the monitor and saw Professor Comstock still holding court with the media on Cassandra's front stoop. "Are you in agreement that we could be dealing with two separate issues, the train shipment and a potential nuclear disaster?"

"I won't put all of my eggs in one basket," Cassandra answered.

"I have no intention of doing that," Smith answered. "But your grandfather stating unambiguously in your dream that 'the load was delivered exactly as planned' has me more concerned about the second part than the first part."

"I suppose," Cassandra said. "But there has to be some kind of linkage for them to appear in the same dream."

Smith sighed. "I agree, but the connection is unclear to me at the moment."

"Need I state the obvious?" Holly Mullen asked with a hint of disdain in her voice.

"That our primary concern at this point should be preventing the loss of any nuclear material," Carrie Finch answered with a touch of venom in her tone. "No nuclear material, no dirty bomb. Duh."

"You little NIA tool," Mullen barked.

"Better to be in the game making a difference, then scampering around on the dark web with a weird haircut," Finch countered.

"Ladies!" Smith said with authority. "Don't make me send both of you to your rooms." When she was sure Finch and Mullen were finished clawing at each other, she continued, "I believe I have a foolproof way to prevent any of the material from being stolen."

"How?" Cassandra demanded.

Smith glanced at her monitor again and smiled. "Ms. Morse, please leave this phone on speaker and take it to where both your uncle and the microphones outside can pick up what I'm saying."

"Okay," Cassandra said reluctantly as she picked up the phone. Cassandra looked at Mullen who just shrugged. Mullen was just as lost as Cassandra.

"Oh!" said Carrie Finch with a satisfied giggle since she had worked it out before Mullen. "Will we have time to make the arrangements?"

"That will be Madison Street's problem, not ours," Smith answered.

Cassandra opened the door and her uncle stopped mid-sentence. "The Assistant Director of the National Intelligence Agency would like a word with you." Cassandra moved the phone so it was close enough to the microphones so that everyone could hear.

"Professor Comstock?" Smith asked.

The mob of reporters fell still as they hung on every word.

"Yes," Comstock answered. "This is Professor Comstock."

"This is Barbara Smith." She paused for effect and she got it. No one moved, a few weren't even breathing. "I would like to challenge you to a debate this evening on the merits of moving the nuclear waste material from the Diablo Canyon facility to the San Onofre facility."

A huge smile broke across Uncle Billy's face. "I accept!"

"Excellent," Smith said casually. "You are more familiar with the local TV markets than I. Do you think you could convince Madison Street to be the moderator?"

"I would be honored," Madison Street shouted from the fence line as every other reporter, print and broadcast, stared dagger through her.

A howl of indignant protests immediately went up.

"Excellent," Smith said. "Ms. Morse, would you please give Professor Comstock and Madison Street one of the phones I sent you so my staff can work out the logistics."

Cassandra Morse bit her lip to keep from laughing out loud in front of the cameras but felt no need for restraint when she was back inside with the door closed.

"Now we know why she sent three phones and not one," Cassandra said with a laugh.

"She burned our asses," Mullen answered.

"The debate was her endgame all along," Cassandra added.

"But to what end?" Mullen asked softly.

"You realize," Smith said over the speaker, "I can still hear both of you."

"Okay, Babs," Mullen said. "What's the game here? This debate is going to cause every person in L.A. County to be lining the tracks when the shipment starts to roll."

"I certainly hope so," Smith said smugly.

"Oh my God! That's brilliant!" Carrie Finch could be heard shouting in the background.

Mullen's nose flared with anger that her NIA rival had figured out something before her. Still, she was not about to admit it.

Cassandra saw the expression on Mullen's face and took point so Mullen wouldn't have to admit she was still in the dark. "You want to enlighten us?"

"If you wanted to assure something wasn't going to be stolen from a train on a two-hundred-and-fifty-mile trip..."

Mullen slapped her forehead. "In addition to having a police escort and possibly the National Guard, have a few hundred thousand people with phone video cameras along every inch of the track."

Chapter 43

JACK LOGAN SAT in a chair next to Tom McMahon and just a few feet away from the seventy-inch 4K OLED monitor on the wall in McMahon's office. After playing the muted raw video from the USS Ronald Reagan of Congressman Donald Warwick's receiving his poisoned drink at normal speed three times, he hit the pause button.

Next, he queued up the spot Ashton had conveniently fast-forwarded through where Rachel Frey was just about to hit the button on her keychain. He took the video off mute. Logan made a note of the time stamp on the bottom of the video on a scratch pad in front of him and hit the play button.

They watched as Frey pressed the button then carefully returned her key fob to her oversized bag. Exactly twenty-one seconds later, the alarms started going off.

"Crap," Logan muttered.

"Double crap," McMahon answered.

Logan leaned back in his chair, interlocked his fingers behind his head and sighed.

"Is there any way we can get confirmation?"

Logan laughed. "I still have some friends I could send this to but they're not stupid. They'll immediately figure out what happened."

"Is that a bad thing?" McMahon asked.

Logan's eyes locked on McMahon. "I guess it depends on where your loyalties lie."

"If that bitch fired a weapon of mass destruction at Reagan Carrier Strike Group 5…." McMahon let that thought linger.

"The Reagan alone has over 5,000 sailors and 60 plus aircraft," Logan added softly.

A heavy silence settled over the office.

"Do you trust your guy?" McMahon finally asked.

"With my life," Logan answered.

"Send it," McMahon said.

Logan attached a copy of the video to an email then put in a cryptic note indicating the time stamp and sent it using his Bathmann Aeronautics email address.

***

A few seconds later, the email landed in the inbox of an analyst at the NIA. When he saw who it was from, he immediately picked up the seldom used red phone on the corner of his desk. An instant later, a matching red phone on the corner of Kevin Meyer's desk didn't buzz. Instead, it forwarded the call to the jet en route to Los Angeles.

"Yes," Meyer said.

"Michael Hicks has blown his deep cover and sent us a video."

"Forward it directly to the A.D." Meyer was on his feet and moving fast. His sudden appearance and interruption startled Carrie Finch and Nick Bergman but A.D. Barbara Smith was nonplussed.

"Hicks blew his cover."

"Really?" Smith asked calmly. "How did he do it?"

"He sent us a video."

Smith pointed in the direction of the monitor on the rear wall of the passenger section of the jet then to Carrie Finch. Meyer didn't need further instructions as he turned Smith's laptop in Finch's direction.

"He sent us a time stamp," Meyer said.

"I can see that," Finch answered as her fingers danced like summer lightning over the keyboard and the monitor came to life. "Who is Hicks?" Finch asked.

"One of my best field agents," Smith answered.

Finch leaned back and her eyes locked on Smith's. "How long has he been in deep cover?" she asked.

"Nearly six months," Smith answered.

Finch raised one eyebrow.

"You weren't the only one who thought the entire Cassandra Morse incident didn't pass the smell test," Smith said.

Smith shifted her position to see the screen better. Paul Rogers, Director of Homeland Security, overhearing what was being said, got up and stood next to her.

"What's going on?" Rogers asked.

"The man I have inside Bathmann Aeronautics just blew his cover. He wouldn't have done it without a very good reason."

"Agreed," Rogers confirmed.

Finch queued up the video to the suggested time stamp and hit play. They all watched as Rachel Frey pushed the button on her key fob and a few seconds later, alarms began to sound.

"What am I looking at?" Smith asked Finch.

Finch leaned back and looked at Smith. "Really?" she asked.

"Okay," Smith said with a chuckle. "What are you looking at?"

"From the date and time stamp, the décor and the people present," Finch said. "This appears to be the officer's wardroom on the USS Ronald Reagan moments before it was attacked."

Paul Rogers was suddenly much more interested and moved closer to the screen. "Play that again."

Smith's eyes twinkled when she saw the response Finch was getting from the Director of Homeland. "What else?"

"This came in from a Bathmann Aeronautics email address, which claims it is from a Jack Logan and not someone named Hicks," Finch said. "Since you said Hicks was one of your best agents, I assume this video is the smoking gun you've had him looking for, so he didn't blow his cover, he completed his mission."

Meyer and Smith exchanged approving nods as Paul Rogers stared open-mouthed at Finch.

"Since there isn't much we can do about the train at the moment, I want you two," Smith said as she motioned toward Finch and Bergman, "to work on this."

"I've tried to investigate this previously." Finch's eyes danced back and forth between the A.D. of the NIA and the Director of DHS. "I've run into nothing but roadblocks and access denials."

Smith glanced at Meyer who immediately picked up his phone and started dialing. Rogers' assistant had started dialing his phone as well.

"It will take a few minutes to process," Smith said calmly. "You'll find you now have unencumbered access to all NIA data."

"And the Homeland Security database as well." Rogers turned to Smith and asked, "Will four be enough?"

"Since she'll be inside my bubble, yes," Smith answered. "When we get back to DC, I'm going to want a full blanket."

"Agreed," Rogers answered. Without being asked, his aide was on the phone again.

For once, Carrie Finch was baffled. "Four what, ma'am?" She asked.

Bergman laughed as he patted Finch on the shoulder. "They just handed you the keys to the magic kingdom which makes you the ultimate high value target for every terrorist and dictator in the world."

Smith, smiling, motioned for Bergman to continue.

"When we arrive in L.A., you're going to have a four-man security detail assigned to you." Bergman turned to Smith. "Will she have her own car?"

"Yes," Rogers answered for Smith.

"Bullet resistant and run flat tires?" Bergman asked.

"Yes," Rogers answered.

"How many cup holders?" Bergman asked. Apparently, he was the only one on the jet who thought that question was funny.

Chapter 44

TOM MCMAHON DROVE and Jack Logan rode shotgun on the forty-five-minute drive from the Bathmann testing facility to the company headquarters in Austin.

"How long have you known?" Logan asked.

McMahon shrugged. "Since about a month after you started."

"What gave me away?"

"You were too damn good," McMahon chuckled. "Most of the guys we hire from the military are head cases or people with questionable ethics."

"So you made a few phone calls."

"Yeah," McMahon answered. "While your fake background was CIA quality, nobody in the Criminal Investigation Division had ever heard of anyone named Jack Logan."

"Interesting," Logan said. "Why didn't you out me?"

McMahon sighed. "This whole thing with what happened on the Gipper didn't sit right with me."

"Why?" Logan asked.

"First off, they kept me out of the loop on the security and Ashton handled it personally."

"That was unusual?"

"It has never happened before or since."

Being a good interrogator, Logan knew when to keep his mouth shut. McMahon was right on the edge of emptying the bag and he didn't want to say or do anything which might cause McMahon to clam up.

McMahon was a good interrogator as well and knew what the silence meant. He had probably gone through some of the same training. He also knew there was more in play here than usual. He understood that the players in the rough and tumble world of defense contracting were not choirboys. Corners were cut, lines were crossed, and "legal" bribes were made every day. It was all part of doing business and Bathmann Aeronautics was no better or worse than the rest of the other jackals. But this thing on the USS Ronald Reagan had stuck in his craw. A dead congressman. A WMD fired on a Navy Strike Group. A competitor's prototype blown out of the sky. After seeing the video any loyalty he had toward the company was gone.

McMahon glanced at Logan and made his choice.

"Ashton, like most Colonels, who had plateaued while in the military, plateaued for a reason. He's a useless paper pusher," McMahon said. "The rumor around the farm was that the Pentagon was about ready to pull the plug on the E-38. Bathmann and Ashton couldn't let that happen."

"You think they planned and executed the entire thing?"

"Yeah," McMahon said. "And I think Rachel Frey was in it up to her pretty little neck."

"Why?" Logan asked.

"Ashton doesn't have the brains and Bathmann doesn't have the balls."

Logan chuckled as he fished a burner phone out of his pocket.

"Who are you calling?"

"My boss," Logan answered.

"Who is your boss?"

"I report directly to the Assistant Director of the National Intelligence Agency."

"Jesus," McMahon said. "Who the hell are you?"

Logan held up a finger to indicate that McMahon should wait. As the phone rang, he put it on speaker.

"Yes?" Kevin Meyer said.

"I need to speak to Ms. Smith."

"No," Meyer answered. "First you need to speak to Carrie Finch."

"This is Finch. The Assistant Director asked me to brief you before she speaks with you."

"I'm on speaker with Tom McMahon…"

"I know who he is," Finch said, cutting him off. To her credit, she didn't ask if McMahon could be trusted. After reading Michael

Hicks's – AKA Jack Logan – file, if he was satisfied, so was she. "We did a full analysis of the video and it appears to be unaltered. Checking the timeline on the video we were able to find a signal broadcast from the USS Ronald Reagan to a signal booster concealed on the flight deck. The broadcast was so short, it had been mistaken for static or possibly lightning. The signal was received by a Bathmann Aeronautics ship roughly forty miles away from the USS Ronald Reagan. The ship, which was supposed to be a simple science monitoring vessel, was actually the command and control center for the Icarus platform which fired at the Reagan."

There was a brief pause.

"This is Smith."

"I like your new girl."

"I do too. Where are you?"

"We're in transit to the Bathmann World Headquarters. ETA of about fifteen minutes."

"Stop and get a cup of coffee. I'll have a team contact you when they're in place."

"Yes. ma'am," Hicks answered. "What do you want me to do with her?"

"Invite her to come chat with me in Los Angeles."

"If she declines?"

"She murdered a congressman and an admiral. Use your persuasive skills."

"There's a Starbucks right across the street from the main entrance," McMahon said.

"Perfect," Smith answered. "Please take me off speaker," Smith said. "I have some instructions for you."

For the next two minutes Hicks listened but didn't say anything other than the occasional, "yes, ma'am."

McMahon and Logan had found a window seat in the coffee shop and waited. They didn't have to wait long as a pair of heavy Black SUVs pulled up to the curb in front of the Starbucks and six very serious men in SWAT gear got out. They all had on helmets and bullet-resistant vests with "DHS" printed in bold letters on the back.

A few of the startled pedestrians pulled out their phones and started videoing.

"Show time," Hicks said as he finished his coffee in one gulp and tossed his cup in the trash as he headed outside. McMahon, a step behind, saw the deference the six men were all showing the man he knew as Jack Logan. He watched as one of the men handed Logan his credentials and a clip-on holster containing a Glock 21 with customized grips and sights.

"Who the hell are you?" McMahon asked.

Logan chuckled and extended his hand. "I told you. My real name is Michael Hicks."

"And your playmates?" McMahon asked as he nodded at the other six men on the curb with them.

Hicks chuckled. "Sometimes my boss has a great sense of humor. When she wants to make an impression, we go full Shock and Awe, baby," Hicks answered with a laugh.

With six heavily armed men, traffic came to a stop when they jaywalked across the street and entered the lobby of the world headquarters of Bathmann Aeronautics. If Barbara Smith had designed the entrance for maximum effect, she had hit the "X" ring. The three men working the security desk froze as Hicks shoved his cred pack in the closest one's face. "I'm the senior agent in charge, Michael Hicks of the United States Department of Homeland Security Anti-Terrorist Division. You will escort me to the office of Rachel Louise Frey," Hicks said in a cold tone. He turned to one of the men following him and pointed at the two remaining, now terrified, rent-a-cops. "If either one of them reaches for a telephone or pushes a silent alarm, shoot them both."

"Gladly," the agent answered as he fed a round into his AR-15 and grinned at the two security guards.

Alarms went off as the team stepped through the metal detectors, but they didn't even slow down. Hicks, McMahon, the remaining five agents and the security guard crowded into an express elevator that took them directly to the top floor.

The door opened to a large reception area where a startled woman was behind a chrome and granite desk. Hicks marched straight up to her and showed her his cred pack. "Rachel Louise Frey."

With shaking hands, she pointed down the hall. "She's with Mr. Bathmann. Last door at the end of the hall."

With a nod from Hicks, one of the agents shoved the security guard who had escorted them upstairs roughly into a chair. "Sit and stay," Hicks said softly. When he heard the phone on the receptionist desk start to ring. "Do not answer that." Hicks pointed at one of his men. "Stay here."

"Yes, sir," the man in SWAT gear said with authority.

Hicks, McMahon and the four remaining members of the team headed down the hall, and without bothering to knock, walked straight into the office of Louis Bathmann IV. Inside with Bathmann were Rachel Frey and Gabe Ashton.

"Logan? What's the meaning of this!" Bathmann shouted as he started to his feet.

"Please stay seated," Hicks said softly. "I'm not Jack Logan. I'm Senior Agent in Charge, Michael Hicks, of the Department of Homeland Security Anti-Terrorist Division." Hicks turned his attention to Frey.

"Rachel Louise Frey, you have the right to remain silent. Anything you say can be used against you in court. You have the right to talk to a lawyer for advice before we ask you any questions. You have the right to have a lawyer with you during questioning. If you cannot afford a lawyer, one will be appointed for you before any questioning if you wish. If you decide to answer questions now without a lawyer present, you have the right to stop answering at any time. Do you understand these rights?"

"Yes," she answered calmly.

"The Assistant Director of the National Intelligence Agency Barbara Smith requested that you come to Los Angeles for an interview."

"And if I decline?" Frey asked with a sweet smile.

Hicks smiled back at her just as sweetly. "Then we invoke the Patriot Act, contact the media and have you do a perp walk in handcuffs and leg shackles out the front door of this building." Hicks smiled again. "Then you still have your chat with A.D. Smith, but it will be at Guantanamo Bay. Oh," Hicks added, "the A.D.'s schedule is pretty tight so it might be a month or two before she can find the time to fly to Cuba."

Bathmann looked at Ashton. "Get Legal up here."

Ashton looked at Hicks for permission.

"Absolutely," Hicks said with a laugh. "Let's get the lawyers involved. Then we'll schedule a press conference."

"What are you proposing?" Rachel Frey asked calmly.

"We escort you home where you pack an overnight bag. We fly you on an NIA Gulfstream to Los Angeles where we put you up in a five-star hotel for the night and you meet with the A.D. at her convenience sometime tomorrow." Hicks's face turned to stone. "Or, we throw you in the back of the next military cargo plane headed to Gitmo."

"Los Angeles is lovely this time of year," Frey said with a confident smile.

Hicks motioned to the four-armed men. "Please escort Ms. Frey home and to the airport."

"Yes, sir," one of the men answered crisply.

After Rachel Frey was out of the room, Bathmann turned on Hicks. "What's going on here?" he demanded.

Hicks turned less aggressive. "A.D. Barbara Smith wishes for me to extend her deepest regrets for this embarrassing situation. While we are not at liberty to discuss an ongoing investigation, every effort will be made to keep your name and the name of your company out of the press."

"Please tell Barbara I appreciate that," Bathmann answered. "Do you have another seat available on your jet?"

"Of course, sir," Hicks answered. "A.D. Smith anticipated you would want to have Ms. Frey represented by legal counsel. She has two rooms already booked."

"That is so like her," Bathmann said warmly. "If you need anything, please contact me directly."

"Thank you, sir," Hicks said humbly as he bowed slightly. "We expected nothing less from a man of your stature."

When they arrived back at the elevators, McMahon wheeled on Hicks. "What the hell was that?"

Hicks answered his question with a question. "What was what?"

"You basically kissed Bathmann's ass back there."

Hicks smiled as the elevator dinged.

"Ah," McMahon said as he caught up. "You want him to think you bought his cover story."

***

After Hicks and the others had left the office, Bathmann looked over at Ashton. "How long before Frey realizes we've thrown her under the bus?"

Ashton shrugged. "It shouldn't be too long." Ashton scratched his head and made a face. "Do you believe all of the sunshine that Hicks guy was blowing up your skirt?"

"No," Bathmann answered. "I'm going to be on the phone calling in every chit I've got."

"Thank God everyone in Washington is a whore."

"Amen to that," Bathmann said as he reached for his phone.

On the sidewalk outside of Bathmann's headquarters, Hicks shook McMahon's hand. "How long before they fire you?" Hicks asked.

"Sooner, rather than later would be my guess," McMahon answered.

Hicks handed McMahon a business card with only a phone number printed on it, no name or other identifying information. "If you're looking for work, call this number anytime 24/7. I won't be the one answering but they'll know how to find me."

"Who the hell are you? Jason Bourne?"

"Naw," Hicks said with a laugh. "Same building; different department." Hicks turned serious. "Fair warning, the only thing worse than the pay are the hours."

"And this would be different how exactly?" Now it was McMahon's turn to turn serious. "Nail these bastards."

"We intend to," Hicks said as he climbed into the rear of one of the SUVs.

As soon as they had pulled away from the curb, he called A.D. Smith. Meyer answered and immediately turned the phone over to his boss.

"Well?" Smith asked.

"I played the beta male to Bathmann's alpha male as well as I could."

"Do you think he bought that I was scared of him?"

"The man has an ego but I doubt he completely bought it. He's going to burn up the phonelines to Washington."

"He's already started," Smith answered.

"That was a masterstroke. I wonder when he's going to realized you've outmaneuvered him?"

"That was my new girl's idea," Smith answered. "Inside the beltway is going to be on fire within the next few hours. Since you got Bathmann to personally make the calls it will not even be considered a rumor since everyone who matters will be hearing it straight from the horse's mouth."

"I would have said the other end of the horse."

"Indeed," Smith answered with a chuckle. "Sit on Rachel Frey until we're ready."

"Yes, ma'am."

Chapter 45

A S THE NIA jet was making its final approach into LAX and the "fasten seatbelt" light came on, Barbara Smith had decided it was time she got to know Nick Bergman. Not wanting to intrude, and not wanting to sit with the Homeland Security people, Kevin Meyer motioned to the empty seat next to Carrie Finch. She put her laptop case on the floor under her seat and he sat down.

"How long have you worked for A.D. Smith?" Finch asked.

"A bit over six years," Meyer answered.

"So, you were around when this whole thing started with Mullen?"

"Yes," Meyer answered.

"Why does Mullen hate Smith so much?"

"You don't waste much time on small talk, do you?" Meyer said with a chuckle.

"No."

"Mullen had an older brother who was a world class hacker. Smith busted him and sent him to federal prison where he was murdered."

"Ouch."

"It really screwed Holly up. She went from the All-American budding genius to what you see now in the blink of an eye."

"So Smith tried to recruit her as penitence for her brother?"

"I was ringside and that's the way I saw it." Meyer pulled out his phone and entered a few keystrokes. "I just sent you the file on Keith Mullen."

"You appeared to have that all queued up," Finch said flatly.

"Guilty as charged," Meyer answered. "With Holly back on the scene, I thought it would be wise if you knew the whole story."

"Okay."

Finch gripped the armrest of the seat and closed her eyes. Knowing most air crashes occurred on either take-off or landing, at this point in every flight she had ever been on, she braced herself for the worst. As the executive jet rolled to a stop at a hangar far from the mail terminal and any other private hangars, she finally started to relax. There was a line of eight SUVs in the hangar. Three each - a lead car, follow car and protected car - were reserved for A.D. Smith and Paul Rogers. The seventh car was Finch's new ride and the eighth was for her security detail.

On the tarmac, Carrie Finch was introduced to her four-man protection detail and given a quick tutorial of the features on her car. Bergman noticed she was only half listening, she clearly had something on her mind.

As they pulled out of the airport to start the drive to the television studio, Finch was deep in the file on Keith Mullen.

"Look at this and tell me what you see."

Bergman began studying the file. "Killed in the prison yard in front of over forty witnesses." He flipped through the autopsy pictures. "Gross," he muttered. "Stabbed over a dozen times." He looked up. "What am I missing?"

"Nothing," Finch answered. "It's perfect."

"I've seen that look before." He looked at the file again. "You think it's too perfect."

"How often do hackers get shanked in a minimum-security prison?"

"How often does anyone get shanked in minimum-security?" Bergman answered.

"Only one time ever," Finch answered.

"What are you thinking here?"

"I need more information before I can form an opinion," she answered.

They both looked up as the convoy rolled to a stop. Finch closed her laptop and reached for the door handle.

"No ma'am," the driver, who had introduced himself earlier as Special Agent Haycock, said politely. "You need to always wait until a member of your detail opens the door for us."

"Us?"

"As the driver, I stay in the vehicle with you with the engine running until we get the all clear."

"I see."

"When you get back to Washington, there will be a protectee orientation training session for you. Until then, when we're moving from one secure location to another, you need to follow our instructions instantly." Haycock turned in his seat and smiled at Finch. "While it is highly unlikely we'll ever have a problem, since you're so small, there is the possibility that if we do have an issue, one of your detail, probably me, might simply pick you up and start running with you in his arms. If that should happen please do not resist."

Bergman leaned in and whispered in Finch's ear. "I love powerful women. Do you have any idea how turned on I am right now?"

Finch giggled then turned to Haycock then pointed to Bergman. "If I asked you to shoot him, would that be a problem?"

The driver sized up Bergman and grinned. "The paperwork whenever we discharge our weapon is brutal. It would be easier for me to just beat the crap out of him and leave him in a heap on the curb."

"So you think you could take him?" Finch asked with a chuckle.

"Ma'am, I think my thirteen-year-old sister could take him."

"I'll keep that in mind," Finch said. "Are you going to be my permanent driver Special Agent Haycock?"

Haycock was a bit surprised Finch had remembered his name. Being a "floater" and not permanently assigned to any one person, most of the people he guarded simply looked at him as the hired help and not someone worth remembering. "No, ma'am. They grabbed me when the call came in. I'm temporarily assigned to the L.A. office."

"Temporary? What is your home base?"

"They move me around a lot."

"Where would you rather be?"

"I grew up in Northern Virginia and I've got family there."

"Would you like to work in Washington?"

"That would be ideal on many levels, ma'am."

The door opened and another member of her security detail, S.A. Alverez, offered Finch a hand to help her get out of the SUV. "All clear, ma'am."

Waiting inside the television studio were Cassandra Morse, Det. Steve Foley and Holly Mullen.

Before Mullen could light into A.D. Barbara Smith, Finch pulled her aside and motioned for Kevin Meyer to join them. "Can you get us a private room?"

Meyer made eye contact with Mullen, smiled, then said, "Yes, ma'am."

Mullen glared at Finch.

Finch sighed and shook her head. "I don't like you. You don't like me."

"I think we can agree on that," Mullen answered with a snort.

"What do you want to talk to me about?"

"Your brother."

"My brother?"

They were rejoined by Kevin Meyer. "I've found you a private office." They followed him to an office that probably belonged to a second-tier manager. The room was small and cluttered but big enough for Finch's purposes. Finch's driver and the man who had helped her out of the car stood at parade rest just outside the door.

Once the door was closed, Mullen wheeled on Finch. "Exactly who the hell do you think you are?" shouted Mullen.

The door immediately burst open and the two men, each twice the size of Holly Mullen, stormed into the room. The driver, Haycock, put himself between Finch and Mullen.

Finch smiled at Haycock. He was funny and willing to take a bullet for her. This guy kept getting better and better.

"Is there a problem, ma'am?" Haycock asked without taking his eyes off of Mullen.

"No," Finch answered calmly. "Please wait outside."

Reluctantly, both men backed out of the room. Before the door could close, Kevin Meyer came in with two cups of coffee. He put a cup of black in front of Finch, then set a second cup down in front of Mullen. "Here you go Holly. Two creams. One sugar."

Mullen took a sip. "Perfect, thanks." Mullen pulled back and started at Meyer. "How did you know how I like my coffee?"

"I read it in your file."

"Oh my God! Could you possibly be any more transparent?" Finch shouted at Meyer and looked ready to explode. "Please tell the A.D. I would like to speak to her at her earliest convenience."

A huge smile broke across his face. "Yes, ma'am."

"What the hell is going on?" Mullen demanded.

Finch, seeing A.D. Smith, followed by Nick Bergman, striding in their direction, held up a finger indicating she should wait.

"Yes?" Smith asked.

"Either you tell her right now or I do," Finch snarled.

"Tell me what?" Mullen demanded.

Barbara Smith burst out laughing. It was a rich, deep-throated laugh. "All yours," she said as she took a step back.

Mullen was staring daggers through both Finch and Smith.

"Your brother is not dead," Carrie Finch said dismissively. "He's in witness protection."

Mullen was stunned and momentarily speechless. She shook her head and turned on Smith. "Is this true?"

"Yes," Smith answered.

"Why fake his death?"

"The people your brother turned on were such good hackers we were afraid if he went straight into witness protection they would have found a way around the safeguards to find him and they would have killed him. After a bit of plastic surgery and a fitness program, I doubt your mother would have recognized him."

"Among others," Finch muttered under her breath.

Mullen glared at Finch then asked. "Who created his new ID?"

"Your brother did. He works for me."

"W-W-What?" Mullen stammered.

"I think what she's saying is," Finch snapped, "that if you hadn't been such a complete horse's ass and had actually shown up in Washington for your interview you would have had your family reunion six years ago."

Smith shrugged. "After you went all over the web bragging about exactly how you had stuck it to the bad old Barbara Smith, I couldn't exactly invite you back in for another visit without raising more than a few eyebrows."

"Where is he?"

Finch rolled her eyes. "Really?" Finch said to Smith. "You actually tried to hire her? I've had this for less than half a day while working on another project and figured it out. She's had it for six years and had a personal interest!"

"Where's my brother?" Mullen demanded as she felt her anger level rising.

Finch motioned dramatically with both hands in the direction of Kevin Meyer.

"Hey, sis," Meyer said.

"Keith?"

"Kevin now," he answered.

Holly Mullen, with her mouth wide open, studied Kevin Meyers then the lights clicked on. She gasped and threw her arms around his neck. "Oh my God!"

"I can't wait for you to meet Joanna and the girls."

"Girls?"

"I have two daughters."

"I'm an aunt!"

Mullen, torn between being furious and delighted, pointed a finger at her brother. "You I'll deal with in a minute." Mullen turned and slugged Finch in the shoulder. "How long have you known?"

"That he was your brother or that there was something suspicious about your relationship with Smith?" Finch asked in a detached monotone voice as she rubbed her arm.

"When did you first suspect?"

"Suspect? The moment your brother started sharing information about you with me. Then he kept dropping tantalizing breadcrumbs in front of me like finding an excuse to sit next to me when we were landing and giving me a file."

"Ahh," Mullen said. "Nobody takes a leak around her royal highness without prior written approval."

Mullen and Finch both turned and looked at Barbara Smith who just shrugged.

"Then I got absolute confirmation…"

"Confirmation? What confirmation?"

"If you would quit interrupting me, I would tell you," Finch said in the same tone a parent might use with an unruly seven-year-old.

Mullen growled then motioned for Finch to continue.

"What do you think are the chances we would need to refresh Barbara Smith's memory about someone who had embarrassed the hell out of her by ditching on a meeting, then going online and bragged about it?"

Mullen chuckled. "Somewhere considerably less than zero."

"Damn," Bergman muttered. "I completely missed that one."

Finch ignored Bergman and glared at Smith. "Especially when your absence blew up what I imagine was a carefully planned and executed meeting which was repaying a debt."

"Debt?"

"Thanks to your brother, some very nasty people were taken out of play. This is pure speculation, but I guess the agreement with your brother and A.D. Smith included a new ID and, since you're his only family, the ability for him to reconnect with you."

Finch and Mullen looked at Smith for confirmation. Smith nodded.

Finch wheeled on Smith and Meyer. "For future reference, I really don't like being led around by my nose."

"Duly noted," Smith answered with a smile. "It won't happen again."

"When did you know he was my brother?"

Finch sighed. "I suspected it on the airplane." She shook her head and pointed to Mullen's coffee. "A few moments ago, I got absolute confirmation. But, of course, you completely missed it."

Mullen growled and held her thumb and index finger about an inch apart. "So close," she said with venom in her voice. "I was right on the edge of starting to like you."

Finch snorted. "Don't bother," Finch answered. "When this is over, I'm sure you'll slither back into whatever hole you crawled out of."

Mullen took a step in Finch's direction but stopped when Smith's voice cracked like a whip.

"Ladies!" Smith said with a low growl. "We don't have all day for this. Ms. Finch, tell her the clue she missed."

"Clues actually," Finch answered. "He always calls me Ms. Finch or ma'am. Twice on the airplane he referred to her as Holly and not Ms. Mullen. Then, out of nowhere, he called a woman he supposedly just met 'Holly'." Finch pointed at Meyer. "Then, he brought you a coffee with two creams and one sugar."

"He said it was in my file, how I liked my coffee."

"I've read your file," Finch said as she used her hand to cover a yawn. "There is no mention of coffee anywhere."

"Damn!" Meyer said as he turned to Smith. "You were right. I didn't think there was a chance in hell she would have caught the coffee thing."

Smith smiled but didn't answer. She was transfixed watching the two young women in front of her mixing it up.

"How the hell am I supposed to know what's in my file?" Mullen protested. "Unlike you, I've never read it."

Finch shrugged. "That's a fair point," Finch conceded. "That moves you from complete idiot to merely dense."

Mullen started for Finch again.

"Ladies!" Smith said as Meyer stepped in between them. "Ms. Finch, please explain why you think Ms. Mullen is dense so we can get on with the issue at hand."

Finch shrugged. "What would you call someone who was standing inches away from a person they grew up with and not recognizing them?" Finch snorted. "I think merely calling them dense is being generous."

Mullen opened her mouth and raised a finger to protest but stopped and bowed to Finch. "Okay. You win this round." She turned to her brother and held out her hand.

Meyer, with a silly grin on his face asked, "What?"

"I want to see pictures of my nieces and the woman dumb enough to marry you." Mullen's eyes started to fill with tears as she pounded her brother on his chest with both hands. "Damn you!"

Chapter 46

SMITH, FINCH AND Bergman left Mullen and Meyer alone in the office to catch up. Through the office window they could see Mullen alternating between slugging her brother and giving him a tearful hug.

Finch pulled Smith into a quiet corner and Bergman tagged along.

"What do you see in her that I'm missing?" Finch asked Smith as she watched Mullen through the glass.

"She's a survivor," Smith answered. "She has great instincts and is fearless and resourceful." Smith's eyes locked on Finch who didn't seem convinced. "Ask yourself this. Would you have been able to walk out of that newspaper office the way she did without ending up with a black bag over your head?"

"Probably not," Finch answered honestly.

"Probably not?" Smith said with more than a hint of disbelief in her tone. "Finch, you're a linear thinker, one of the best I've ever seen. She is a non-linear thinker. To you, she is an undisciplined kook. To her, you're an anal-retentive tight-ass who has never had a creative thought in your head. In today's world the NIA needs both of you."

"Judge the results and not the person nor their technique," Finch answered softly. "Interesting."

"For the past six years she has quietly become one of the top hackers in the world," Smith continued. "She can gain access to people and places on the dark net you and Nick don't even know exist. If we could bring her onboard and make her a team player, it would be a major coup for the agency and for your career."

"Ah," Finch said softly.

"Ah?" Bergman asked. "Ah what?"

Smith motioned to Finch to bring Bergman up to speed. "Twenty-four hours ago, I was a nobody working the Bulgarian desk. Now I have the highest security clearance available for the NIA, a security detail and I'm the new protégé of the A.D. If I can bring Mullen into the fold, something A.D. Smith failed spectacularly to do six years ago, not only will no one question my promotion, I'll be the new flavor of the month, heir apparent to take A.D. Smith's job when she retires or is forced out."

"You're going to be making a lot of enemies in a hurry. It wouldn't hurt to have a few friends. Especially one who is just as capable as you with a diametrically opposite worldview."

Bergman shook his head. "When I'm around you two, sometimes I feel like I'm playing checkers while you two are playing 3-D chess."

"It won't be easy to get her onboard," Smith continued while ignoring Bergman. "She is definitely the Yin to your Yang. I want you to give her a chance to prove herself. I think you can learn a lot from each other and make a formidable team."

"It doesn't mean I have to like her," Finch stated flatly.

"We have an old saying inside the beltway. If you want a friend in Washington, get yourself a dog."

They turned when they heard a commotion behind them and saw Professor William Comstock and his two-person entourage enter the television studio. With Comstock was Jeffrey and an equally handsome but more intense version of Jeffery. In his mid-twenties he could have been Jeffery's younger brother. The new arrival was thin and just under six feet tall and had a fast-retreating hairline with the rest of his hair pulled back into a tight "man bun".

They were intercepted by a young and harried producer who was in charge of getting the debate arranged on short notice. The producer was in his mid-twenties, and like a million others in Hollywood, had a low-wage job he was vastly over-qualified for but offered enough flexibility to allow him to make auditions. He was handsome and fit with quick eyes that indicated his IQ was well above average. His most noticeable features were a dazzling set of teeth and perfect skin. He guided team Comstock in the direction of the conference room and waved for Smith, Finch and Bergman to join them.

"What about us?" Cassandra asked.

The producer looked at A.D. Smith for her opinion.

"The more the merrier," Assistant Director Smith said as she walked over and gave Comstock a sisterly hug. "Hello Bill," she said.

"Barbara," Comstock answered.

"How long have you two known each other?" Cassandra asked.

"I've known Bill for more years than I would care to admit," Smith answered.

Between the Comstock and Smith trios, along with Morse, Foley and the producer, it was a snug fit. While there was an eight-person conference table and a credenza with water and stale pastries on top, there wasn't much room for walking around.

Cassandra and Foley, both feeling like third wheels, moved to the corner the furthest from the door and left the chairs for the others. Just before the discussion began, Mullen and Meyer appeared in the doorway. Since the last remaining seat at the table was next to Finch, Mullen refused to sit down and instead walked over and stood next to Cassandra.

"Madison is in a meeting with the station owners," the producer offered apologetically. "She should be with us shortly…"

"I don't want to blindside you, Bill," Smith said as she cut across the producer. "I told you the shipment would be moving through Los Angeles tomorrow night…"

Carrie Finch sat up straight. "What do you mean you told him?" she demanded. Her linear mind had obviously kicked into overdrive with this new bit of information.

Smith ignored her. "We've moved the shipment date up to tonight. The spent rods have already been moved from the trucks to a train, and the train left the San Luis Obispo depot over an hour ago."

Jeffery morphed into his Mr. Hyde persona and slammed his fist down on the table and shouted. "I told you we couldn't trust her!"

Comstock's face was ashen as he put his hand on Jeffery's arm to try to calm him. "You said tonight would be a trial run."

Smith pointed to Cassandra. "You have to agree, the situation has changed. If anyone is planning on attacking the shipment, we will catch them by surprise and have the material safely at San Onofre before they can make an adjustment."

"When will the train reach L.A. County?" Comstock asked.

"With a lead and trailing train and National Guard positioned at key points along the track, it is moving at an average speed of around 30 mph," Smith answered. "It should be in Los Angeles County in approximately three hours."

"Of course!" Jeffery said as he threw his hands up in disbelief. "You change the day and now you have it coming through L.A. in the middle of the night instead of on Saturday afternoon as you promised." Jeffery turned to Comstock as he rose to his feet. "We need to get out of here, Professor. If not, all of our planning will be wasted."

Professor Comstock slowly shook his head. "I'm afraid I have to agree with my young friend. We had some spectacular things we had spent months planning for scheduled for tomorrow and now we'll have to scramble to implement them." Comstock shook his head as he rose to his feet. "I'm disappointed in you, Barbara. The debate is off."

The producer bolted from the room.

"Don't be silly," she said dismissively. "You should be thanking me. All of the interest Ms. Morse has generated, and a primetime debate will allow you to rally your troops better than a phone tree or email blast. It will triple your turnout."

"True," Comstock answered with a sigh. "But I'll be needed elsewhere."

Madison Street burst in the room on a full run. "I understand we may have hit a small snag," she said with a forced smile.

"The train is already on its way to Los Angeles and I need to leave immediately to help organize our protest."

"I see," Street said. "I'm sure you have someone else capable of articulating your position."

"I need Jeffery with me," Comstock answered. "This is Alex Hodge; he is both knowledgeable and well-spoken."

"I would rather stay with you and Jeffery," Hodge protested.

"We need to think of the greater good, Alex," Comstock said calmly.

"I won't debate him," Barbara Smith said with a note of finality in her voice.

"Why on earth not?" Comstock demanded.

"Yes. Why not?" Street seconded.

"The public would see Professor Comstock and me as equals. While I'm sure Mr. Hodge is well-spoken and knowledgeable. However, if I were to debate an unknown, it would be a no-win situation for me. If I mop the floor with him, I will look like a bully. If he were to pull a David to my Goliath, he becomes the hero and I would look the fool." Barbara Smith sighed. "I have to agree, the debate is off."

"I have a suggestion," Carrie Finch offered.

Every head in the room turned in her direction.

"We have someone who is already well-versed and knowledgeable on the subject and would not require any prep time. Plus, she would be viewed as in the same weight class as Mr. Hodge."

"She?" Holly Mullen asked. "Are you talking about me?"

"In the past forty-eight hours you've created a complete dossier on nuclear power generation and the safe handling of nuclear waste material." Finch shrugged. "Like any good debater, I think you could take either side of the issue and make a case."

"Forget it!" Mullen said flatly. "Not going to happen."

"Humor us for a moment," Finch said as she turned to Hodge. "How would you present the issue of nuclear waste?"

Hodge shrugged. "The average nuclear facility generates up to thirty metric tons of waste every year that has a half-life of over 20,000 years."

Finch motioned to Mullen. "The counter argument."

"All of the nuclear waste generated in the entire world in the last seventy-five years could fit in six Olympic sized swimming pools with room left over. It could be safely stored in a remote and geologically stable site for the next million years."

"The danger lies in transporting nuclear waste through heavily populated areas," Finch said.

"Obviously," Hodge answered. "There is always the risk of a derailment or sabotage."

Finch motioned to Mullen.

"In seventy years of transporting nuclear waste there has never been a leak," Mullen answered.

"Your strongest argument," Finch said as she motioned to Hodge.

"Fukushima Daiichi, Chernobyl, Three Mile Island. Nuclear power is a disaster just waiting to happen."

She turned to Mullen.

"The San Andreas, the Hosgri and the Shoreline Faults are all in the area around the Diablo Canyon storage area. It is insanity to keep large quantities of nuclear waste in a geologically unstable area when there is a reasonable alternative only a few hundred miles away."

"I do not see that we're working at cross purposes here…" Finch started to say before she was interrupted by Mullen. Instead of snapping at Mullen, she bit her tongue.

"Oh, I get it," Mullen said. "If not for the issues of cooling the core and how to deal with the waste, nuclear power would be an environmentalist's wet dream. A reliable and pollution free unlimited source for electricity."

Hodge snorted. "I wouldn't be so flippant about the dangers of the meltdown. They are very real and potentially disastrous."

"That is exactly why the Nutty Professor and the Princess of Darkness have teamed up on this. They're both smart enough to see the risk and reward." Mullen pointed to Comstock. "Being a marine biologist, he is both horrified and offended that Diablo Canyon uses seawater for their cooling systems. That's why he has been such a strident foe of the facility from the beginning."

Comstock smiled. "While I do not appreciate your 'Nutty Professor' analogy, your analysis is correct. I am not as anti-nuclear as my young friends here." Comstock motioned to Jeffrey and Hodge. "I think for the last seventy years too many bad decisions have been made by greedy politicians and people looking to line their pockets without regard to the risks."

Barbara Smith smiled. "While hardly original on your part, I like being called the 'Princess of Darkness'. My concern is, and always will be, keeping nuclear material out of the hands of terrorists so they can't make a dirty bomb." She motioned in Comstock's direction. "Bill has his agenda and I have mine. Since our interests do not conflict, we've worked together to shine some light on this too often ignored issue many times before. Ms. Morse has gotten the public all riled up, which can benefit both sides."

Comstock smiled. "Brilliant as usual Barbara. Both sides make their case; preaching to the choir if you will."

"Agreed," Smith answered.

Mullen shook her head. "Pass."

"That's unfortunate," Smith said without bothering to argue as she turned to Finch. "How long will it take for you to prep?"

"Dear God!" Mullen shouted. "You'd put that cold fish on television?"

"You don't leave me any choice," Smith said as she started to her feet.

Finch nudged Meyer's foot under the table where no one could see. He got the message.

"It's for a good cause Holly," her brother said.

Mullen glanced at her brother out of the corner of her eye then held her hands up in mock surrender. "I'll do it."

Hodge looked at Mullen, still dressed in the wardrobe she had borrowed from Cassandra, and clearly was not impressed. "I'm game," he scoffed with a smug smile.

Cassandra, still standing behind Hodge, patted him on the shoulder and chuckled. "Bring your own body bag."

"What does that mean?" Hodge asked while looking over his shoulder.

Finch shook her head. "You just agreed to debate a woman who has spent the past six years making a monkey out of the Assistant Director of the National Intelligence Agency. If you try to embarrass her on live television, she is going to verbally emasculate you and laugh her ass off while doing it."

Chapter 47

WHAT HAD BEEN billed as the "Great Debate" and had put a gleam in the eye of Madison Street, quickly devolved into the least watched program on the air in Greater Los Angeles that night. With, as one of the competing channels called it, the "Train of Death", rumbling through town and protestors filling the streets, two unknown millennials debating the merits of nuclear power was hardly compelling television.

It was a fairly civil affair with both Mullen and Hodge being polite and professional. Since Hodge never laid a glove on her and Mullen had rocked him a few times, all of the judges had Holly Mullen leading on their scorecards. But, since this was all for show and not for dough, she never delivered a knock-out punch.

Mercifully, they pulled the plug after only fifteen minutes and went "live on the scene".

The live coverage of the movement of the waste material was possibly even less compelling than the debate. The FAA had closed the airspace over the train tracks to only allow military or law enforcement aircraft. This meant all of the reporting had to be done at ground level. With the National Guard, the bulk of the security team from Diablo Canyon, and what appeared to be every law enforcement officer in Southern California out in force, it was impossible to even get close to the railway. Plus, the train was moving, so the best a reporter could hope for was a long-range glimpse of a dark train on a dark night.

The "usual suspects" protesters were caught completely off guard and most needed Google maps to even find the train tracks. The "protests" were a disorganized joke. With no logical or easily accessible gathering points and all of the streets that crossed the tracks blocked by either the LAPD or the L.A. County Sheriff's Department, the epicenter of the protests were around the TV live broadcasts.

Carrie Finch and A.D. Smith had watched the "debate" shoulder-to-shoulder from the rear of the studio with Bergman and Meyer lurking in the background.

"Okay, that was pretty impressive," Finch said as she watched the stage crew unclipping Mullen's microphone.

"Could you have done better?" Smith asked.

"No," Finch answered flatly.

"Can you work with her?"

"Yes."

Smith chuckled. "I see we've moved from pedantic to cryptic."

Finch shrugged. "There was no dry run. You always planned to move the shipment tonight and not tomorrow."

"Yes."

"Who is cryptic now?"

"Touché."

"What would be the hierarchy?" Finch asked.

"Like Bergman, she'll report to you."

Hearing his name, Nick Bergman joined the conversation. "What are we talking about?"

"Hiring Holly Mullen," Finch answered.

"Outstanding!" Bergman said with a laugh. "I know you don't like her but I can count on one hand the number of people you do like."

Finch ignored Bergman. "Will Meyer be an issue?" she asked Smith.

"While their paths will cross, Meyer works for me."

"Will I be able to fire her?"

"Not without my approval," Smith answered. "Is that a problem?"

"No." Finch answered before turning to Kevin Meyer. "What are the odds I can convince your sister to come work for us?"

Meyer pointed to Smith. "For her, a thousand to one. For you, even money."

"Why do I get such better odds?" Finch asked.

"You didn't hear this from me, but Holly is an idealist and a dreamer. She always wanted to work for one of the alphabet intelligence agencies to make the world a better place. But she is also stubborn.

Because of her history with A.D. Smith, it will take a miracle to get her to work directly for her. You, on the other hand, brought me back from the dead and, while she would never admit it to your face, she is very grateful."

"Okay," Finch said as her eyes fluttered and she drifted deep into thought.

A.D. Smith started to say something, but Bergman touched her on her sleeve and shook his head. "Give her a minute," he said softly.

Smith leaned back and looked at Bergman with fresh eyes. He didn't notice since his full attention was focused on Carrie Finch. Smith knew that people comfortably in the upper end of the genius range like Finch could be erratic and had a high burnout rate. If Bergman was the touchstone that could keep Finch from going off the rails, the value of his stock at the NIA had just gone through the roof.

Finch closed her eyes and drew in a deep breath through her nose. After about fifteen seconds, she opened her eyes and slowly exhaled.

"What can I offer?" Finch asked Smith.

"Back up a Brinks truck," Smith answered.

Her eyes locked on Holly who was just leaving the stage.

"Mullen," Finch said as he waved her over.

"Yeah," Mullen answered.

"I want you to come work with me."

"In your dreams."

Finch ignored her answer. "You'll be working on special projects with Nick and me." Finch motioned in Smith's direction. "You will never have to deal with her. You'll liaison either through me or your brother."

"I'd still have to deal with you."

Finch shrugged. "Do you have a problem with him?" She asked as she pointed to Nick Bergman.

"Not yet, but give it time," Mullen answered.

"He would be the only one you would ever need to talk to. We can put you on a different floor and give you a private office. I'll even rent you a secure living space where you never even have to come into the building if that's what it takes."

Mullen grunted but didn't walk away. She looked at Smith for confirmation and the A.D. nodded her agreement. "I'll be damned,"

Mullen said as she turned her attention back to Finch. "Define special projects."

"Whatever tweaks your interest."

"Total autonomy?"

"Yes."

"I'm listening," Mullen said cautiously.

"We need a changing of the guard at the NIA. People like you and me can see a risk others miss. Combining our very different worldviews could give us a fresh perspective. We can make a difference."

"I'll think about it," Mullen said.

"We'll rent you a house in your brother's neighborhood so you can get to know your nieces."

"That's devious," Mullen said with a laugh. "You've got real potential."

"Thirty-day trial?" Finch asked.

"I walk away any time I want?"

"Yes."

"Signing bonus?"

"If you last a year," Finch said as she extended her hand. "Do we have a deal?"

Mullen shrugged then accepted Finch's hand. "Deal." Mullen leaned in close and whispered in Finch's ear. "While you think I was dense for missing all the clues about my brother, you're no better than me."

"I don't understand," Finch said with a puzzled expression on her face.

"You're standing right next to a guy who is madly in love with you and you've completely missed it." Mullen nodded in Nick Bergman's direction.

"We've never even gone out," Finch said softly as she leaned in even closer, so she was not overheard.

"How many times has he asked you out?"

"More than once."

"All of your weird quirks and mood swings haven't sent him running to the exit," Mullen said. "For women like us, to find a good-looking guy with any social skills, rudimental personal hygiene who completely gets us and is willing to put up with our nonsense, makes him a keeper." Mullen patted Finch on the arm. "If you don't want him, I'll take him."

Finch blinked a few times then looked first at Mullen then Bergman.

"What?" Bergman said as he gave Finch a playful hip bump and an even more playful smile. "Come on? What?"

"Damn," Finch muttered.

"Whose dense now, bitch?"

Before they could continue their discussion, Cassandra Morse wandered over with a concerned look on her face. "I've been watching all of the other television station feeds in the breakroom and I haven't seen my uncle on any of them. It's out of character for him to not be the center of attention." Morse looked at Smith. "I assume you have a tail on him?"

"Of course," Smith answered as she glanced at Meyer who was already on his phone.

Meyer's call was brief. "They followed him for a bit over three hours north to the Morro Bay Marina. There he immediately got on a boat, and they lost him after he set sail."

"Why weren't we informed?" Smith asked.

"They called it in but, since they were moving away from the train and not toward it, no one thought it was worth kicking upstairs."

Cassandra slapped herself on the forehead. "What was the name of the boat on that old TV show 'Gilligan's Island' ?"

"The Minnow," Foley answered slowly, not sure where this conversation was heading.

"That's the name of my uncle's boat. He's the Gilligan from my dream."

"Are you saying what I think you're saying?" Smith demanded with concern etched on her face.

"Yes," Cassandra answered. "My uncle is a terrorist, and the train was just a diversion. The real target is the Diablo Canyon Nuclear facility."

Chapter 48

"I 'VE KNOWN YOUR uncle since before you were born," Smith said.

"How long have you known his sidekick, Jeffery?" Cassandra asked.

"Damn," Smith answered as she turned to Finch and Mullen. She didn't need to give them any instructions, they were already on the move in the direction of the conference room where they had left their laptops.

"What assets do you have in place near Diablo Canyon?" Cassandra asked.

"None," Smith answered. "Everything we've got is already more than a hundred miles south of here. Including every law enforcement helicopter in Southern California."

"Even if you turned the helicopters around right now, they would have to be refueled and would be more than an hour behind us," Cassandra said. "What about at Diablo Canyon?"

Smith shook her head. "A skeleton crew at best. Probably the absolute minimum required to keep the plant operational. Everyone else is on the train. We've got nothing."

"Other law enforcement?"

Smith shook her head. "Same thing. This was an all hands on deck operation…."

"Which left your flank completely exposed," Cassandra finished.

Madison Street seeing the flurry of activity wandered over. "What's going on?" She asked.

"Your news helicopter is a Bell 412 EPI," Cassandra stated, not asked.

"If you say so," Street answered with a baffled expression on her face. "Why?"

"Did they add extra fuel tanks?"

"No idea," Street answered. "Again, why?"

"We're going to need to borrow it."

"Excuse me," Street said with a startled expression on her face. "The station paid over ten million dollars for that helicopter."

"The National Intelligence Agency will guarantee its safe return or replacement," Smith said.

"What the hell is going on?" Street demanded.

"We need to get to the Diablo Canyon Nuclear facility as quickly as possible and your helicopter is our only option," Cassandra said then nodded toward A.D. Smith.

"If necessary, I'll declare a national emergency and seize it," Smith added.

"That won't do you any good," Street said. "With the airspace over Los Angeles closed, our pilot and crew have all gone home."

"That won't be a problem," Cassandra said as she held out her hand. "I can fly anything. Keys."

"Only if I go with you," Street said.

Cassandra glanced in Smith's direction. "Your call."

"Go." Smith answered without hesitation.

"Does your security detail have any ordinance?" Cassandra asked.

"Sidearms arms only," Smith answered. "All of our snipers and long rifle personnel are with the train."

Foley cleared his throat. "You've got me," he said.

"Meaning?" Smith asked briskly.

"I have my M-24 in the trunk of my car, and I passed the seven week course at Ft. Benning."

"Why do you have a sniper rifle in the trunk of your car?" Cassandra asked.

"I put it there right after you told me about your damn dream."

"Just go," Smith said.

Cassandra and Foley started trotting toward the door leading to the helipad with Madison Street and a cameraman hustling to catch up. Foley detoured to his car and came back with a heavy black carrying case, stowed it in the passenger section then climbed into the co-pilot seat.

Foley leaned in toward Cassandra. "Do you really know how to fly this thing?"

"In theory."

"Good lord," Foley said as he put on his headgear.

Cassandra made a face as she flipped some switches and the rotor began to turn. "Piece of cake."

Chapter 49

"I'M GETTING NOWHERE," Bergman said. "All of my normal dark web sites are locked up tighter than a convent." He glanced first at Finch then Mullen. Both were staring so intently at their screens, he was pretty sure neither one heard him.

A.D. Smith walked into the room. "Update?"

Neither Finch nor Mullen looked up.

"Finch isn't ignoring you, ma'am," Bergman said. "Let me touch her on the shoulder."

Kevin Meyer, who had accompanied his boss into the room, grinned and said, "Same applies to Holly."

Bergman touched Finch and Meyer touched Mullen. Both women instantly snapped out of their trances.

"Update?" Smith repeated now that she had her two top analysts' full attention.

"You go first," Mullen said. "What I found can wait.".

"There is a vulnerability at the Diablo Canyon Nuclear facility," Finch said. "There are four primary water intake valves. If they become clogged, it will restrict the cooling capacity. Professor Comstock knows this since he was previously called in to clean the filters after a kelp blockage."

"So he would know the exact location to inflict the maximum damage."

"Yes," Finch answered.

Smith sighed. "Morse's dream now makes perfect sense. Gilligan and Comstock both named their boats the SS Minnow and the toilet plunger was needed to clean the pipes. How did we miss that?"

"Gilligan's Island had been off the air for over twenty years before I was even born, ma'am," Finch answered. "I had to Google it."

"Me too," added Mullen.

"They have underwater barriers to prevent any boats from getting into the area," Finch said. "So that should minimize the damage."

"Had," Smith corrected. "Someone at Diablo has manually lowered the barrier and so far we've been unsuccessful in overriding the command remotely."

Finch closed her eyes and shook her head. "I assume if the flow is restricted, there is an automatic shutdown procedure."

"Apparently," Smith said. "some of Comstock's people have seized the control room and barricaded themselves in. They can't completely override all of the safety protocols but if the rate of flow of the cooling water drops below fifty percent, the core will melt."

"It gets worse," Mullen said softly. "Jeffery Nelson is quite the nut job. I figured out his numerous aliases and tracked his footprints on the dark web. He is virulently anti-nuclear and worse…" Holly Mullen drew in deep breath through her nose, puffed out her cheeks and released the air. "I hacked into his personal server. He has written a rambling manifesto which was set to be automatically released Sunday morning."

"Oh God," Finch muttered as her face turned ashen.

"What?" Smith demanded.

Mullen motioned to Finch to continue.

"The only reason he would put it on auto-release is because he doesn't expect to be alive on Sunday." Finch motioned to Mullen.

"This is not a publicity stunt," Mullen continued. "This is a suicide mission and he plans to take Southern California down with him."

Smith turned to Meyer. "Wake the President."

Chapter 50

AS THE MINNOW chugged through the Morro bay inlet and out into the Pacific Ocean, Jeffery Nelson was supervising the operation of four college students. They were a scruffy, motley crew who all looked malnourished and wild-eyed.

"Remember," Jeffery said. "Two diving weights per garbage bag so they sink fast. Also be sure all the bags are tightly sealed, so they don't let water in before they get ripped open in the intake flow. Otherwise, the ducks will just bob along the surface and be useless."

After dropping two diving weights in the bottom of an extra-strength tear-resistant thirty-gallon plastic garbage bag, the four college students began adding gallon Ziplock bags full of the tiny ducks into the larger bag.

"Get as much air as you can out of the bags," Jeffery said. "We want them to sink quickly when we're over the intake area."

With the Minnow now safely in blue water and chugging toward the Diablo Canyon site, Comstock, on the bridge, set the compass point on the auto-pilot and headed down the steps to the deck and pulled up short. After doing a quick count of the bags, he turned to Jeffery. "I thought we decided that six bags would be enough to restrict the flow and allow them time to shut down the reactors?"

"There has been a change of plans Professor," Jeffery said with an evil grin on his face as he nodded in the direction of one of the college students who immediately grabbed the professor and pulled his arms behind his back. A second student put a pair of plastic double restraints over his wrists and cinched them tight. "Instead of dropping these bags outside the security perimeter and hoping enough get sucked into the cooling system to cause a temporary shutdown, we're going to get inside the restricted area and drop them right on top of the intakes."

Comstock protested. "If you drop all of those bags directly over the intakes, when the ducks expand, it will completely clog the cooling system and there will be a total meltdown."

"That's the new plan," Jeffery answered smugly. "Thank you, by the way. If you hadn't sold out and taken that little cleanup job a few years ago, we wouldn't have known exactly where to drop the bags to do the most damage."

"You'll never get past their security."

Jeffery laughed. "Oh, you mean all of the security which is currently on a train well south of Los Angeles with the waste material?" Jeffery patted Comstock on the head. "Thanks again, old man. Because of you, every eye is focused on the train."

"You still have to get through the inlet gate," Comstock said with more confidence than he felt.

Jeffery smiled again. "We have people controlling the security gate and it is already down. We've also taken over the control room."

"But why?" demanded Prof. Comstock.

"As Eldridge Cleaver said, 'you're either part of the solution or you're part of the problem'. You and your generation spends all of your time reminiscing about meaningless college sit-ins and anti-war marches. None of you will risk your paycheck or retirement funds much less put any skin in the game. Your day has passed, old man," said Jeffery. "Take him below."

Chapter 51

HAVING BEEN IN the air for nearly an hour, the cameraman was in the co-pilot seat busy giving Cassandra Morse a crash course on controlling the nose camera.

"You have a monitor here that displays what the camera sees," he said pointing to a twelve-inch HD screen mounted on the dashboard of the helicopter. "You control it with this joystick. Right button is zoom in; left is zoom out. Got it?"

"I think so," Morse answered.

The cameraman shook his head and grinned. "If Madison can figure it out, I'm pretty sure you can too. It has a built-in stabilizer that will minimize the movement and vibration. Point and shoot. In a few minutes, we'll be linking up with the satellite and we'll be live. From that point on, anything you say into your headset or comes in over the radio will be heard live back at the studio and is probably being broadcast worldwide."

"Roger that," Cassandra answered.

He unbuckled his seat belt and weaved his way back into the passenger section where he turned his attention to Foley. "We've got a tripod in the door which I normally use to mount my camera. Obviously in this case, you'll get priority and I go hand held. Okay?"

Foley fed the five-round clip into his M-24 and nodded.

Madison asked the cameraman, "Are all of the cameras on?"

The cameraman tapped his earpiece. "All internal and the external cameras and microphones are hot and we're on the air."

"This is Madison Street reporting live from just outside the Diablo Canyon Nuclear Power Station where terrorists are currently launching a brazen attack. If they succeed, it will make the movie *The China Syndrome* look like a kiddie cartoon."

The radio crackled. "Valkyrie this is Smith."

Street whispered into her microphone. "Let's listen in on the conversation between heavily decorated former Naval combat pilot, Cassandra Morse, known as Valkyrie, whose dream predicted this nightmare and the Assistant Director of the National Intelligence Agency, Barbara Smith."

"Status?" Cassandra asked. She ignored the cameraman filming her from behind.

"From our satellite imagery, you should be on the target in less than two minutes," Smith said calmly. "Heat signatures indicate there are six hostiles onboard. Our team has concluded they plan to drop weighted waterproof plastic bags into the area directly above the intake valves which will be shredded, releasing your uncle's rubber duckies and clogging the flow."

"Can't they simply power down?" Cassandra asked.

"Hostiles currently hold the control room and they've put enough barricades and obstructions in place that will prevent us from breaching the room in time."

"Backup?"

"Heavy backup is en route," Smith answered.

"Rules of engagement?" Cassandra asked.

"First fire, lethal fire authorization has been granted personally by the President of the United States," Smith answered. "Foley, if you have the shot take it."

"Yes, ma'am," Foley answered.

"You heard it here first," Madison Street whispered in the microphone. "The president has given the shoot to kill order for these terrorists. Thankfully, also onboard is former Army sniper and current LAPD detective, Steve Foley. At the moment, these two brave souls, Morse and Foley, are all that stands between us and the total devastation of the State of California."

"There it is!" Foley shouted as he saw the boat idling near the Diablo Canyon facility with its running lights off. The college students had just thrown the last of about a third of the plastic bags they had filled overboard and were watching them sink. They looked up when they heard the helicopter approaching. When they saw the television station logo painted on the side, instead of ducking or taking evasive action, they smiled and waved.

Foley opened the side door of the helicopter and braced himself for the wind and vibration of the fast-moving helicopter as he rested his M-24 on the tripod.

"Hardly ideal," Foley said to Cassandra.

"When we get closer, I'll try to give you a better platform."

The cameraman gave Foley a nudge and he trained his camera on the Minnow.

"Do you mind?" asked Foley.

Cassandra flipped on the helicopter's spotlight that captured the boat in its light.

"This is the LAPD. Turn off your engine!" Cassandra announced over the helicopter's public address system.

Instantly, the boat began to move at full throttle to the next drop off site.

"The targets have dropped their first set of bags," Cassandra said to Smith.

"One of the intakes blocked is not an issue but two will be problematic."

"How long until they reach launch point two?" Morse asked.

"Ninety seconds."

Cassandra brought the helicopter in close and parallel to the boat and matched its speed. "This is as good as I've got," Cassandra said.

Foley fed a round into the breach and fired. The round ripped through a half dozen bags and they exploded. In rapid succession he fired four more rounds, all of them pulverizing the bags sitting on deck scattering thousands of dehydrated rubber duckies. Almost instantly, when the wave spray the Minnow was creating began hitting them, the deck area began to fill with the rapidly expanding rubber duckies.

The four students dove for cover and pulled out an assortment of handguns and opened fire on the helicopter. A lucky shot glanced off the windshield, leaving an impressive crack. Another hit the body of the helicopter but didn't cause any damage.

"Tell me you got all that," said Madison Street.

The cameraman gave Madison a thumb's up.

"Interesting target choice," Cassandra said as she continued to match the speed of the boat.

"Moving helicopter and moving targets," Foley answered. "I'm happy I hit the damn boat."

"Can you take out the engine?" Cassandra asked.

"Maybe, but we're got a problem."

"What?"

"I only have five rounds left."

"Seriously?"

"It's a sniper rifle and it's built for quality not quantity. Besides," Foley added, "the ammo is over three bucks a round."

"We may have better luck if we take out the bridge."

Cassandra zipped ahead of the boat which had just about reached the second drop zone and was slowing down.

Foley fired his five remaining rounds into wheelhouse but it didn't disable the Minnow.

"There is only one way to stop them," Cassandra said.

Foley knew what she had in mind.

Cassandra hovered the chopper to where it was only inches above the water and Foley grabbed the emergency life raft. He pulled the ripcord and it was nearly inflated before it even hit the water. Next, before he could react, Foley threw the startled cameraman overboard.

"Oh no you don't," Madison Street said as she saw what was coming and started to put up a fight.

When Cassandra saw Foley near the open door with both of his hands on Street and struggling to keep his balance, she jerked the stick and the helicopter listed instantly to the right.

With no grip, both Foley and Street lost their balance and tumbled into the Pacific.

Chapter 52

CASSANDRA MORSE BLEW past the Minnow and when she was about a half mile ahead, she banked the helicopter and did a one eighty turn. She dropped the helicopter down until its landing skids were only a few inches above the water. She aimed her nose at the approaching boat and gave the bird full throttle.

Collision course.

She adjusted the camera so the world could see what was coming.

"Heavy is on the way, Lieutenant!" Smith barked.

"We're out of time and we're out of options, ma'am," Cassandra said without even the slightest quiver in her voice.

Every cable and broadcast channel in the free world had broken into their programming and were broadcasting the live feed from the nose camera.

Over one hundred million people were watching and, as the word spread like wild fire about what was happening, that number was growing by the second.

Carrie Finch and Holly Mullen were standing shoulder-to-shoulder watching the live feed with tears streaming down their cheeks.

"Goodspeed, Valkyrie," Smith said gently. "Godspeed."

Cassandra glanced over to the co-pilot seat and smiled at her grandfather. He was in his Vietnam era flight suit and was beaming with pride.

"You really should say something," he said as the distance between the helicopter and boat was closing fast.

"Not on my watch, you bastard!" she shouted.

The admiral waved his hand. "Not exactly Gandalf and the Balrog, but it'll do."

Just moments before impact she heard a familiar voice with a slow southern drawl in her ear.

"Valkyrie, this is Underdog. We are ninety seconds out. What is your status?"

Cassandra pulled back hard on the stick and the news helicopter began to quickly gain altitude. One side of the landing gear clipped an antenna on the top of the bridge of the Minnow but did no damage to the chopper.

"We have three friendlies in the water, Underdog."

"Roger that, Valkyrie. The Coast Guard is en route and nine minutes out."

"We need to stop a boat from depositing their payload."

"Affirmative, Valkyrie. We have you on our radar. You might want to give us some space to operate."

"Roger that, Underdog."

Morse banked away from the Minnow.

"The whole world is watching," the admiral said. "Let's show them what the Navy can do."

Not wanting to be heard talking to the ghost of her grandfather, she nodded.

She put the chopper about a quarter mile off of the Minnow's bow and paced its speed. When she was satisfied, she reached over and grabbed the controls of the live television feed camera and focused on the four red dots closing fast on the Minnow.

"Valkyrie, this is Underdog. We will be making a pass to get their attention in ten seconds."

"Roger that," Cassandra said as she tried to keep both the helicopter and the camera steady.

A pair of F/A-18 Super Hornets came into view of the camera at most thirty feet above the Pacific. When their M61A1 Six-barrel Gatling Guns opened fire, they kicked up water only inches from the Minnow and lit up the sky. The percussion of heavy weapons fire and jet wash caused the helicopter to vibrate and Cassandra had to fight the stick to keep it steady.

The Minnow, with Jeffery at the helm, did not slow down. Cassandra focused the camera on the deck of the Minnow and gave it maximum zoom. The four college students and her uncle, with his hands now untied, could all clearly be seen jumping over the handrail and into the ocean.

"Underdog," Cassandra said. "There is only one soul left on that vessel and I don't think he's planning on surrendering."

"Understood, Valkyrie."

Cassandra, knowing what was coming, pulled back on the zoom so the entire boat and the area around it was visible to the television audience. The pair of F/A 18 Super Hornets that had peeled off earlier were the first pair to arrive. Collectively they fired over three hundred 20mm rounds into the Minnow. Almost immediately a sixty-foot-high fire ball engulfed the boat and what was left of it started to slow down.

The second wave, the pair that had fired the warning shots, roared in and finished the job. The Minnow vanished beneath the waves.

"Go Navy!" Cassandra shouted.

Cassandra moved the helicopter so it was over the debris field and she noticed something odd. First a handful, then a few dozen, then thousands of the rubber duckies began floating to the surface.

For the first time since she had been blown out of the sky in the SV-1, Cassandra Morse started laughing.

Chapter 53

THERE IS AN old saying, success has many fathers, but failure is an orphan.

It was Father's Day at the Los Angeles Federal Courthouse. Every elected official in California was jockeying for a position if not on stage at least at a place where cameras might see them. As demand for press credentials had grown, they had changed the venue of the 2 p.m. press conference three times. It had gone from the normal press room, to the largest courtroom in the building to where it was now, in the auditorium that could seat six hundred. They were expecting a full house with standing room only and potential angry gate crashers.

Cassandra Morse and a collection of others directly involved in what was being called "The Diablo Canyon Incident", were in the "Green Room" just off the stage. It seemed that everyone wanted to offer their congratulations have their picture taken with Cassandra. She was delighted when she was rescued by Carrie Finch.

"A.D. Smith would like a private word."

Finch directed Morse to a quiet corner where Smith was chatting with a distinguished looking man who looked vaguely familiar.

"Ah," Smith said. "The lady of the hour. Let me introduce you to Attorney General Christopher Gardner."

Gardner extended his hand and she accepted it. She smiled when there was no connection. After her experience with her celebrity attorney Briner, she was starting to think the null contact was a lawyer thing. Either they were soulless, or she inherently didn't trust anyone who had ever set foot in law school.

"We would like to have you join us upstairs after the press conference."

"Why?" Cassandra asked.

"We're planning on charging Rachel Frey of Bathmann Aeronautics with the murder of your grandfather," Garner answered. "All things considered, we felt letting you be a witness was the least we could do."

Glancing over the A.G.'s shoulder, Cassandra saw her grandfather dressed in a World War II sailor uniform like Gene Kelly in "Anchors Aweigh" and dancing a jig.

"That would be excellent," Cassandra answered with a smile.

"The President is arriving on Air Force One around midnight local time to bring you and everyone else involved in the Diablo Canyon Incident to Washington tomorrow. He plans to award you and Detective Foley the Medal of Freedom in the Oval Office."

"Thanks, Chris," Smith said. The A.G. took his cue, bowed slightly and left the two women alone.

"Would you like a bit of advice?" Smith asked.

"Do I have to follow it?"

"No." Smith chuckled. "This was a big win. Epic. Everyone knows what you did, hell, half the world saw it live. This is the time to be gracious and self-effacing." Smith's eyes twinkled mischievously. "Even funny if you have it in you."

"Okay," Cassandra answered tentatively.

"Share the spotlight. It will only make you look better, and you will never have another opportunity this big to get yourself some major IOUs."

"Why would I need IOUs?" Cassandra asked.

Smith shrugged. "You could live another sixty or seventy years. You never know when they might come in handy."

"Will you be onstage with me?"

"Absolutely not, and I greatly appreciate it if my name and the NIA never come up. On the other hand," Smith pointed in the direction of DHS Director Paul Rogers who was standing by himself looking forlorn. He looked as radioactive as Diablo Canyon might have been if Jeffery Nelson hadn't been stopped. No one wanted to be close to him. "The Department of Homeland Security, after the kidnapping incident and missing the threat to Diablo Canyon, could use a win. And you would have a friend for life."

"You're really good at this, aren't you?"

"I live in a world of moves and counter-moves. It is important to not get so immersed in the details you miss the bigger picture. You should always maximize opportunities when they are presented."

"*Carpe diem*," Cassandra said with a small smile.

"Exactly."

"How many people should I bring on stage with me?"

"Foley, of course, next to you and no more than four or five behind you. Any more than that and it loses its impact."

They turned when they heard a female voice shouting.

"You son-of-a-bitch." Madison Street came in through the side door, looking absolutely radiant and made a beeline for Det. Steve Foley. "I can't believe you threw me out of my own helicopter!"

Foley pulled away then pointed his thumb over his shoulder in Cassandra Morse's direction. "I can't believe she dumped me out with you."

They both turned and pretended to glare at Cassandra who just shrugged.

When she turned back to continue her conversation with Smith, she was gone. Looking around, all she caught was a glimpse of Smith's back heading to a rear exit with her entourage and away from the spotlight.

Cassandra wished she could join her. Right now, the only place she wanted to be was asleep in her own bed. While the two-hour nap she had grabbed when she went home to change clothes had recharged her battery a bit, she was still way below full capacity.

Cassandra sighed and headed to the refreshment table set up in the corner to get a bottle of water. Before she arrived, a terrified intern with a clipboard in his hand approached her. "The governor is ready to introduce you now…"

Cassandra's demeanor instantly changed.

Showtime.

She wheeled and started pointing to people. Lt. Blanche Harrison of the LAPD. Madison Street. Grant Olsen. And finally, Paul Rogers of DHS. "I want you all standing directly behind me," Her tone indicated it was not a topic open for discussion.

She grabbed Steve Foley's arm. "You're with me. I want you beside me the whole time."

Cassandra smiled when she saw Barbara Smith had waited in the doorway to see if she had taken her advice. Smith nodded her head maybe a quarter of an inch then vanished.

The door to the auditorium opened and Cassandra stepped out first, followed by Foley then by the other four Cassandra had selected.

As soon as she was visible, the room exploded and she got a standing ovation from every member of the media. Cassandra, with Foley as her wingman, checked over her shoulder to be sure the quartet she had selected was where she wanted them on stage. Satisfied, she motioned for silence and immediately got it. Everyone in the room wanted to hear what she had to say.

"Before I take any questions, I would like to introduce a few people." She pointed to Grant Olsen. "This is Grant Olsen from the *Los Angeles Guardian*. If he doesn't get a Pulitzer Prize if for nothing else than being a colossal pain in the butt, you should all be ashamed of yourselves." Laughter rippled through the crowd.

Next, she pointed to Madison Street and made a face. "I'm really sorry about all of the bullet holes in your helicopter, Madison." More laughter. "And I'm really sorry we had to throw you into the ocean." Cassandra paused and looked at the mob of reporters. "But I'm pretty sure everyone in this room has felt like tossing you overboard more than once."

The hall exploded with laughter. Madison Street, smiling so big, she looked at risk of dislocating her jaw, waved.

Next Cassandra pulled Lt. Harrison forward. "This is Lt. Blanche Harrison of LAPD. She is a perfect example of why we need more women in positions of authority. She's smart and cool under pressure. When the chips were down, she made the right call and assigned Det. Foley to help me. I cannot properly express my gratitude for her cooperation and the support of the incredible men and women working under her at the Pacific Division."

Foley rolled his eyes and shook his head but didn't say anything. Harrison was stunned and speechless as she returned to her spot.

Cassandra put her arm around Foley and pulled him close. "Speaking of Detective Steve Foley, this is the man who has always believed in me and risked his life to save the lives of everyone in this room. If not for him, things would have been very, very different this morning."

The room exploded again.

Cassandra motioned for quiet

"All I can say, old friend," she paused for effect and the room fell completely silent. "Thank God you can swim!"

The room exploded even louder this time.

Foley, who looked like he would rather be a thousand other places, just shook his head, waved and sighed.

Cassandra motioned for quiet again and the smile vanished from her face.

"All kidding aside," she said. "We dodged a bullet this morning." Cassandra pulled Rogers forward. "This is Director Paul Rogers of the Department of Homeland Security. He and his department took a great deal of heat for kidnapping Grant Olsen off the street." Cassandra paused. "With the research Grant was doing for me, he looked like he had information about an imminent terrorist attack on the City of Los Angeles. To their undying credit, the DHS made the proper decision that the lives of possibly millions of people were more important than inconveniencing an annoying reporter for a few hours." Cassandra stepped back and started applauding. "I say Bravo! Well Done! I sleep better at night knowing fine men like Paul Rogers are manning the wall protecting all of us!"

The rest of the room joined in. Cassandra leaned and whispered in Rogers' ear. "Barbara Smith sends her regards."

Chapter 54

WHILE THE LOS Angeles satellite office of the National Intelligence Agency located in the Federal Courthouse was a tiny fraction the size of the Washington DC office, it had similar security. When Michael Hicks, AKA Jack Logan, escorted Rachel Frey and one of the Bathmann Aeronautics lawyers into the security room, she immediately saw a German Shepherd sitting passively in the corner. She smugly asked, "May I pet your dog?"

"Be my guest," one of the four security guards answered. "But decide which one of your hands you never want to use again."

"You really need to be taking this more seriously," said Russell Rhodes, associate legal counsel for Bathmann Aeronautics. "You're in big trouble."

Frey shrugged. "We'll see."

After a thorough pat down and sniffing, the hidden door leading to the NIA conference room opened. The table inside this conference room would only seat twelve instead of the twenty in DC. Rhodes pulled up short when he saw who was in the room. At the end of the table was the Attorney General of the United States, Christopher Gardner. To his immediate right was Barbara Smith, Assistant Director of the National Intelligence agency and to his left was Cassandra Morse. Also at the table were Carrie Finch, Holly Mullen and Nick Bergman.

"All for me?"

Cassandra Morse's eyes narrowed when she saw Michael Hicks.

He smiled when he saw the recognition on her face. He blew her a kiss and waved at her the same way she had done to him on Venice Beach. Barbara Smith, the only one with a clear view of the interplay between Morse and Hicks, chuckled. The others at the table were mystified but chose to ignore it.

"Rachel Louise Frey," the A.G. said, as he rose to his feet. "You have the right to remain silent. Anything you say can be used against you in court. You have the right to talk to a lawyer for advice before we ask you any questions. You have the right to have a lawyer with you during questioning. If you cannot afford a lawyer, one will be appointed for you before any questioning if you wish. If you decide to answer questions now without a lawyer present, you have the right to stop answering at any time. Do you understand these rights?"

"I do," Rachel Frey answered calmly.

"Is the man with you your lawyer?"

"He is not." Frey shot Rhodes a dismissive glance.

"Who is he?"

"He is Russell Rhodes, legal counsel for Bathmann Aeronautics, and he represents their interests and not mine."

"Would you like Mr. Rhodes to represent your interests in this matter?"

"I would not," Frey replied. "I waive my right to have an attorney present for this interview."

The Attorney General motioned in the direction of two of the security guards who had followed Frey and Rhodes into the conference room. "Please escort Mr. Rhodes out of the room."

"I strongly object!" Rhodes shouted as the MPs bracketed him and started herding him to the door.

"Noted," answered the A.G.

After the door closed, Rachel Frey took a seat at the opposite end of the table. Michael Hicks positioned himself directly behind Frey. "First," Frey said, "this conversation is completely off the record and purely hypothetical."

"I don't think so," A.G. Gardner stated flatly.

Frey shrugged. "In that case, I'm invoking my right to remain silent."

"You're in no position to be dictating terms, Ms. Frey."

Frey laughed but didn't answer.

Gardner looked at Smith who shrugged then said softly, "What could it hurt?"

"Okay," Gardner said. "For the moment we're off the record."

"What do you think you have on me?" Frey asked coldly.

"Apparently Mr. Bathmann didn't trust you." Gardner pushed a button on a remote and the HD screen behind began playing the video of Frey preparing the flask and glass which was used to kill congressman Warwick.

Frey chuckled. "I've already gone over this with Jack, or Michael, or whatever he is calling himself today." Frey put her hands in her lap and smiled sweetly. "You really don't want me on a witness stand."

"Why is that?" Barbara Smith asked.

Rachel Frey's persona instantly changed. She morphed from a confident businesswoman in the middle of a tough negotiation to a quivering tearful mess. "I didn't know what was in the flask," she said with a terrified tone in her voice as tears streamed down her cheeks. "I was just doing what my boss, Mr. Doorman, told me to do." In less than a heartbeat, she returned to herself. "You really think a jury would believe a pretty twenty-five-year-old woman, only out of college for eighteen months and the lowly assistant to a vice president of the company would conceive and execute something at this level. Please."

"We also have video of you pushing a button on your keychain that activated Icarus," Gardner said.

"Same answer," Frey retorted. "Boohoo, pity poor me. Evil men abusing a young woman. Do you think for one minute a jury would buy that I would knowingly pushed a button that would likely kill me? I'd be your worst nightmare." Frey eyed Smith and Gardner and smiled again. "Ah. You already knew that. You want me to roll over on Bradley Doorman and Louis Bathmann." Her eyes narrowed and she turned deadly serious. "What's in it for me?"

"Witness protection…"

"No deal," Frey said firmly. "I have no intention of living in some pissant backwater town with U.S. Marshals keeping an eye on me."

"If you prefer, we could reserve you the Jeffery Epstein holding cell in a Federal detention center somewhere until Bathmann and Doorman can figure out who to bribe to have you assassinated."

"First off," Frey said with a dismissive wave of her hand. "Doorman is an idiot. While he totally bought in on the program, it was all Louie the Fourth and his butt-boy Ashton who did the actually planning."

"You can prove that?" Gardner asked.

"I can," Frey answered firmly.

When she saw the stunned looks at the other end of the table, she smiled again. Like so many before, they had underestimated her.

"You have more than the flask and glass?" Smith asked.

"So much more, even one of your bush league Justice Department lawyers could get a conviction against Bathmann's team of two-thousand-dollars-an-hour attorneys."

"What do you propose?" Gardner asked.

"You make a wire transfer of ten million dollars to a bank of my choice and when this is over, I walk away, and you never see me again."

As a heavy silence settled over the room, Cassandra Morse fought the urge to explode out of her seat and strangle Frey. The woman was up to her neck in the conspiracy that killed a powerful congressman, her grandfather and very nearly her. She could see from the body language and questions from Smith and Gardner where this was headed. The A.G. was looking to land the big tuna, Louis Bathmann IV. If it meant letting a few minnows get away, so be it.

Cassandra couldn't let that happen.

"Do you still have the flask and glass?" Gardner asked.

"Before you answer that," Cassandra said. "Do you mind if I touch your hand?"

This question drew odd looks from everyone in the room. Attorney General Gardner was about to object but Barbara Smith put her hand on his arm and stopped him. She had no idea what Cassandra was doing, but she wanted to see it play out. "Again, what would be the harm, Chris?" she asked softly.

A.G. Gardner cleared his throat and asked. "Would you object to Cassandra Morse touching your hand while we continue the questioning?"

"Knock yourself out, Dream Lady." Rachel Frey let out a cackle that would have been perfect for a witch stirring a cauldron on Halloween. "I've always wanted to take part in a séance."

Cassandra moved to the chair next to Frey and as soon as their hands met, there was a static electric shock as the connection was made. Cassandra smiled and motioned to Gardner to continue.

"Do you still have the flask and glass used in the murder of Congressman Warwick?" Gardner asked.

"I know where they are, and if we can come to an agreement, I'll tell you," Frey answered as she glanced at Cassandra and smiled.

Cassandra returned the smile.

"You look like you're dying to ask me a question." Frey rested her other hand on top of Cassandra's. "Knock yourself out."

"Why did you order them to perform the surgery on me?"

"That was all Bathmann," Frey answered.

"No," Cassandra said gently. "It was all you. Bathmann wanted to put thirty pounds of diving weights on me and toss me overboard."

Frey had a startled expression on her face. "Where did you come up with the number thirty?" she demanded.

"We'll get to that," Cassandra answered sweetly then her expression turned sad. Cassandra looked around the room and shook her head. "That's disappointing. I was just a test to see how far you could push Bathmann. You didn't care about the experiment. It was just a power play with me as a pawn."

That comment stopped Frey cold.

"That's pure speculation on your part," Frey protested half-heartedly.

"How did you get the glass and flask out of the building?" Cassandra asked.

Frey shrugged but did not answer.

"Ah, I see," Cassandra said. "You knew they would insist you turn over the evidence as soon as you disembarked the Reagan. Realizing what a powerful bargaining tool you had, you gave them a duplicate set and not the real ones you had used. By the time Bathmann had discovered he had been double-crossed, it was too late. You had already hidden the real flask and glass."

"You couldn't possibly know that," Frey said with a hint of alarm in her voice. "You're just guessing."

"Am I?" Cassandra smiled. She was enjoying herself. "What happens to your get out of jail free card when I tell them where to find the glass and flask?"

"You're bluffing," Frey said now with full blown panic in her voice.

"You were right. That would have been the last place anyone would have looked." Cassandra turned her attention in the direction of A.D. Smith. "Do you have people in the Lake Como region of Italy?"

"This is some kind of a trick," Frey said as the last drops of her confidence began to evaporate.

"Unfortunately for you," Cassandra said with a broad smile, "the little experiment you ordered done to me worked."

"Explain." Frey demanded

"Like Dr. Frankenstein, the monster you created has come back to destroy you. Since you let me touch you, I now know everything you know about the box and how you got it out of Bathmann World Headquarters." Cassandra smiled. "You really should have taken witness protection when you had the chance. Now that I have everything you know, your best case scenario is an 8x10 cell for the next fifty years or so."

Seeing all of her leverage going up in smoke, Rachel Frey looked down at her hands still encasing one of Cassandra's. A light clicked on as she realized what was happening.

Frey jerked her hand away from Cassandra's and leapt to her feet.

Cassandra, knowing exactly what was coming, was half a beat faster and ten times tougher.

Frey lunged for Cassandra's throat as she shouted, "You bitch!"

Cassandra easily sidestepped Frey's attack and drove a vicious right hand into the charging Frey's solar plexus. With the addition of Frey's momentum moving into the punch and the precision with which the blow was delivered, Frey's feet actually came off the floor at contact. All of the air rushed out of her lungs as she crumpled to all fours on the carpet, pawing the ground looking for oxygen.

"That was for my grandfather," Cassandra said as put her left index finger under the helpless woman's chin and forced the gasping and helpless woman's head up so they were making eye contact.

Cassandra, with a wicked smile on her face, drew back her fist and launched a massive roundhouse right that caught Frey squarely on the nose. "That's for me."

Chapter 55

APPARENTLY, SOMEONE HAD pushed a panic button and the four men from the security room bursted in. Michael Hicks gently pulled Cassandra away from Frey before they arrived but when she offered no resistance, he released his grip. Frey, with the wind still knocked out of her and her face a crimson mask, was lying face first on the floor. Two of the security men attempted to lift the groggy woman to her feet but she was completely deadweight and would have to be carried.

Hicks chuckled. "A head butt would have been better."

Cassandra flexed her right hand and grimaced. "Undoubtedly," Cassandra answered.

Hicks took her hand to examine it. When she normally made a connection she felt something like a small static electricity spark; this time it was like she had stuck her finger in a wall socket.

"Oh," she said as her eyes flew open in surprise but didn't pull her hand away.

"Nothing broken," Hicks said with a smile.

While other voices whispered in her head, Hicks's voice was like rolling thunder. Having witnessed what had just happened during the interrogation, she suspected he knew exactly what he was doing. He was watching her reaction to their contact with an intensity she felt was both exciting and a bit unnerving.

Cassandra Morse studied Hicks closely. Coming from a military family and being a combat pilot, she had spent her entire life around alpha males and Hicks certainly fit the profile. He was a real man; a warrior and not a poser or pretender. She knew intuitively there was nothing phony or deceitful about him. He was the kind of man who would be up and out of bed instantly to investigate that strange noise in the kitchen in the middle of the night without being asked. If he said something, he meant it. If you crossed him, you'd regret it. If he considered you a friend, and if needed, he would drop what he was doing and travel halfway around the world to help you, no questions asked.

After seeing what had happened with Rachel Frey, he clearly suspected she could read his thoughts and he was doing his best to try to block her. His thoughts were mostly gibberish. He was thinking about the weather and baseball scores but occasionally his real feelings were slipping through.

He wanted her.

After years of wandering in the wilderness, this alpha male had finally found his alpha female.

Cassandra blinked a few times and felt her knees starting to go weak.

She wanted him too.

She reclaimed her hand and broke their connection, otherwise she might have thrown him on top of the conference table, torn off his clothes and ravaged him while not caring who might be watching.

Looking over her shoulder she saw the admiral grinning from ear-to-ear and fanning himself. "Hot stuff," he said.

Hicks smiled when he saw the look on her face. He knew she knew how he felt. "Your hand is going to be sore for a few days."

"Thanks for not stopping me."

"After spending time around her," Hicks said as he motioned toward Frey, "I wanted to jump in to help but it looked like you had everything under control."

Cassandra dropped her eyes. "Coffee later?"

Hicks smiled. "That would be as good a place as any to start."

"Meaning?" Cassandra asked.

"After six months undercover they owe me at least a month off. I'd like to spend it with you."

She felt her knees starting to go weak again then couldn't believe the word that came out of her mouth.

"Okay."

Chapter 56

THE SECURITY DETAIL had given up on Frey walking out under her own steam, each of them grabbed a limb and looked around for instructions.

"Place her in a holding cell," A.G. Gardner said. "Then get her a doctor."

After they had removed Frey, Barbara Smith wheeled on Cassandra. "Do you care to explain what just happened?"

"Maybe we should have this conversation in private," Cassandra said.

"None of us can unsee what we just witnessed," Smith snapped.

Cassandra drew in a cleansing breath and released it. "Let's deal with the missing flask and glass that were used in the murder the congressman first. Frey knew the value of those items since she had used them to maneuver Bradley Doorman out and take his place. She was smart enough to realize Louis Bathmann wanted those items under his control and not hers, so she had to hide them. Aware that her every move was being watched she anticipated her office, residence, and any place she visited would be searched. She put them in the last place anyone would ever look."

"Oh my God!" Carrie Finch blurted as she was the first one to catch up.

"Lake Como!" Holly Mullen said as she slapped herself on the forehead.

Finch and Mullen looked at each other than burst out laughing.

"That's brilliant," Finch said as she wiped a tear from her eye.

"How could I have missed that?" Mullen said as she pounded the palm of her hand on her forehead.

"Missed what?" Smith thundered as she was starting to lose her patience.

Carrie Finch and Holly Mullen exchanged glances and Mullen indicated Carrie should continue. "You got there first."

Carrie Finch nodded. "She was moving into Doorman's old office," she said. "Doorman was escorted out of the building and was not allowed to take anything with him."

"Oh My God!" Nick Bergman said with a wide grin. "No one would look for the smoking gun there."

"Humor me," Barbara Smith growled as she turned to Morse. "Where are the flask and glass?"

"When they were boxing up Doorman's personal possessions from his office," Cassandra said, "she slipped them into one of the boxes."

"She wanted to get them out of the building and couldn't do it herself, so he had Bathmann do it for her," Finch added.

Now it was Smith's turn to laugh. "That's inspired."

"Wasn't that a bit risky?" A.G. Gardner asked. "What if Doorman had opened the box and found them?"

"There were multiple boxes and Frey put them in the bottom of a box marked 'Misc. junk'," Cassandra said. "Then she covered them with other stuff. Even if Doorman opened the box, he'd see the junk on top and it was unlikely he would have ever gotten to the bottom. Even if he did, she left a note for him." Cassandra's eyes twinkled. "In addition to the flask and glass there are several thumb drives with enough damning information to bring down Bathmann Aeronautics. She offered to form an alliance for a hostile takeover."

Attorney General Christopher Gardner straightened up. "Are you saying there really are confidential files that could implicate Louis Bathmann IV?"

"Bathmann and about half of the members of congress and a good hunk of the Pentagon," Cassandra answered.

Gardner glared at Cassandra. "You know this how?"

"After Bathmann blew the SV-1 out of the sky, I landed, unconscious and barely alive, in the water just off the bow of the Bathmann ship which was controlling Icarus. They didn't want to be discovered so they jammed my automatic rescue signal beacon and pulled me on board. They initially planned to just toss me overboard then Rachel

Frey decided to use me to test exactly how much leverage she actually had over Louis Bathmann." Cassandra chuckled. "There is a certain symmetry here. It was the experiment Frey ordered performed on me that would be her downfall. If she had just killed me the way Bathmann wanted, she and everyone else would be free and in the clear."

"What was the procedure?" Barbara Smith asked.

"Are you familiar with the work of Dr. Tanner Dawson?"

"Dawson is a part of this?" Smith asked with a startled expression on her face.

"No," Cassandra answered. "He was duped into performing the procedure. He thought I was someone else with a different name and medical history. It wasn't until he saw my picture in the newspaper that he realized what had happened."

"What are we talking about?" asked A.G. Gardner.

Smith motioned to Cassandra. "You're probably more up to speed on this than I am."

"Dr. Tanner Dawson has been doing some minimally invasive micro-surgery where he makes a tiny hole in the skull then sends in a probe to stimulate a portion of the brain."

"He is getting some miraculous result on people suffering from PTSD and other mental issues," Smith added.

"The DOD wanted him to start doing the procedure on healthy people, particularly front-line troops and pilots, but Dr. Dawson has refused."

"Why?" Gardner asked.

"The side effects. Psychotic episodes, sleep disruption, nightmare, headaches, delusions…you name it," Cassandra answered.

"Won't those idiots ever learn?" Smith said disgustedly. "They keep trying to build the super soldier."

"How did you get past all of that?" Smith asked.

"As you can tell from my dreams, I'm still working my way through it," Cassandra said as she winked at her grandfather. "After Dr. Dawson explained what was happening to me, I'm starting to wrap my head around it much better."

"What I just witnessed was one of the most remarkable things I've ever seen," Gardner said. "So this procedure allows you to read people's minds?"

"Sort of," Cassandra answered. "It doesn't work with everyone, but with some people when I make skin-to-skin contact, I can read their current thoughts. I can't read their memories and, thankfully, it appears to be a one-way street. I can read their thoughts, but they cannot read mine."

"Ah," Nick Bergman said. "That was why you wanted to touch her when she was being questioned about the flask and glass."

"Exactly," Cassandra answered. "Not being on her guard, when asked a question, she would naturally think about it." Cassandra pointed at Hicks. "You came really close to blocking me. With a bit of practice, you would have it."

"I think we should work on that," Hicks said with a grin.

"I think we should," Cassandra answered with a silly expression on her face.

"I think you two should get a room," Mullen muttered mostly to herself.

Carrie Finch had a faraway look on her face. "Let me guess, you made physical contact with the arsonist when he was thinking about burning down his building…"

"And the homeless guys who were thinking about getting off of the street for the night," Mullen finished.

"Wow!" Carrie Finch said as she put both of her hands on the top of her head as if trying to keep it from exploding. "Since you hadn't figured out what was going on yet, those thoughts went straight to your sub-conscious and made a dream."

"Bingo!" Cassandra continued. "The same thing happened with the nuclear material…"

"You weren't even aware you had touched your uncle and his assistant, so your conscious mind never considered them as suspects. Everything pointed to the guy in the bar," Mullen finished for Cassandra.

"Just like you're reading my mind. What happens next?" Cassandra asked.

The Attorney General cleared his throat as he rose to his feet. "Barbara, I'll leave it to you to tidy this up."

"Thank you for coming in, Ms. Morse," Smith said. "We'll have a driver…"

"Bravo Sierra," Cassandra barked as she fell back in her seat. "I understand the Attorney General's need for plausible deniability, but that doesn't apply to me. These assholes killed my grandfather, tried to kill me and fired on the 5,000 crewmen on my ship." Cassandra Morse's eyes locked on Smith. They were cold and emotionless. "What are you going to do about it? Or…" Cassandra paused. "Do I need to deal with this myself?"

"How would you deal with it?" Smith asked.

"With all due respect ma'am," Morse answered as her jaw tightened and all emotion drained out of her body. "All I would need to do is make two or three phone calls and the wrath of God would hit Bathmann and everyone involved with this."

"I see," Smith answered.

What's going to happen to Rachel Frey?" Morse demanded.

"She'll be on the next plane out to Guantanamo Bay," Smith answered. "There she'll be tried by a secret military tribunal for the murder of a senior naval officer and a sitting congressman and attempted mass murder by firing a weapon of mass destruction at the USS Ronald Reagan Strike Group."

"What is the penalty if convicted?"

"Being a military court, she will have the choice of death by firing squad or hanging."

"If she opts for the firing squad and you need a volunteer, let me know," Cassandra said as she glanced at Hicks who had a smirk on his face and couldn't take his eyes off of her. She shook her head and turned back to Smith.

"What about Doorman?"

"As soon as he catches wind of what is happening, he'll be on the next plane to a country without extradition to the US."

"Which is good news for us," Smith said.

"Why?"

"He's going to be in such a hurry to get out of Dodge, if he hasn't found the stuff Frey sent him, it will be there when we come looking for it."

"That makes sense. But doesn't that mean he's getting away with murder?"

"I didn't say that," Smith said as she glanced at Michael Hicks. "But there will be other considerations."

"Ah!" Morse said. "You want to see what's on the files Frey sent to Doorman. Smart."

"Very perspective," Smith answered. "If they contain what I think they contain, there are going to be an awful lot of people in Washington who will want to see Louis Bathmann and his crew go away before they can get in front of any microphones much less a grand jury."

"Excellent!" Morse said as she started to her feet. "I'll give you a week."

"Or?"

"They fired on the USS Ronald Reagan," Cassandra Morse answered with steel in her voice. "I have a few friends over at the United States Naval Special Warfare Command and Seal Team 6 that might take that personally."

"You're all right with that?" Smith asked with a bemused expression on her face as she glanced at Michael Hicks who was having trouble keeping the grin off of his face.

"My only problem, ma'am," Morse answered through gritted teeth. "I might not be the one who gets to pull the trigger."

"Understood," Smith answered as she glanced at Hicks again. "I believe this situation will be contained before you get back from your meeting with the president in three days."

"Are we done here?" Cassandra asked. "I need a shower, a change of clothes and some sleep before Air Force One arrives."

"One more thing," Smith said as she grabbed Cassandra's hand.

Cassandra's eyes flew open. "You can't be serious!" she said with a laugh. "Me working for the National Intelligence Agency. Not even in your dreams."

Chapter 57

WHILE CASSANDRA MORSE, Detective Steve Foley and the four pilots had flown to Washington with the President on Air Force One, the return trip wasn't as dramatic. While hardly commercial coach, the sixteen-seat jet on loan from the State Department was quite a step down.

Morse and Foley, in the Oval office, each received the Medal of Freedom. And, not to be outdone, at the same ceremony the Navy had decided that despite her "medical discharge" she was still a commissioned officer and, along with the four pilots, deserved The Navy Cross. Then, to her surprise, instead of the President or SECNAV making the presentation to her, they had her father present the medal.

To see one Morse in tears was a rarity. To see two at the same time was unprecedented.

Det. Foley wasn't onboard; he had never been to Washington before and wanted to spend a few days looking at the sites. Lt. Max Underwood was sitting next to Cassandra in the aisle seat, so he had more legroom. "I heard a rumor that the Navy offered you your wings back," Underwood said with his soft drawl.

"They made the offer," Morse answered.

"And?"

"And I turned them down."

"Why?" Underwood asked.

Cassandra laughed and shook her head. "It was tough enough having three admirals on the family tree and being a female. As soon as anyone did a web search and found the "Dream Lady" article it would be a nightmare."

"Fair enough," Underwood said.

"What about you?"

"In addition to the Navy Cross, an immediate promotion to Lt. Commander and my choice of assignments."

"Wow!"

"Apparently, thanks to our little fireworks display, Navy recruitment has gone through the roof in the past few days."

Cassandra pointed in the direction of the three other pilots who were huddled near the galley sharing a laugh. "What about them?"

"Same deal." Underwood chuckled. "I think they all plan to name their first-born Cassandra."

"That could be rough if their first born was a boy," she said with a laugh. "Your pick of assignments, huh? Where are you heading?"

"Gina is from Reno and really likes Fallon since it is close to her family," Underwood said as he nodded in the direction of his wife and an adorable two-year-old little boy asleep in her arms.

"That's quite a noble sacrifice on your part," Cassandra said with a laugh. "I'm assuming you'll be at the Naval Fighters Weapons School."

"It's an ugly job, but someone has to do it," Underwood answered with a straight face.

"Any of the other three going to Top Gun?" Cassandra asked.

"One definite, one maybe and one no."

They were interrupted when a steward approached them. "We received a message from a Michael Hicks who recommended you turn on cable news."

"Please turn on the television," Cassandra said.

The steward pushed a button and the three televisions spread around the cabin all sprang to life.

Above the "Breaking News" banner a well-groomed clone of Madison Street was doing a live report from Austin, Texas. "We now have confirmation that Louis Bathmann IV, long time CEO of Bathmann Aeronautics, was found dead this morning in his sprawling estate just outside Austin from an apparent self-inflicted gunshot wound. Also found was Bathmann's chief of security, Gabriel Ashton. With Bathmann a lifelong bachelor, there had been speculation that he and Ashton were lovers."

"Nice touch," Cassandra Morse muttered before bursting out laughing. She waved the steward back over. "You don't happen to have any champagne in the galley?"

"Funny you should mention that," the steward answered. "A.D. Barbara Smith had a case delivered just before take-off."

"Of course she did," Morse said with a smile. "Please ask the other Naval officers to join us."

"Yes, ma'am."

"And please bring champagne for everyone."

"Right away."

"What's going on?" Underwood asked.

Cassandra held up her finger and waited until the others arrived. "This is highly classified and need to know, but I thought you all needed to know." She pointed to the TV screen. "That's the Mike Foxtrot that killed my grandfather, Admiral Henry Morse, and fired on the Gipper."

"Outstanding!" proclaimed Max Underwood as he accepted a glass of bubbly.

Cassandra, seeing her grandfather grinning at her from one of seats across the aisle, asked the steward for another flute of champagne. While he fetched it, she lowered the food tray in front of her grandfather and instructed the steward to put it in front of the admiral.

Cassandra held her glass in the direction of her grandfather. "To those who are no longer here but will always be with us."

After a moment's hesitation, the other four pilots knew what Cassandra was doing. They all raised their glass in the direction of the empty seat and Underwood spoke for them all. "To Admiral Henry Morse!"

✳✳✳

By the time the jet landed at LAX, more than half a case of the champagne had been consumed and no one in Navy blue was fit to fly or drive.

Waiting at the bottom of the steps for Cassandra was Michael Hicks. When he saw her glassy eyes and unsteady gait, he smiled and offered her a hand which she gladly accepted and got her usual jolt. "I see you got my message."

"You've been a naughty boy," Cassandra said as she released her grip on his hand and hugged his arm instead.

"Is this Hicks?" Underwood asked. Now that he was safely at the bottom of the stairs of the jet, he relieved his wife of the dead weight of their sleeping son.

"He is indeed," Cassandra answered proudly.

After introductions and handshakes all round, Morse motioned in the direction of six cars with drivers idling a few hundred feet from the jet and made a face.

"The steward called ahead that the Navy, as usual, needed ground transportation. Come on," Hicks said as he guided Cassandra in the direction of the lead car. "I'm going to get you home and tuck you in bed."

Cassandra pulled Hicks closer. "Tuck wasn't the word I had in mind, but it's only off by one letter."

"How much have you had to drink?"

"Just one," Cassandra said as she batted her lashes at Hicks.

"One what?"

"One bottle." Cassandra scrunched up her face. "Or was it two?"

After Hicks poured her into the backseat of the Escalade, he climbed in beside her and had to help her with her seatbelt. The driver apparently already knew her address and didn't bother asking questions.

Cassandra leaned heavily on Hicks and rested her head on his shoulder. "I should never drink champagne, especially when I'm this tired."

"Apparently," Hicks said as he brushed her hair out of his face. "Do you want the good news, the good news, the good news or the good news?"

"Let's start with the good news."

"The smoking gun files Rachel Frey had on Bathmann were exactly where you said they would be."

"How deep are the files going to be buried?" Cassandra asked.

"There would be a better chance of someone digging up Jimmy Hoffa than those files ever seeing the light of day." Hicks grinned. "The Armed Services Committee announced this morning it was pulling the plug on the F-38 and going with the SV-1. Combined with the death of Louis the Fourth, Bathmann Aeronautics stock cratered this morning."

"That's a crying shame." Cassandra motioned for him to continue. "What else do you have for me?"

"Bradley Doorman was killed last night by a hit and run driver."

"These things happen," Cassandra said. "What else?"

"The Bathmann research ship that pulled you out of the water then held you drugged up for three weeks had an explosion."

"Explosion? What kind of explosion?" Cassandra asked.

"Apparently, the type of explosion you get when a vessel takes a direct hit from a cruise missile in the engine room," Hicks answered. "It sank so quickly; all hands were lost and it went down in such deep water there is no chance of salvage."

"I assume you saved the best for last."

"I did," Hicks said cheerfully. "Rachel Frey didn't make it to Gitmo. She fell out of a helicopter over the Gulf of Mexico yesterday morning and her body was not recovered."

"I wonder why?" Cassandra asked innocently.

Hicks shrugged. "The thirty pounds of diving weights strapped to her might have been a contributing factor."

"How high was the helicopter?"

"Eight thousand feet."

"Was she conscious?"

"Yes."

Being a pilot, Cassandra was still sober enough to quickly calculate the terminal velocity of falling 8,000 feet. "So she had over twenty seconds to consider the error of her ways before impact."

"I thought it was the least I could do."

Cassandra pulled Hicks even closer. "Man! You really know how to sweet talk a girl."

"We need to get you home and to bed…"

"My thoughts exactly."

"We need you to be awake at 0300."

"Why?"

"We're going to walk down to the beach and see the light show."

Cassandra leaned back and gave Hicks an odd look. "I'm not tracking."

"Around 0330, a satellite is going to explode about three hundred miles off of the coast of California." Hicks grinned at Morse.

"Considering its size, it will be pretty impressive as it burns up on reentry."

"Icarus?"

"Yes."

Epilogue

"JERK," CASSANDRA GASPED as she fell heavily on the blanket near the water on Venice Beach. Michael Hicks tossed her a towel as she laid on her back with her arm draped across her face shielding her eyes from the sun as she tried to regain her breath.

In the month they had been together their relationship had evolved from white hot passion to competitive. As would be expected, with her being Navy, she destroyed him in the water. With him being Army, he destroyed her on land.

Hicks checked his watch. "Sub-six minutes per mile in the sand, not bad for a Navy brat. Especially a girl."

Cassandra playfully kicked him. "I thought I was going to have to ask the lifeguards to go out and look for you yesterday since you were so far behind."

Hicks pulled a bottle of water out of their ice filled cooler and nudged Cassandra's bare skin between her sports bra and running shorts with it. She jumped when the cold bottle made contact. "Jerk," she repeated as she pulled herself up into a sitting position and accepted the reusable container.

During their time together they had fully synched and Cassandra no longer needed to be in physical contact with Hicks to be on the same wavelength. They had a no Bravo Sierra relationship. She had never trusted anyone the way she did Hicks. They were like an old happily married couple who knew what their partner was thinking and could finish each other's thoughts.

Between their ten-mile early morning beach run, three-mile late afternoon ocean swim and nightly sexual marathons, Cassandra was easily in the best shape of her life.

After a month with Hicks, Cassandra was now two pounds below her best Navy weight and her skin was a deep bronze. With her sun-streaked blonde hair, killer tan and killer bod, she looked like the kind of California Girl the Beach Boys wrote songs about.

For others, life went on.

Cassandra's Uncle Billy, Professor Comstock, humiliated but still alive, dodged a bullet. Since the government wanted The Diablo Incident forgotten as soon as possible, he was allowed to quietly retire from public life and not stand trial.

Blanche Harrison got her captain bars and Foley turned down the lieutenant offer. He preferred working the streets to working a desk.

Grant Olsen had taken his dream job. Thanks in no small part to a personal letter of recommendation from the Director of Homeland Security combined with a Pulitzer Prize nomination, he was now a reporter for *The Washington Post*.

Carrie Finch had been promoted to Deputy Assistant Director for the National Intelligence agency and was lovingly referred to as Barbara Smith's "mini-me". Seldom was one seen without the other. Cassandra had been surprised and flattered and immediately accepted when Finch asked her to be in her bridal party. The date was uncertain since Finch wanted to complete her conversion from being a non-practicing Methodist to being a non-practicing Jew. The switch didn't mean much to her but apparently it meant a great deal to Nick Bergman's mother.

"Let me ask you something," Cassandra said seriously.

"Sure," Hicks answered.

"Would you be willing to give Dr. Newman a DNA sample?"

Hicks burst out laughing. "Why? Are you pregnant?"

"No," Cassandra answered quickly. She thought about it for a moment then repeated even more firmly, "No."

Hicks propped himself up on one elbow and his eyes locked on Cassandra's. "What's going on?"

Cassandra sighed. "That day in the conference room with Frey you weren't the least bit surprised that I could read her mind."

Hicks fell back on his blanket and laughed. "Of course I wasn't surprised. I've been dealing with stuff like that my entire life."

"Yeah, right," Cassandra said.

"Sweetie, no offense, I know you and Newman think you're hot stuff in the mind reading department. Compared to my mom, you're playing t-ball while she's the MVP of the Major Leagues." Hicks pulled another bottle of water out of the cooler. "I never got away with a damn thing when I was growing up and don't get me started on my aunts and sister," Hicks said as he took a sip of water. "If they had been born a few hundred years ago they probably would have all been burned at the stake."

"That might explain it," Cassandra said as she took another gulp of her water.

"Explain what?"

"I can only read the thoughts of certain people. Usually when I connect with someone I get a mild shock, kind of like static electricity. When I touched you for the first time, I was almost knocked to the floor."

"Damn," Hicks said with a laugh. "I thought it was my animal magnetism and raw sexual power."

"This is important to me," Cassandra said seriously. "Dr. Newman thinks the reason I connect or not depends on if the person I touch has the psychic gene. In your case, you would appear to have it in spades." Cassandra's eyes locked on Hicks. "The better I understand all of this the better it is for me."

"That's good enough for me," Hicks answered. "Tell Dr. Newman I'm in and I'll ask my mom, and aunts and sister for samples too."

"Thank you," Cassandra said softly as she fell back on the blanket and closed her eyes. "Does your mother know what you do?"

Hicks laughed. "I've never said anything but, like you, she's impossible for me to keep anything from."

"Does she approve?" Cassandra asked softly.

"According to her, I'm doing what I was born to do. That's why she named me Michael."

Cassandra laughed out loud. "So your mom thought she was giving birth to an Archangel?"

"Apparently."

"I need to meet this lady."

"Be careful what you wish for," Hicks said then pointed toward the street. "Incoming."

Carrie Finch's driver and now body man, S.A. Glenn Haycock was headed in their direction. Finch had been so taken with him on her earlier visit to L.A., she had requested his permanent assignment as the head of her security detail. He had the perfect temperament for dealing with Finch. He took his job extremely seriously but Finch not so much. Instead of being annoyed, he found her pedantic abruptness a refreshing change from the normal self-important blowhards he had driven around previously. Obviously armed and in a dark suit, Haycock could not have possibly looked any more out of place on Venice Beach.

Hicks got to his feet and brushed off as much sand as possible. Next, he held out a hand and offered it to Cassandra.

She felt the spark, but she didn't need the connection to know what was going on. They had moved well past that.

Duty calls.

Vacation time was over for Michael Hicks.

Picking up their cooler and blanket, Hicks started walking in the direction of a trio of Cadillac Escalades idling at the curb. A half dozen no-nonsense men had established a perimeter around the heavy SUVs. When they reached the middle car, Cassandra noted it sat lower than the other two because of the additional armament. Carrie Finch was now considered a high value target by bad people around the globe.

When one of the members of the security team opened the rear passenger door, as expected, Finch was in the middle seat and on the phone. Next to her, Cassandra saw possibly the last person she expected. Holly Mullen. The facial piercings were missing, the purple hair was gone. She now had a bootcamp style buzz cut and was wearing a black pantsuit. The long sleeves of her white silk blouse and well-cut jacket covered most of her ink.

Hicks sat the cooler and blanket on the curb then kissed Cassandra like he meant it. He gave her a hug and knowing no words needed to be spoken, he climbed into the SUV.

Finch waved but kept talking on her phone.

"Damn Girl!" Mullen said as she admired Cassandra's new look. "Buff City!"

"I'm surprised to see you with Finch," Cassandra said.

Mullen shrugged. "The enemy of my enemy is my friend kind of thing."

Cassandra chuckled.

"Speaking of enemies," Finch said as she finished her call and handed her phone over her shoulder without looking to Nick Bergman, who was sitting directly behind her in the third row of seats. "We've got a problem that could use your unique skillset."

"Excuse me?" Cassandra asked with a puzzled expression on her face.

"We want to get the old band back together," Mullen said brightly.

"Are you coming or not?" Finch asked.

Books by Rod Pennington
Available on Amazon.com

The Family Series
A dark comedy about a dysfunctional family
of four of the world's best assassins.

Family Reunion
Family Business
Family Secrets
Family Honor
Family Debt

Stand Alone Books

Indweller
Cassandra Files: Genesis

Books by Rod Pennington & Jeffery A. Martin
Available on Amazon.com

The Fourth Awakening Series:
A woman overcomes her mid-life crisis
by going on a vision quest with an enigmatic billionaire.

The Fourth Awakening
The Gathering Darkness
The Fourth Awakening Chronicles I
The Fourth Awakening Chronicles II
The Fourth Awakening Chronicles III
The Fourth Awakening Chronicles IV

Stand Alone Books

What Ever Happened to Mr. MAJIC?
Better Choices

www.ingramcontent.com/pod-product-compliance
Lightning Source LLC
Chambersburg PA
CBHW071255250626
47159CB00004B/1186